WHITE LILIES

By

GARRY. P. BAKER

While all the places mentioned in this novel do exist, all names and events are totally fictional.

Chapter One

Sara Jane Gray, twenty-two, slim built about five foot six inches tall, and very attractive, with shoulder length mousy brown hair.

Smartly dressed in a grey trouser suit she made her way to her third job interview in as many weeks.

Sara was desperate to get a job, possibly a job with prospects and one that paid well, money was short.

She was the second daughter to Eileen and Jack Gray, wealthy landowners in the area where they live, Bourne, a small market town in Lincolnshire. Neither Sara nor her sister Christine, had what one would call, a happy childhood; their father totally ignored them, only acknowledging their presence, with cruel and meaningful comments. Although never witnessed by Sara and Christine, cruelty from Jack towards their mother was of a different nature, it was certain that this house did not contain one vital family ingredient, love. Jack Gray was a ruthless businessman, despised by many and hated by all.

Jack had no time for his wife and children, he was a bitter man.

At eleven Sara was sent off to boarding school in the city of York, where Christine, had been for the previous two years. She and her sister only went home at Christmas and two weeks during the summer break, the other four weeks of the summer break were spent with their grandparents in Penrhyn, Cornwall. They were their Mothers parents; both their father's parents had died before Sara and Christine were born.

It couldn't be said that holidays in Cornwall were happy times, they were old people and lacked patience, most of the time, was spent in their bedrooms watching television, they were not allowed to play in the house and most of the time Christine was left in charge of Sara.

At the age of seventeen Sara, who was far less than innocent, left boarding school, not completing her education. She moved to the small but growing town of Spalding in Lincolnshire only eleven miles from her parent's home.

Unknown to them Sara rented a rather grubby bed-sit. Sara and Christine's parents had completely disowned them; these two pretty sisters had blossomed into two beautiful young ladies.

Their mother would not dare mention either of them in the presence of their father. He said they were an embarrassment to him, to make matters worse, Christine was rumoured to be having a relationship with girls, one girl in particular, a very pretty girl of the same age, called Sam, they were said to be very open about their sexuality.

Christine and Sam rented a flat in the town of Selby, Yorkshire, keeping in regular touch with Sara; they visited her on many occasions.

Sara now nineteen and more financially stable decided it was time to give up her bed-sit and go for a mortgage, this she did on a one bedroom flat overlooking the River Welland.

The River Welland flows through the top half of the town, with its well maintained sides and its springtime flowers it helped enhance the view from the veranda of Sara's flat, a flat where she had entertained several men, who were obviously only interested in one thing. Sara wanted more than what these men had in mind, and she had by now given her self somewhat of a bad reputation, which was growing.

Sara applied for and got a job at the local food factory trimming lettuce, but after a relationship with her supervisor and a smack round the face from his wife, who also worked there, she was asked to leave.

Unemployed and back on the job market, Sara decided she would apply at the local newly opened super market stacking shelves at night, after a successful interview was offered the position, but it wasn't long before she was using her womanly guile's to gain promotion. Much to Sara's delight, she soon got what she wanted and was promoted to supervisor. She was put on the day shift, but Sara became more than friendly with the Managing Director and it wasn't long before she was promoted to deputy shift manager.

Sara was climbing the promotion ladder at one hell of a speed, but then the ladder gave way, it was announced the company was in a financial mess and the receivers had been brought in.

After a few weeks and no buyer had been found, Sara along with twenty or so others was made redundant.

Although unemployed Sara had, out of this mess, gained one thing managerial skills, which she could use to make a much needed change to her life, so without further ado she started sending copies of her self styled, C.V to local companies, although it didn't quite read true it got her three promising replies. She quickly replied to all three and was offered an interview from each.

The first interview was for a manager at a fruit shop; however, she soon realised that they were not looking for a shop manager, but a shop assistant, come dog's body.

The second interview was for an assistant manager in the delicatessen department, in a leading supermarket chain at a store in Peterborough. The interview went well and Sara was certain in her mind, of a good result, she received a letter a few days later asking her to attend a further interview. On this occasion things didn't go as well as Sara had hoped for, the gentleman interviewing her decided to check some of the facts on Sara's C.V only to find out that she had been rather economical with the truth and that her references were false.

Not all was lost, there was still the third interview although in a very different direction and with no real choice, she attended the interview.

This position was for Office Manager in a small family firm of estate agents, Gardener and Son.

Mr Alf Gardener and his son Tom interviewed Sara at the Spalding shop, although the position was for their King's Lynn premises. The position involved meeting customers, helping with sales and ensuring the office ran smoothly. Freda, Alf's sister, was currently doing the job, but was retiring shortly and the successful applicant would be her successor. Sara was offered the position after a second interview and readily accepted, although it wasn't really, what she wanted.

Sara soon settled in to the role and she found Mr Gardener a widower of fifteen years a very pleasant employer, He gave her the use of a company car, for pleasure as well as work. After about six months of Sara being there, Mr Gardener, a very heavy smoker became ill with lung Cancer, placing him off work; this also meant Tom too spent a lot of time off work looking after his father. Sara was left to run both shops, which she managed with a limited amount of problems.

Mr Gardener took a turn for the worse and after four months, he died. As a sign of respect, both shops were shut for a week. Tom now had to decide what to do with the business, him being sole heir to his father's estate. Not wanting to go against his father's wishes he decided to keep the business going. Sara was asked by Tom to run the Kings Lynn shop and Tom would run the Spalding shop, she was given the title of Branch Manager and a pay rise plus the full use of the company car but, she was manager, manager over who? She had no staff but despite her earlier reservations, this had been the break she needed.

That night Sara spoke to her sister Christine on the phone, as they did every night, and much to Sara's delight Christine and Sam were looking to move to Spalding.

When Christine and Sam told Sara of their intentions this gave Sara an idea, she was finding running the Kings Lynn shop on her own tiring she desperately needed more help and had already suggested to Tom they should employ two extra staff, Tom too had been finding it tiring running the Spalding branch alone so she told him of Christine and her partners intentions, she asked him if it might be a good idea to offer them the jobs

"To be honest with you Sara I was seriously considering advertising, but if you think they are suitable, go ahead ask them I'm prepared to give them a chance".

Sara offered the positions to Christine and Sam they were more than happy with the idea. Within weeks they arranged to rent a flat in Spalding; five minutes walk from the shop.

The arrangements were that Christine would work at Spalding with Tom and Sam work at Kings Lynn with Sara. This worked without problems, lifting the pressure off Sara and Tom giving them both more time to themselves. Tom had also realised he had started to take notice of Sara not only as an employee.

Tom a tall well built thirty-year-old bachelor, average in looks and always smartly dressed; his parents were always kind and showed him a lot of love but, never spoilt him, leading him through the right paths in life. Tom loved his parents very much, becoming very close to his father, more so after the sudden death of his Mother in a road accident one January morning, Tom was just fifteen. Tom's father bought the business thirty years previous to his death having worked there since himself leaving school turning it from a mess into a very profitable business.

Tom hadn't been that lucky with the opposite sex, in fact he had only had two girlfriends; one only lasted a week the other, lasted eighteen months, Pat a local girl, at the time she worked for his dad as a personal secretary.

Tom and Pat never had sex, she told him she wanted to save herself until they were married only to find some local farmers son had been seeing to her. He had no idea until one night Tom was out jogging and passed a car parked down a lane, being almost dark it wasn't until he got closer he realised it was Pats car thinking it to have broken down he went to investigate, on approaching the car he noticed some movement, on a closer inspection the movement was obvious it was Pat he could hear her screams of pleasure and getting closer still he could see a bare arse going up down, he lost his temper pulling open the door and dragging her half naked lover out and beat shit out of him still in a temper he then smashed the car windows. Tom later found out this affair had been going on for two years starting six months before they met, she had been using him for money and Tom had plenty. From that day on Tom never set eyes on Pat again she didn't turn up for work again, she wrote a letter to him resigning her position and requesting her P45 a reference plus all moneys owed. After this, Tom lost interest in women and buried himself in work. That was until Sara, her slender figure, her pretty face enhanced by the way she wore her hair she was always dressed smartly, without doubt she was a beauty. What could Tom do, he was her boss he shouldn't be feeling like this, after all if he made a move towards her or told her his feelings, she could very well get upset and that would put stress on their working relationship that and wouldn't do, so he decided to keep his thoughts of Sara to himself,

Tom knew he was going to find this hard, almost impossible Tom had no idea that Sara was feeling the same way. She was scared, she too could feel a strong attraction growing between them, but she was too worried to make the first move, after all Sara had made enough mistakes with men to last her a lifetime, and just say if she came on to Tom and he wasn't interested she could very well land up making a right fool of herself and that could upset their very good working relationship. Sara decided to push her feelings for Tom aside, she also thought that if Tom was interested in her he would surely have made a move by now, apart from that she knew nothing of Tom or his personal life, only as a boss. Sara wasn't sure if he had a girlfriend, he'd never mentioned one, but why should he? It wasn't any of Sara's business. She couldn't stop thinking of Tom as much as she tried, she was falling for him in a big way, but what did he think of her, or did he just look on her as a colleague and not as a woman?. All Sara could think of was Tom. She saw him in her dreams; her mind was full of images of him. Her head was telling her to leave things as they were, but her heart was telling her to go after what she wanted.

Chapter Two

Christmas 1998 was fast approaching arrangements were made for the staff meal. Tom agreed the meal and drinks would be paid for by the business, they would all go for a meal at a restaurant in Spalding then go on a pub crawl Sara booked them all a table at an Indian restaurant on the Winsover Road fortunately the restaurant had a licensed bar so the drinks flowed freely. Both Tom and Sara were rather tipsy, whereas Christine and Sam stuck to soft drink.

In the restaurant that night, on the other side of the room were Christine and Sara's parents who were sat with some friends, Mr and Mrs Ingamells. Both groups were unaware of each others presence until Christine got up to go to the loo and saw them, not wanting it to be said that she had ignored them decided in her wisdom to go over and be pleasant, asking them if they were well, Jack seeing her coming immediately got out of his seat and started shouting at Christine and calling her a dirty dyke. Sara as did everyone else in the restaurant saw and heard what was going on but she unlike Christine was worse for the drink, couldn't help herself she got up from her chair staggered over to them and gave them what for, her father retaliated calling her a drunken common whore, Mr Ingamells found this very amusing and started laughing Sara didn't appreciate his laughter and hit him with a clenched fist right on the nose, this wiped the grin off his face knocking him off his chair, he was covered in blood and somewhat embarrassed, they quickly upped and left.

Tom and Sam just sat there gob smacked deciding it was time to grab Sara and Christine, pay the bill and make a quick exit before they were all thrown out, Tom couldn't stop laughing

"I think it best not to book next years meal lets get out of here, pity really that was the best Indian I've ever had".

Sara was so embarrassed over the whole situation she wanted to go home but Tom insisted on going to another pub. Feeling she had done the night harm and not wanting to do anymore, she decided it best to go for another drink with Tom and try to apologise. Sam and Christine agreed to have one more drink then they would be off home. Once Sam and Christine had gone home and Tom and Sara were alone Tom asked Sara about the incident in the pub earlier Sara told him the full story of who the people were and how they were treated as children also how they reacted at finding out that Christine was a lesbian. Tom changing the subject asked her if she had a boyfriend. Sara noticed a change in Toms voice and the smile when she told him she hadn't, Toms voice became softer and he seemed to want to know all about her, asking her about past boyfriends and jobs, she decided to tell Tom the full story of her past hiding nothing.

This wasn't like Sara she had always been rather economical when it came to the truth, but not this time, Sara wanted Tom to know the real Sara, from Sara and not from someone else who might just add a bit more for interesting listening. Sara couldn't take any more let downs, her past relationships had been total disasters, so if there was the slightest chance of having a relationship with Tom she wanted it to be based on honesty and not lies.

Sara needed to put her past to bed; she knew she had grown to be a different person. Tom listened to her story without commenting, when she had finished he said to her that it was time he came clean with her and told her how he really felt.

Tom said to Sara

"I'm in love with you Sara; I have been for some time"

Tom told Sara he had wanted to tell her this for ages but was worried of what her reactions would be. Sara was speechless she had been secretly in love with Tom all this time not aware of the fact Tom was in love with her, she was ecstatic, she threw her arms around him and they kissed, that first kiss seemed to last for ages,

"I love you to Tom and you don't know how much I've wanted to tell you",

They kissed again; people around them could easily mistake them as one.

Tom and Sara decided not rush things taking each day as it came. They returned to work on the Monday as usual; they never mentioned anything about their newfound love to Christine and Sam although it wasn't long before Sam overheard Sara talking on the phone. Sara not realising Sam was behind her ended the conversation saying

"I love you too Tom"

When Sara turned round and saw Sam grinning at her she realised she had heard her. Sara confided in her asking her not to mention anything to anyone but Christine had overheard Tom's side of the conversation, Tom finished his phone call to Sara by saying

"I love you sweetheart I'll be round for seven".

Tom also realising Christine had over heard him, told her the full story. Christine was delighted for them, she waited for Tom to go for his dinner and rang her sister to congratulate her and tell her how pleased she was.

That week seemed to drag by Tom asked Sara to spend Christmas day at his house, which she readily accepted. Sara had only seen Tom's house from the outside. She had often wondered of its hidden secrets.

Tom lived in a large Victorian property; it was situated in the village of Pinchbeck, a suburb of Spalding. Although he lived on his own, the house was immaculate and the garden was perfect, it was obvious he took pride in his home. If you didn't know Tom you would swear blind there had been a woman's touch about the house, but this was how Tom lived.

Tom cooked the dinner, cooking was one thing Tom was good at and enjoyed doing. The meal comprised of turkey, roast potatoes, brussel sprouts, carrots, cauliflower and homemade stuffing followed by home made Christmas pudding. The table was laid out to perfection and Tom had even made a Christmas cake obviously in a hurry the icing was still soft this made Sara laugh. He had put a bottle of good champagne in an ice bucket, the table was set fit for a queen and Sara was his queen. Tom had put up a Christmas tree and a few decorations, something this house hadn't seen in fifteen years since the death of his mother. Tom was going to make Christmas 1998 a Christmas to remember.

The meal was a great success, Sara couldn't get over what a good cook he was, and that champers definitely washed their meal down.

After the meal they sat and chatted, Tom produced a present from beneath the tree. The present, a gold locket with a diamond tipped arrow engraved on one side and on the other side the words, Sara I love you, this would be something she would always treasure. Sara embarrassingly gave Tom his present from her it was a shirt and after-shave; there was no need for her to be embarrassed Tom was more than happy with his present.

Sara stayed until about eleven o'clock and decided it was time to go home she had had a wonderful time, Sara left promising to ring him when she got to her flat. She might just as well have stayed there; they were on the phone until two o'clock Boxing Day morning talking about nothing. Sara was so happy she had finally found a man who wanted her and not just her body. He hadn't made a single move towards her sexually nor she him, this was a record for her, every other boyfriend she had she had slept with on the first night. It had been at least two years since Sara had slept with a man and for a young woman of twenty-three that's a long time.

Tom also was so happy to have Sara as his girlfriend and he was certain he was going to keep it that way. He wanted Sara more than he could tell her he had strong sexual feelings for her but there was no way he was going to risk ruining their relationship over sex he was sure they would both know when it was right.

Tom still a virgin had no idea of sex, only what he had read, sex was never talked about in the Gardener home he wasn't sure how to satisfy a woman, where as Sara had had several sexual relationships, Tom was worried, could he be a good lover and satisfy her sexual needs.

Tom and Sara arranged to meet on Boxing Day afternoon and go out for a ride. Tom picked Sara up around one in the afternoon and they drove over to the coast heading first for Cromer, Sara had made a few sandwiches, which they ate before then moving onto Wells next to the sea where they did some window-shopping.

Tom had many good memories of Wells, his mother and father once had a cottage there, where they spent many weekends. His dad had a small boat and would take him fishing and crab catching; the only thing they caught was colds but at least there was not a shortage of shops to buy crab from. He also had sad memories of Wells, the day he and his Father spread his Mothers ashes on the beach, this was something his Mother always wanted to happen and Tom had the dreadful job of spreading his father's ashes in the same place. Tom placed some flowers on the beach.

Tom never talked much of his childhood although if the truth was known he had never had any reason to talk about it as, no one had shown any interest in Tom Gardener as a child. As they walked back from the beach along the raised wooden path onto the cold windy bank, Sara asked him about his childhood Tom seemed a bit reluctant at first to talk about his past but Sara was insistent she wanted to know everything about him. Once Tom started talking there was no stopping him, he told her how he missed his mother and how he would love to talk to her, the holidays together as a family, the hurt he felt after her sudden death, the emptiness afterwards. His father seemed to cope very well, but Tom found out from his aunt after he died that he hadn't coped very well at all in fact his dad never got over her death he had spent many hours crying alone, on one occasion his aunt Freda had walked in finding him very upset and she insisted he confided to her. This upset Tom immensely

"I should have seen dads grief and helped him but I had been too blind, I sometimes think if I hadn't have been so selfishly tied up in my own grief I would have recognised dads hurt, anyway it's too late to change things as much as I would love to".

This was the first time Tom had spoken to anyone about this sad business. Sara asked him about his school days. Tom told her that he went to one of the primary schools in the town which he loved, then onto the local Grammar school, he told her how he was bullied regularly by a gang of lads from his school they would take money off him so that they would leave him alone that was until one day he hadn't brought any money with him and the lads beat him black and blue his dad demanded to know where he got the bruises from, he finally told his dad and gave him their names his dad knew their parents, his dad never said a word he just left the house and came back an hour later with four pounds and gave it to Tom without saying a word, when Tom took the money off his dad he noticed his dads knuckles were cut. The next day when Tom went to school he found out his dad had called round on the bullies parents and demanded his sons pocket money back explaining to them that if Tom was bullied again he would be back, one of the fathers told Alf to fuck off, Alf not liking his choice of words, hit him, obviously this method worked, he came away with Toms money and the bullying stopped. Tom then went on to say how he stayed at grammar school until he was eighteen taking his 'O'levels then his 'A' levels after that he got a place at, Nottingham University where he gained a degree in science. After leaving University, he couldn't find a job so he started work for his father and was soon made a partner at which point a certain young lady by the name of Pat who worked for his dad started to show an interest in him. He told her how he caught Pat with another bloke and that he hadn't had another relationship since and was very lonely.

Tom never really mixed with other people; he had friends although his only real friend had been killed on a motorbike when he was only twenty. Tom didn't go out drinking or to nightclubs, it just wasn't his scene, if he felt like a drink, he would have a beer at home and he enjoyed a good film. Tom admitted to Sara he was very much a loner also admitting he didn't like that, but after the experience with Pat just couldn't bring himself to trust anyone at this Sara interrupted him

"Do you still love Pat?"

"No not now, I did love her or at least I think I did and I missed her"

"Can you trust me Tom?" asked Sara

"I think so" replied Tom

"Good because I promise you, you can, I'm not Pat, I love you and I'm sure of that" said Sara turning towards Tom to kiss him.

Time was getting on and the light was fading so they decided to head home. They were only five minutes into their journey from Wells when a car coming from the opposite direction was overtaken by another car which was travelling at one hell of a speed hit Toms car head on, the people in the car which had been overtaken fortunately, for them managed to avoided the accident, they got out of their car and ran to check on all parties. Tom and Sara were still conscious and both were trapped, although Tom was fading into a state of unconsciousness; Sara seemed very calm although her left arm was giving her some pain. The people in the other car were not so lucky one of them lay on the side of the road and was obviously dead.

All emergency services soon arrived, both Tom and Sara had to be cut out of the car the remaining person in the other car was pronounced dead at the scene, as was his mate. They were two young lads from the nearby town of Fakenham. One of the lads, the passenger, obviously had not been wearing a seat belt, he had been thrown through the front window and the driver was crushed on impact. Both cars were unrecognisable it was hard to believe how anyone survived by their state.

Tom and Sara were taken to Kings Lynn Hospital, it soon appeared Sara had escaped with a broken left arm, whip lash and small cuts to her legs and face they told her she would be kept in overnight she was more concerned as to how Tom was, she had been told he had been sent down to theatre but not to worry he was going to be O.K. Sara wouldn't be happy until she had seen Tom for herself. Sara was taken to have her arm put in plaster and her cuts sorted and then taken to a ward.

After about two hours a nurse came into see Sara

"Mr Gardener is going to be fine, see we told you, you had nothing to worry about".

Apparently a piece of metal from the car had cut into his stomach area and he needed a small operation to remove it also his leg was broken that needed to be put in plaster and he also fractured two of his ribs, at least he would be all right and she had been told she could see him shortly.

The Police arrived in the ward to take a statement off Sara, they ask her if Tom had been drinking, he hadn't this was confirmed later with a blood test. Sara asked the Police about the two boys in the other car they wouldn't give her any details only that the witnesses at the scene backed her statement and were waiting for blood test results and for the accident investigators to complete their job at the scene telling her she would be informed as soon as they had put everything together. The Police asked Sara if she wished to inform anyone she gave them Christine's home address and Tom's aunt's address.

Eventually Tom was brought onto the same ward as Sara and put in one of the side rooms; he looked a mess his face was badly bruised, his stomach in bandages and his leg in plaster. He was still unconscious and a drip had been attached to his hand. This upset Sara intensely, she couldn't bear to think that Tom had to go through this,

Sara burst into tears she, just wanted to hold him, hug him

"What have them two bastards done to you Tom? I'm pleased they're dead after all they had no respect for our lives",

When she had calmed down, she felt guilty for thinking this way.

Christine and Sam arrived obviously very upset, they sat with Sara all that evening, they were just pleased they were both still alive. Tom eventually came round asking for Sara, he was still in a lot of pain, he cried when saw her he was so worried that she had been hurt, he tried to move to put his arms around her but the pain was too much to take. Tom asked her about the people in the other car, Sara told him, and this upset him,

"I can't really remember much about it all, I could see this car coming towards us then that horrible noise" said Tom.

Having had a very uncomfortable night's sleep, Tom woke sore and stiff he was still in a room on his own and wanted to be put onto a ward with Sara, this was not allowed. Tom couldn't eat anything he was still on a drip mind you looking at the food he wasn't missing much, Sara left hers, as did most other patients, she was in hurry to see Tom. When Sara entered Toms room she could hear that he had the television on it was showing the local news, they were showing the accident. Sara sat on the chair near Tom's bed; she couldn't believe what she had seen the state of the two cars beyond recognition. The Police officer on television said he was surprised anyone had survived.

Later that day the Doctor came to visit them telling Sara she could possibly go home on the Monday if they thought she was up to it although Tom would be kept in.

It wasn't long before the Police called on Tom asking him, what if anything could he remember, Tom couldn't tell them much only he saw the car coming out from behind a car heading straight at them and that was it. Tom asked the Police whether they had any news about the two lads, they said they were not really allowed to give out any information on the other the party but unofficially the car had been stolen and both lads were thought to be drunk. Tom wasn't surprised he and Sara had been talking between themselves earlier and Tom said either they were plain stupid or pissed out of their minds it appears they where both. Selfish as it may seem Tom was relieved at what he had been told, deep down he wouldn't be able to live with the thought of having killed two people as it was they chose to do what they did putting their lives and others at risk, a risk that cost them dearly.

Sara was getting rather concerned that Tom's aunt Freda hadn't been in to see Tom the Police said they would contact her as she lived on her own not far from where Tom lived perhaps they had called and she was out. Sara decided to give her a ring but there was no reply Sara tried several times but with no luck, she rang the Police they told her they called but there was no reply and the next-door neighbour had seen her going out earlier that week. This baffled Sara; Tom had always said she hardly ever leaves her home unless Tom takes her shopping.

Monday morning arrived and the Doctor came to visit he said Sara could go home although she didn't want to leave Tom in the Hospital she was relieved to be going home and in any-case Tom was feeling a lot better his ribs still ached and he hadn't tried to walk but at least he was comfortable. Sara rang Christine and asked her to collect her later that day as she was going to spend some time with Tom.

Tom and Sara needed to sort out what they were going to do about work should they stay closed or open, if they opened both shops they would have to provide Christine and Sam with a car and that wouldn't be cost affective so they decided to open Spalding shop on Monday, Tuesday and Wednesday and Kings Lynn shop on Thursday, Friday and Saturday until they were sorted. They also decided not to open either until the New Year this seemed the only thing to do in the present circumstances. So it was agreed Christine and Sam would work together at each shop and Sara would do what she could.

On the Tuesday Christine took Sara to visit Tom as Sara couldn't drive in her present state, Sara asked him if he had heard from his aunt when he said he hadn't she told him that the Police had called on her but got no reply Tom seemed concerned and asked Sara to go and check on her Tom gave her a front door key for his aunts house that he kept in his wallet. Seeing how concerned Tom was she decided to make her visit a short one and go straight to his aunt's house? On arriving at her House Sara and Christine noticed all the curtains were shut, when they opened the door the smell hit them. They first shouted her name then searched the house they found Toms Aunt Freda dead in her bed. They called the Police; an undertaker was called to take her away. How the hell would Tom take this, 1998 was definitely leaving with a bad taste. The Police asked Sara if she would be present when Tom was told, she said she would.

The Police took Sara back to the Hospital as soon as Sara and the two Police walked in Tom knew it was bad news. Sara had never seen Tom so upset and angry. It appeared the Police had called a total of three times noting all the curtains were closed, it also appeared the neighbour they asked was known to be not quite the sandwich, she wouldn't know what day it was, let alone if she had seen Freda, she had been taking a dog for a walk for the past seven years and yet she had never had a dog, obviously the police were completely unaware of her condition. Tom was furious; Tom's aunt Freda had possibly laid dead in her bed since the last time he had spoken to her on Christmas day.

Chapter Three

Tom had a lot to sort out but being in a hospital wasn't going to make it very easy, he asked Sara if she could arrange the funeral, she said she would, Tom also wanted to see his aunt but she lay in the morgue at Boston Hospital. Tom needed to be out of Hospital he was hoping to be released on the Wednesday.

On Wednesday the Doctor made his usual morning ward visit, he told Tom that under the circumstances providing he had someone to look after him and he felt he could cope with his crutches he could go home, so he rang Sara and asked her if she could arrange for Christine to collect him.

Christine and Sara arrived to collect Tom at about one thirty and by two thirty they were at the Chapel of rest in Boston Hospital to see Toms aunt,

"Doesn't she look peaceful?" Tom said,

This was a question that required no reply. They stayed at her side for about half an hour, Tom was obviously upset. Sara tried to make polite conversation

"How old was she Tom?" asked Sara

"Sixty-nine, no age and I always thought she was in good health".

Before he left Boston Tom rang the Coroners office, they asked him if he could pop in to see them, when he arrived. a man introduced himself as the Coroner

"Your aunt died of a Heart attack"

"But I had no idea she had a bad heart" said Tom

"Yes, she was on medication from the doctor"

"Would she have died in pain?"

"It's quite possible she passed away in her sleep, and the time of death is thought to have been Boxing Day morning".

Tom had no more questions.

Christine drove them both back to Tom's house and left them there. He hadn't been that close to his aunt but she had always been there for him especially when his mother died. Aunt Freda had been a widow since she was thirty and hadn't had any children of her own, Tom always felt rather suffocated in her presence.

Sara had arranged for the funeral to take place on the following Monday at Boston Crematorium, that being the fourth day of the New Year, there wouldn't be any New Year celebrations this year.

The Monday arrived, a total of eleven people turned up at the funeral, Freda never mixed with many people, so it was just Tom, Sara and a few neighbours. Tom invited every one back to his house for a few sandwiches. Once every one had gone home Tom had to decide what he had to do next, there was the Will to be read, if Freda had written one, the house had to be sorted and what did she want done with her ashes, things were going to be hard. Both Sara and Tom not being able to drive and they couldn't expect Christine and Sam to drive them all over for free, apart from that, the car Christine drove was well past its sell by date. If they were going to taxi them about they would need a decent and reliable car and the insurance from the accident wouldn't be rushing so Tom suggested to Sara that he should get them a company car and pay them extra to drive them around, Sara put Tom's suggestion to Christine and Sam who were more than happy to help especially with the thought of having a new car.

Tom contacted his solicitor and asked him to find out if Aunt Freda had a Will as luck would have it Freda had used the same solicitor as Tom and she had only just recently had her Will done, so they set a date for the Will to be read.

The solicitor asked for Tom and Aunt Freda's neighbour, Mrs Mann, to be present. The Will was simple everything was to be sold apart from odd personal items and Mrs Mann was to receive ten thousand pounds for herself and Mrs Mann's granddaughter was to have a further ten thousand to place in trust for her daughter until she reached the age of twenty one and finally her ashes were to be spread on her late husbands grave in Spalding Cemetery by Tom. Tom collected her ashes and did as she requested. Tom had never realised how wealthy his aunt was it was just something he hadn't thought about. Freda had several bank accounts in the town, monies totalling up to one hundred and thirty thousand plus and then he had to take the house into account and that hadn't yet been valued, Tom had no idea his aunt had this amount of money, so what with the money his father had left him plus the house along with the business and now all this from Freda's, Tom had been left one very wealthy man.

Tom now had the job of sorting through his aunt's belonging's he ask Sara to help him. Sara emptied all her bedroom drawers putting her clothes into bin bags. Under her bed, Sara found an old toffee tin she opened it and inside she found it to be full of love letters.

Sara called Tom upstairs to see what she had found they sat on the bed and read the letters some of which were very sexually explicit. Tom never heard Freda talk much about his uncle and he definitely never looked on her as having a sex life she was just plain old Aunt Freda to Tom, he couldn't believe what he was reading. In one of the letters Toms uncle had said how much he had enjoyed making love on their last meeting, then the penny dropped these letter weren't from Tom's uncle, aunt Freda had had a secret lover just after his uncle had died and no one knew; this took the morbidity out of the whole situation the room was full of laughter. Tom was so intrigued, he needed to know more, here was a woman he knew, respected loved and she was just the same as every one else with her own skeletons in her cupboard and Tom and Sara and had just opened her cupboard door, there were a lot of questions Tom needed to answer, was this man still alive? If so, did he live locally? When did the affair end? Did it end? Was he disguised as one of the neighbours at the funeral? Is he married? Does he know she's dead? The biggest question he had to ask himself was, did he really want any answers and just remember her, as he knew her, intriguing as it seemed Tom decided to go for the latter but he kept the letters just in case he changed his mind.

Freda's house was put on the market and after several viewing's a buyer was found and the house was sold, so once death duties had been settled Tom had been left with a substantial amount to do with as he wished.

Sam and Christine agreed to try and run the two shops between them only when they arrived to open the King Lynn shop they found it had been burgled and wrecked, they called the police, who after looking around gave Christine a crime number and left, Christine rang Tom, he went ballistic

"I've had enough Chris by the sounds of it this is obviously kids"

They hadn't just stolen computers and other odd bits they smashed the office up and shit on the floor these were animals and this was the seventh shop to be done in the area within the last six months. Tom rang Sara asking her to go with him to so he could look for himself.

"What a mess" said Sara

They couldn't believe what they were seeing.

"What did the police say?" asked Tom

"The Police never really commented only to say they would make enquires and handed me this number" replied Christine,

"I've had enough of this, they can take that bloody number and stuff it" said Tom angrily

"Calm down Tom" insisted Sara.

Tom after a lot of discussion with Sara, Sam and Christine decided to close the Kings Lynn shop and sell the lease but they would expand the Spalding shop or even if need be look for bigger premises, so no one would lose their job. As it was business wasn't over good at Kings Lynn so what little there was could be done from Spalding under one roof, this suited all of them, no more travelling and they all would be under one roof.

The whole situation worked extremely well. Tom and Sara did as much as possible keeping to the office and Sam and Christine did the valuations between them, in all they were a good team.

Six weeks had passed since their accident, and they both had to go for x-rays, Sara's x-ray showed her arm to have healed, but Tom's leg, although it was doing fine, the Doctor decided it best to keep it in plaster for a further two weeks Tom was well pissed off, a further two weeks of plaster and then physiotherapy for god knows how long.

Valentines Day was fast approaching. Tom wanted to arrange something special for Sara. He would have loved to have taken her away to Paris for a couple of days, but the state he was in it wouldn't have been very romantic, Tom needed to think of something soon. The relationship between Sara and Tom couldn't have been better although nothing sexual had happened between them, Tom was scared of making a move towards Sara in case it scared Sara off and Sara felt the same about moving towards Tom, so as far as sex was concerned it became a stalemate and both were gagging for it, yet in all honesty with the way things had been recently sex would have been very difficult let alone exciting.

Toms love for Sara was growing daily and he wanted to show her how much he loved her, he knew what he wanted to do, but at the same time he didn't want to scare her off, but if she loved him as much as he loved her she would at least think about what he was going to ask her. Tom decided to go for it, he didn't say a word to anyone, and he asked Sara if she would like to go to round his house for a meal on the evening of Valentine's Day, Sara readily accepted, this was to be a meal Sara would never forget or want to forget.

Chapter Four

Sara arrived at Tom's house at about six on the evening of Valentines with Tom meeting her at the door. Sara dressed in a silvery grey trouser suit looked stunning, and around her neck, she wore the locket Tom had bought her for Christmas Tom kissed her on the cheek noticing the smell of her perfume

"You look lovely sweetheart and smell gorgeous kissing her again only this time on the lips, I Love You".

Tom could feel a sensation in the lower region of his body that she noticed only to well. Although Tom had always showed his feelings for Sara, often commenting on her good looks and her dress sense, tonight Sara sensed a difference in Tom's behaviour.

As Sara entered the house, she couldn't help but notice a strong sweet smell mixed in with the smell of food cooking. Tom took hold of her hand leading her to the lounge on opening the door Sara couldn't believe her eyes, Tom had covered his carpet in red rose petals, the room was a mass of different flowers, the ceiling could hardly be seen for heart shaped balloons with ribbons hanging from them it wouldn't have surprised Sara if the house roof didn't lift off Tom wouldn't have cared. He covered the table in a mass of flowers, even the plates were placed on a bed of rose petals. The room was lit by thirty or so heart shaped candles floating in glass water filled bowls placed around the room, soft music was playing in the background. Sara thought she was in a dream this couldn't be true, no man had ever shown so much romance to her, the thought, the time and effort Tom had gone to, Sara could never be more sure of Toms love for her. She was so overwhelmed, she threw her arms around Toms neck and their lips met they kissed for what seemed ages

"I love you Tom Gardener"

"I love you too Sara Gray".

Tom led Sara to the table pulled back a chair for Sara sit on, Tom went into the kitchen soon returning carrying a tray with two servings of garlic mushrooms cooked in a cream sauce, this was followed by roast chicken surrounded by roast potatoes, leeks and carrots in white sauce, Tom opened a bottle of red wine. The meal was undoubtedly a great success. Sara had wondered why Tom hadn't wanted to see Sara the night before not giving her a reason, she thought he had possibly gone off her, now she new the real reason Tom had been to busy setting all this up.

After the meal Tom cleared the table and the pair of them settled down to a second bottle of wine, Tom put a fresh C.D on and sat next to Sara. He put his arm around her,

"That was lovely Tom, thank you" said Sara kissing him after which Tom looking very serious at Sara said

"Sara I know we've only been together as a couple since Christmas, although I sure you must agree it has been quite an eventful time, you Sara have made me the happiest man alive and Sara—well um will you marry me?"

Sara burst into tears throwing her arms around Tom and said

"Yes Tom, there is nothing I want more"

They were now both in tears.

Sara stayed at Tom's house, they both fell to sleep on the sofa this was the first time they had slept in the same room together, although nothing sexually happened.

The next day, a Monday. Tom left Sara asleep on the sofa, quietly rang Christine and Sam telling them him and Sara wouldn't be in to work. When Sara finally woke Tom made them breakfast

"Sara sweetheart I've rang your sister and asked her to look after the office today, I thought if it was O.K with you, we could go out"

"That sounds good to me, but where to?"

"My surprise sweetheart, (reaching over the table taking Sara's hand in his and kissing the back of it) and it's more important than work so ask no more" said Tom smiling.

After breakfast, Tom washed up while Sara used Tom's bathroom after which they headed straight for the bus stop that took them to the train station at Spalding where they caught a train to Peterborough. Once there Tom, holding Sara's hand, led her into a jeweller,

"You don't waste your time" said Sara smiling as she realised what Tom was up to,

"You needn't think I'm going to give you chance to change your mind do you?"

Tom insisted she choose whatever ring she wanted money was to be no object, telling her they had all day. After visiting about six jewellers, Sara found a ring she liked. The ring she chose was a diamond solitaire, before she could have the ring, it had to be sized to fit Sara's finger, so it would be at least two weeks before they could collect it. Tom had been expecting to pay more for the ring, so when Sara had nipped to the toilet he bought her a gold watch arranging to collect it with the ring. After the jewellers, Tom took Sara to a travel agent,

"What are we here for Tom; don't you think you've spent enough?"

"I thought it would be nice to celebrate our engagement with a weekend break in Paris"

"You old romantic, come here" said Sara pulling Tom towards her giving him a kiss.

They couldn't get a booking for four weeks, but at least there was a good chance his leg would be out of plaster and on the mend. Tom didn't want anything to ruin their special day.

By the time they had got sorted at the travel agent it was time to find somewhere to eat after a lot of hunting they decided to go to one of the all day fast food outlets for one of Toms favourite fast food meals, chicken and chips. Once they had finished their meal, Tom suggested they had another walk round the shopping centre; He had a good reason for this. He told Sara he wanted to buy them both some new clothes to go on their holiday with,

"Tom you've spent enough money on me today, just get yourself some"

"No Sara I insist"

"Will I really need any clothes for this holiday?" said Sara laughing.

"I hope not, but just in case come on" replied Tom.

They looked round several clothes shops trying on numerous outfits until they were both happy with what they had chosen. They had spent all day in Peterborough, it was time to head back to the station and catch the train back to Spalding.

Back in Spalding, they made their way back to Sara's flat. Sara made them a sandwich, just as they sat down to eat it; there was a knock on the door,

Tom answered the door to find Sam and Christine standing there, Tom let them in.

"Come on then sis, what's going on, what are you two so secretive about and don't tell us that you're not up to anything we won't believe you" said Christine,

"Tell them Sara, they're not daft" said Tom

"O.K" said Sara

Sara told her sister and Sam their plans, Tom put the kettle on and made them all a drink, Sara describing the ring and showed them the brochures on the hotel in Paris. She showed off the clothes, Tom had bought her. Christine had never seen Sara so happy and obviously very much in Love with Tom, looking at Tom there was no getting out of it the feeling was mutual. Christine and Sam were more than pleased to hear such good news for a change. Having told them how pleased they were for them and saying how they were not in the least bit surprised.

"It looks as though it's been a good day for us all Sam and I have some good news too, we have decided to find out about having our relationship blessed and if we can we would like you two to be our witnesses", said Christine

"We would love to, wouldn't we Sara?" said Tom

"Yes Sis we would, I think that's lovely" and Sara hugged her sister then gave Sam a hug.

"This calls for a celebration," said Sara; Tom suggested they all went out for a drink.

Being a Monday night and not wanting to go far they decided to go to the Pub just up the road from Sara's flat. They walked to the pub, an attractive old white building with a thatched roof set on the corner of a cross roads near to the town bridge that crosses over the river Welland, popular to the towns quieter drinkers but a place Tom, not being much of a drinker, had never visited before. Being a Monday seats were not a problem there were only a few customers in. Once they sat down Tom ordered a bottle of Champagne for them all.

"What's up with you sis?" asked Sara

Christine didn't reply, she had noticed, sitting in the opposite corner were her and Sara's parents friends Mr and Mrs Ingamells. They tried to ignore them, but it wasn't long before Mrs Ingamells noticed them and walked over to their table, she asked Christine and Sara if they where O.K at the same time totally ignoring Tom and Sam. Christine's replied that they were and so were the other two people sat with them Tom and Sam, Mrs Ingamells embarrassed apologised to them saying she didn't mean any offence, she asked if they knew that there father was very ill and had been for some time. They had no idea and if they had there wasn't a lot they could, he had made it quite obvious how he felt about Sara and Christine so why should they bother about him. However, this played somewhat on both their minds and put a bit of a shadow on the evening, they decided to finish their drinks and go back to Sara's flat. Once back at the flat the conversation soon revolved round what Mrs Ingamells had said and although their parents had made it quite obvious of their feelings for them Sam and Christine still couldn't bear the thought of anything happening to them and decided that first thing in the morning they would ride over to Bourne to see them and perhaps try and bury the hatchet.

The next morning bright and early, Sara called round to collect Christine, Bourne being only about a twenty minute ride from Spalding by car they didn't really have much time to plan what they would say, bearing in mind the last time they spoke was at Christmas and the discussion revolved round slagging each other off and Sara hitting out at Mr Ingamells, so they decided that no way would either of them be drawn into another situation like that. Having arrived at their parent's house at about ten, Sara rang the door bell, after about what seemed ages but was only minutes, the door was opened, standing there was their mother and behind her was their father wearing his dressing gown. Sara was first to speak

"Hello could we have a chat?" asked Sara

"Go on then! Chat" instructed Jack arrogantly

"Well dad, mum, Christine and I feel it's time to bury our differences and at least try to get on"

Before Sara had time to say, anymore Mr Gray butted in shouting at them,

"You must think I'm fucking daft You pair of bastards are only here because you have heard that I'm about to snuff it, and you thought you would come along here for the pickings, well you can sod off back to the gutter you came from".

Christine was non-too pleased with her father's response to their visit and she definitely wasn't going to take this off him, even if he was ill and in no uncertain terms, she gave him what for. She told him he was an arrogant stuck up piece of shit and that he should rot in hell she also told him that she had never at any time in her life had the slightest bit of respect for him and she hated him. Sara stopped her telling her, she had said enough but Christine persisted going on to say

"I wish you weren't my father. To be a bastard would in this case be a good thing, (Christine then looking at Sara said) if the truth was known Sara you wish the same don't you?"

Sara never commented, looking at her father, she saw him smirk and soon found out why.

"Well I am pleased to tell you both that you won't be disappointed then because bastards you both are, in the true meaning of the word!" Jack said

Their mother started crying and shouting at her husband saying "You promised you would never tell them, you bastard Jack, You bastard" and Eileen ran upstairs.

Sara and Christine stood there gob smacked they had no idea they were illegitimate, this man they knew as their father wasn't their father after all, in one way they found it hilarious they had often

39

talked among themselves about how they wished they had had a different father, someone who was kind and caring like other kids dads. Still standing at the door staring at this man was Christine and she was determined to get the last word in

"Well you fucking pig let me tell you something, that's the best news I've had in ages, just make sure when you snuff it I can be informed so that I can be the one who pushes your body into the furnace"

Sara laughed at her sisters comments adding she would be there to help her sister, the pair of them started laughing at him as he slammed the door.

"Well sis that wasn't quite the family sort out I had in mind" said Sara

"No, but at least it does explains why the pig had shown such a dislike towards us especially in the later years".

The big question now was if this man wasn't their father who was, both Sara and Christine knew the only person who could answer this was their mother and there was no way she would speak to them now. They made there way back to Spalding where Tom and Sam were waiting for their news on how the visit had gone.

Once in the shop Tom put the kettle on,

"Come on then what happened?" Tom asked

"Did you get it all sorted?" asked Sam

"Yes we can definitely say we sorted it can't we Chris", Sara replied

"Oh—yes there is nothing as sure as that, it has been confirmed by Mr Jack Gray that Miss Sara Gray and Miss Christine Gray are bastards and I hasten to add a bastard in the true meaning of the word" replied Christine.

The room was full of laughter,

"I take it that neither of you have sorted a thing out" said Tom

"You could put it like that" laughed Christine.

Once the laughter had died down Sara and Christine told them word for word what had been said. Neither Sam nor Tom seemed surprised, a few years earlier Sam had asked Christine if she thought there could be a chance he was not their real father because of the way he was with them. At that time, Christine brushed it off saying,

"No he is just a pig".

But Tom said he had also found the fact that any dad should want to totally disown his two daughters hard to take in. Tom asked what if anything they were going to do about the whole situation, they couldn't answer him, they had no idea what to do, Sara said she would love to know who her real father was, but they didn't even know if he was alive and if he was, did he know that he was their father. Were they the result of a sordid passionate affair if so it must have lasted at least two to three years as there is two years between Sara and Sam, is he married, could he have other children, they could have some brothers and sisters Christine butted in jokingly

"That means more bloody Christmas presents" they all laughed

"Then of cause there is the worst scenario of all we could both have different fathers", added Sara

The whole situation definitely gave the whole of that day a talking point. Tom asked them if they could remember a man in their past, they both said that they couldn't neither did they know when their parents had married or if they were married at all, but then again both their names were on both their birth certificates it gave mothers name as Eileen Gray and fathers name as Jack Gray so they must have been married, or was this just a cover up from the sordid truth. This was going to bug them, Sara said this whole situation didn't bother her, she was annoyed that she hadn't been told earlier then she would have had some understanding as to why, this man she thought to be her father had been so rotten with her and Sam, but why had their mother allowed him to have been cruel to them in their later years and why she had hidden this from them?, it explained why he didn't want them about in their earlier years. Christine agreed with what Sara had said she to found them both to be bloody hypocrites they were always preaching to them the rights and wrongs of life, the evils of gay living and their moral standards

"It's obvious they had no standards themselves perhaps this means they could be human after all" laughed Sam

"I doubt that's the case" replied Sara.

Both Christine and Sara although pleased that this pig of a man wasn't their real father, in their hearts they were a little sad.

Sara twenty three, Christine twenty four soon to be twenty five and to find out you're a bastard in the true meaning of the word does have an habit of making the strongest of people sit up and think especially if you have a sister and you're not sure if you share the same father the only consolation they had was, that they both disliked this man enough for it to become a relief finding out the truth, but did they know the truth, all they knew was their dad wasn't their dad and someone else was and the only one who could give the truth was their mother and no way would Jack (as they were now calling him, although Christine being Christine had used many other names some of which were unrepeatable), would allow their mother to speak to them. Neither Tom nor Sam could accept this, Tom said

"You have the right to know if you want the truth, and we will get it one way or another" Sam agreed,

"You just don't know our mother and how much control Jack has over her" said Christine

"Surely no one has that much control over anyone. We know you didn't have a very loving childhood so what were things like".

There was a tense silence Sara looked at Christine and said

"How would you describe our childhood Chris?"

"I don't really know there's a question Sam has asked me several times haven't you Sam"

"Yes Chris but you've never really given me a proper reply" replied Sam

"The thing is I don't really know" replied Christine,

Christine looked at Sara and said

"Come on little sister you try, you're better at putting things like this into words"

"Thanks a million big sister (Sara said in a sarcastic tone) but the thing is when you're a child things that might be strange now seem the norm then, until you start mixing with other children, so I suppose it wasn't until we went to secondary school and that being a boarding school we had even less contact with them. Although I could never understand why I suppose you notice other children were ringing their parents two or three times a week we didn't, we were not allowed home at weekends and only two weeks were spent at home during the school summer holiday and the Christmas holiday. The rest was spent at our grandparents on mums side we only went home then because Nan and Granddad went on holiday for a fortnight and when we did eventually go home they had no time for us in fact dad was a right pig and mum wasn't a lot better and as our teenage years progressed we were left to our own devises then you Chris had that massive row with them, (Sara looked at Christine) what was that row over?"

"God knows but one thing was certain that row ended by me telling that old bastard that I was a lesbian, thinking about it now that should have made me think something wasn't quite right, because he just laughed and said that just shows you're no daughter of mine but mum actually said if that's the way I wished to live my life she was happy for me and mum said she wasn't surprised, at that point the old git slung me out, but he didn't realise I was leaving that day anyway"

"Yes Chris I remember that day well, because I came home to find that pig teasing mum about her daughter being one of those bloody lessees, he asked me if I knew I said I did and asked him what of it, he looked at me with anger and said that you are sick and sad, I lost my temper with him and told him a few home truths I told him he was the sick one and he was one very sad man",

"So you weren't scared of him then Sara?" asked Tom,

"Looking back now I couldn't have been, his cruelty was mental never once was he ever physically abusive towards us" replied Sara

"The only time he showed us any attention was when they had their friends round and that wasn't very often" added Christine.

Sara went on to say how she remembered the day they threw her out, she walked out of school and decided that she wasn't going back.

"I had enough of the place, I went home and he wanted to know why I was home, I told him and he said well you can fuck off back, I told him I wasn't going, he told me to get out and stay out and find a gutter to live in along with your fucking sister then he made some sarcastic remark saying or is it your brother"

"By the sounds of it you're better off out of there to say the least he doesn't sound a very nice person" said Sam,

"Not a very person! that's a rather polite way to describe him" Christine remarked, they all laughed just then the shop door opened and a customer entered that ended the discussion, business began this subject didn't raise its ugly head again that day.

Tom had spent a further two weeks in plaster and it was time to go for a further x-ray, this time the news was good and the plaster would be removed.

"What a relief (said Tom to the doctor) I couldn't be more pleased at hearing you say that, I couldn't bear another day carrying that plaster"

Once they removed it, his leg looked a right mess it was all dry and flaking, but Tom wasn't bothered he just wanted to get it off go home and have a bath, he had forgotten one small thing, he couldn't walk on it his leg was too weak he would need physiotherapy.

Over the next week or so Tom attended physiotherapy on a daily basis until his leg was back to what Tom classed as normal, in all honesty he should have a few more weeks of treatment but Tom being Tom couldn't be doing with it and apart from that their big holiday was fast approaching and he still had a lot to do. Tom had not yet got round to collecting the ring and watch up, the jewellers had rang him to tell him that they were ready, so now his leg was better he could go over to Peterborough and fetch them without Sara knowing, so it was important he made this trip alone.

Toms business was booming although Tom was not at all happy in his work and had discussed this with Sara and often said how since his Dad had died the job didn't seem the same, Tom wanted a challenge, he was bored with selling houses he wanted a different direction when Sara asked what direction he meant Tom said

"I don't know but I need a change, work is becoming a bore and as things are I could sell the business as a going concern after all trade is more than good",

Tom and his dad had once witnessed a drop in the house market and that nearly finished them, but his Dad hung on and the good times returned

"At least at this time the business is worth a nice tidy figure, I own the building so that can be sold with the business"

Tom went on to say, he had had another local estate agent interested, also one of the bigger national companies had approached him wanting to buy him out. Sara asked why he hadn't mention this before, he said

"I didn't want to worry you or the other two because when the time is right we will all sit together and discuss this as a team, as what ever we decide will involve you all"

"What do you mean Tom?"

Tom looked Sara straight in the face.

"If I sell the business and set up something else (Tom paused) no I mean if we sell the business we will need staff to help run what ever new venture we as a team decide on, so if I thought that selling the business would mean losing you, Christine or Sam then we can forget the whole idea"

"When do you think you will sell?"

"I don't know, I suppose sooner rather than later"

"You've obviously made you're mind up, well Tom you have my full backing" said Sara putting her arms around his neck and saying

"I Love you Tom Gardener"

"I Love you too" Tom replied

"So Tom when do you intend telling Christine and Sam?"

"When do you think I should?"

"Sooner rather than later news soon fly's round this town, so as not to upset things and before anyone else tells them you should put them in the picture". Tom agreed saying

"There's no time like the present we'll close the shop for an hour over dinner go up the pub and discuss it".

Sara told Christine and Sam that Tom wanted to have a talk with them about business and that they would all be going out for dinner obviously this caused a look of concern on there faces aware that something big was on the move and causing them to be worried for their futures.

They all arrived at the pub, which was packed Tom ordered their drinks and they all ordered their food Tom insisting on paying then before Tom had chance to say anything Christine looked at Tom and said

"So Tom, when are you selling out to Greens?"

Tom was gob smacked he didn't know what to say he thought he had been so careful so as not to worry them but it appeared that Mr Green had let it slip, possibly on purpose he had said to them that he had an interest in the business and that if Christine and Sam were interested and any deal went ahead their jobs would be safe. This was the last thing Tom wanted to hear, he was furious.

"Let me try to explain",

He told them what he wanted to do and how what ever was decided would be decided between all of them and the only thing that was certain was none of them would be out of job because he wanted them to join him with the new venture what ever it may be. Tom added

"I think our Mr Green is in for a bit of a shock, there's no way Gardeners estate agents will be selling out to Greens, not after this".

There was a great look of relief on the girl's faces,

"When Christine told me what Mr Green had said I couldn't believe it, I said that there was no way I would work for that cunning pig and Christine said she felt the same, so Tom, what are your intentions?" asked Sam

"Well if you come up with some ideas and working with what budget we have we will take it from there, I think we should aim towards the fast food industry, so start thinking and then when Sara and I return from our holiday we'll set the ball rolling and in the mean time we'll keep our friend Mr Green hanging on letting him think he's still top on the list for buying us out" they all agreed.

Chapter Five

The big day came, Tom picked Sara up at about six o'clock on the Friday morning they drove down towards London, calling in at the services on the A.1 for some breakfast then onto Stanmore where they left the car and boarded the under ground. This took them through to Waterloo Station where they boarded Le Shuttle, that took them through the tunnel to Paris the capital city of Love and if any two people were in Love, undoubtedly Tom and Sara were. Once they arrived in Paris, they got a taxi to their Hotel.

Their Hotel was situated about a mile from the City centre, quite a modern Hotel and tastefully decorated in the style of the British Victorian era. Both Tom and Sara were more than happy with the look of the Hotel. Tom collected the keys for their rooms and said

"Before we go to our rooms lets have a drink in the Bar",

Sara sat at a table in the corner of the lounge, there weren't many other people in the room only two or three other couples Tom fetched the drinks and sat down, Sara asked Tom what he had meant when he said rooms, Tom told her he had booked them into single rooms Sara looked annoyed. Tom explained

"I didn't know what to do I didn't want to seem forward and I didn't want to put you on the spot after all Sara, what if I had asked for a twin room and you hadn't wanted to sleep with me"

Sara interrupted

"Shut up Tom, go to the reception tell them you've made a mistake and ask them if they could change the single rooms for one double room or it could be very awkward in a single bed"

Tom smiled and said

"What could be awkward?"

"Just do it" said Sara smiling

"Yes Miss, anything you say Miss"

Tom went and asked the girl on the reception if they had a spare double room and if they could swap, the girl called her manager he said they had got a spare double room, but if they changed, they would have to pay for one of the single rooms as well; Tom said he didn't mind this. So that was sorted. Tom went to Sara and told her the good news. Tom was very nervous, he would be sleeping with this beautiful twenty three year old girl he absolutely adored and him still a virgin at almost thirty one, he hadn't even seen a naked woman before only in books and in films in fact it had been implied by some people in the town that Tom was possibly gay, this was very far from the truth. Yes Tom had his fantasies about making love to a beautiful woman as do most men, but it just never happened, so yes he had sexual feelings towards the opposite sex but now he was to make love for the first time in his life to a woman he was head over heels in love with, Tom was worried, could he meet up to her expectation of him, would he satisfy her? Would he be as good in bed as her previous lovers? What about Sara what was she thinking, the truth of it was all Sara could think about was being with the man she loved, lying in his arms her and Tom making love together, Sara wouldn't be judging Tom on his performance Sara just wanted Tom and wasn't prepared to wait any longer for him.

The time was now getting on it was about four o'clock so they decided to go for a walk being March it was still a bit chilly outside and there had been a bit of rain but this didn't stop them, they walked for miles stopping odd times for a kiss, they were a picture of love Tom suggested as they were not tied down to having their meals at the Hotel they could find a little Pub somewhere and get something to eat, Sara agreed. They found a pub on the side of the river at the point a bridge crossed over, neither Tom nor Sara could speak French so they couldn't read what the board said they presumed it said The Bridge because there was a picture of a bridge on it, things got worse inside Sara sat down, Tom went to the Bar and tried to ordered the drinks but no one in the Pub spoke English so after about ten minutes Tom finally decided to get two beers of any type and two bags of crisps thinking it best to forget about the food and wait until they got back to the Hotel, in one sense this pleased Tom, he was relived to leave the pub this wasn't the place Tom wanted to propose to Sara he wanted everything to be right every minor detail, and knowing Sara had agreed to marry him Tom hadn't yet placed the ring on her finger . If Tom had had any fears of Sara changing her mind, this was not even a thought for Sara she was so much in love with Tom she would have been quite prepared to have got married there and then and as for detail Sara wasn't bothered with that she just wanted Tom and she was going to have him no matter what. Sara found amusement in the serious side of Tom's character, but Tom wanted everything to be right, so he got agitated when things went wrong, Sara just laughed it off she had her sister's sense of humour but not her out spoken temper. They drank their drinks and ate their crisps deciding to make their way back to the Hotel as time was now getting on and they didn't know what time they served food till.

On their way back to the Hotel they found themselves lost, after about an hour of trying to ask local people for directions they finally found a lady who could speak English and she put them back on the right track for the Hotel. By the time they reached the Hotel it was already eight thirty but as luck would have it food was still being served, so they made their way to the restaurant and found a table free in the corner. Tom asked for Lasagne and fries, Sara chose Spaghetti Carbonara and Tom asked for a bottle of their best Champagne, once they had finished a violinist appeared and started playing Tom knelt down on one knee took hold of Sara's hand and softly said to her,

"Sara you know I Love you and I know you've said you will marry me. Now I want to make it official"

Tom removed a box from his pocket opening it he took the ring out at the same time took hold of Sara's left hand and placed the ring on her third finger, Tom then handed her a small gift wrapped package, Sara quickly removed the paper and opened the box

"Oh Tom that's lovely thank you"

She threw her arms around his neck if she had hugged him any harder she would have made him choke,

"Well come on then sweetheart put it on" insisted Tom

"Yes Tom I will" said Sara placing the watch on her right wrist.

Once the mood of excitement had settled Tom opened the bottle of Champagne poured out three glasses one each for him and Sara and one for the chap playing the violin, looking at Sara Tom said

"Sara I love you" and kissed her softly on the back of the hand and they toasted their love.

Back across the water in sunny Spalding, Christine and Sam were also enjoying themselves they too had got engaged and had finally found a Vicar who would be prepared to bless their relationship, so it was good news all round, they just had to make the final arrangements. To celebrate their good news they decided to go out to the Chinese Restaurant near to the Town centre for a meal Christine ordered the house special Chow Mein plus a portion of Rice and Sam went for the King Prawns and a portion of Bamboo shoots all soaked in sweet and sour sauce washed down with a bottle of red wine, this was both their favourite meal of which they had had on several occasions only usually as a take away. Once they had finished their meal also consuming a bottle of wine between them they decided to call for a drink at an Irish Pub that had recently opened on the edge of Town. Both Christine and Sam soon reached a rather intoxicated or you could say totally pissed state, the thing is when Sam gets drunk she goes very quiet where as Christine gets rather mouthy and doesn't give a toss what she says or does, so when a couple of brave young lads saw them holding hands and kissing on their way back to their flat after leaving the pub they thought it clever to take the piss, although at first Christine ignored their insults but this made them braver, Christine then advised them to piss off, but they had to go a little bit further, so when the mouthier of the two tapped Sam on the shoulder and asked her if she had a licker licence for her friend, Sam never said a word she let go of Christine's hand turned round to face this gobby lad and punched him straight on the nose knocking him to the floor. There was Blood everywhere his mate started to shout abuse at them, Christine soon shut him up hitting him in the face and then kicked him straight in the nuts he fell next to his mate, by now a crowd had developed and were cheering the girls on, it wasn't long before the Police arrived but needless to say the lads didn't want to admit that they had just had a good hiding from a couple of girls and told the Police they had fallen over the Officer in charge laughed at them and left, the crowed cheered and some of them took the piss out of the two lads who were by now in a state of total embarrassment and were beginning to regret their behaviour so they decided without further ado to make a quick exit but were stopped by a couple of lads who insisted on them making an apology to Christine and Sam before they left, bruised and embarrassed they apologised and the crowd dispersed leaving Christine and Sam to thank the two lads.

The two lads introduced themselves as Paul and Simon explaining how they had heard the two jerks, teasing Christine and Sam from the other side of the road and were just about to cross the road to help them when Sam hit the first one and they realised help didn't appear to be needed, but they hung about just in case. They told Christine and Sam they knew them to be gay because of the comments from the lads telling them they too were gay and for years had had to put up with sick crap from pratts like those two lads and only just recently had they started hitting back now they found, people like those two never bothered them and if anyone did they would take matters into their own hands. Paul and Simon invited them back to their house for a drink and Christine and Sam accepted.

Paul and Simon lived about half a mile from Christine and Sam on the same road near where the Winsover Road became Bourne Road so not being too far and the night being dry they made their way. Once there they noticed a For Sale board in the small front garden of this small Terraced house Simon and Paul explained how they were in the process of selling and were planning to buy one they liked just up the road at Pode Hole, a small village adjacent to Spalding on the way to Bourne the only problem was just when they thought they had sold their buyers dropped out this had happened twice up to now and they were worried whether when they did finally sell, if the house they wanted would still be there. All four went inside Simon took Christine and Sam into the living room, Paul asked them how they took their drinks before going to the kitchen and putting the kettle on, he wasn't long before he turned up with a tray of Coffees and a plate of biscuits which they all tucked into.

Simon explained how he and Paul had lived there for the past three years completely modernising the house but with it being a terraced property there is only so far you can go Paul agreed and said that the house had cost a lot of money to put right as when they bought it, it was just an empty shell, the previous owner was an old man who had lived there all his life right from being a child with his parents until they passed away and for the last twenty years in the house he hadn't shown it a paint brush, the old chap was now in a nursing home somewhere near town as he could no longer cope on his own, so as you can imagine the house was in a hell of a mess but time, lots of patience and expense has brought it to this and it was now time to move on. Simon went to the cupboard and brought out some photos of the house in the state it was in when they bought it showing them to Sam and Christine both couldn't believe it was the same house they both commented on the massive change in appearance and how lovely the house was.

Time was getting on it had just turned two in the morning and Christine and Sam needed to go home so they made their excuses and left. On their way home, Christine asked Sam what she thought to Simon and Paul's house she said she thought it was lovely, asking why Christine put it to Sam that they might, if she was willing put in an offer if the price was right. Sam said that this was a great idea and that first thing in the morning they should contact the Lads estate agent.

In Paris, Tom and Sara were having a great time; they had drunk more champagne than enough and were rather tipsy, although still very much in control of themselves. They finished their drinks, Sara looked across at Tom and held out her hand, and Tom reached across and took it, and after a short pause led her up to their room.

Tom unlocked the door, took Sara in his arms and carried her to the bed, kissing her passionately. He laid her down and slowly began to undress her, and she him. (Tom not having seen a naked woman before, he was trying hard to control himself, at the same time worrying as to whether he would satisfy her). He started to kiss her, starting with her face, down her neck, her chest and stomach until he reached her most intimate spot. The excitement was too much for

Sara, who shuddered with excitement and orgasm, but Tom hadn't finished yet and quickly brought her to yet another orgasm and again, Sara had never felt so fulfilled. She took Tom into her arms and kissed him more passionately than before, she kissed and caressed him and brought him to an orgasm.

They lay in each other's arms completely at one and both thinking about how much sleep they wouldn't have that night.

It wasn't until about five in the morning when they fell to sleep with Tom being the first to wake around ten he quickly had a shower before making Sara a coffee waking her with a kiss on the cheek telling her how much he loved her she returned the kiss, she soon drank her coffee then insisted that Tom joined her in the shower, although he had only just dried from one shower he didn't need asking twice and joined Sara knowing she had an ulterior motive to get him in the shower and how right he was, they made love in the shower and then in the bed, before agreeing it was time to get dressed and have a bit of very late breakfast.

After breakfast with the time now getting on for eleven thirty Tom suggested they did a bit of sight seeing and added that they should ring Christine and Sam to see how things were at home, Sara objected to this saying they had only been gone for one night but Tom being a worrier insisted.

However things at home were far from well, Christine and Sam had been woken early that morning seven thirty to be precise to the sounds of someone knocking on there door and when Sam opened the door it shocked her to see a Police man and Police woman standing there Sam invited them in called to Christine they all went into the lounge and sat down, the Police asked Christine if her sister was in London Yesterday with a friend, Christine said yes but as far as she knew they caught a train to Paris, she then asked why they wanted to know the Police then said that their car had been involved in a serious road traffic accident on the M25 and the two people in their car had been killed, Christine became hysterical and uncontrollable the Police said until they had a definite identification they couldn't be sure it was Tom and Sara, hysterically Christine insisted she was to be the one to identify them, the Police left saying that they would make arrangements and would be in touch later that morning, on leaving the Police woman seeing the state Christine was in asked Sam if she wanted her to ask Christine's Doctor to call, Sam said she would sort it and shut the door returning to console Christine who was still in a very tearful state. Sam called the Doctor, he gave her some Tranquillisers to help her calm down.

The morning seemed to drag for Christine and Sam, waiting for a phone call and when the phone finally rang around Ten Sam took the call it was the Police woman telling them arrangements had been made for Christine to go and identify the two bodies asking Sam if she would accompany her, Sam said she would and the Police woman said a car would pick them up around midday, Sam put the phone down and told Christine what the Police had said. No sooner had Sam finished telling Christine than the phone rang again Sam answered it and when she heard the voice on the other end Sam dropped the phone and shouted for Christine, Christine rushed into the hall way where the phone laid, Christine still in shock herself

"What's up Sam?"

Sam couldn't get the words out, Christine picked the phone up and when she heard who the caller was she burst into tears Sam who by now had got control of herself took the phone off Christine and spoke to the caller who happened to be Tom. Tom couldn't weigh up what was going on all he could hear was two hysterical women and when

Christine finally told him the whole story he couldn't believe how this sort of mistake had happened Tom was furious

"Why hasn't anyone thought to check if we had arrived at the Hotel in Paris?"

Tom wanted some questions answering, he put the phone down to Christine after he had finally convinced her that everything was fine and they hadn't been involved in an accident and as far as Tom and Sara were concerned, they were very much alive and the whole thing had been one very big mistake and he would be ringing the Police himself to ask them what the hell had happened.

Having put the phone down Tom told Sara what had been going on Sara was absolutely furious and upset to think Christine and Sam had been put through so much because of someone's incompetence.

Sara suggested they paid a visit to the Police in Paris Tom agreed so once they had got directions to the Police station from the hotel reception they made their way. Once there they had no problem finding a Policeman who could understand, Tom told him the whole story the French Police then contacted the Police in London they had a bit of a job finding the department who had been dealing with the incident, but once through they got the whole mess sorted out.

The Police told Tom and Sara that their car had been involved in a serious R.T.A with another vehicle and all involved had been killed.

In the car they found Sara's driving licence, the car was registered to a Mr Tom Gardener from Spalding obviously Tom had no next of Kin but they found out through a neighbour of Toms that he had a girl friend called Sara whose driving licence they had found and it all pointed to Tom and Sara being the two bodies found in the wreckage of the car, but now it seems that this couple had stolen Toms car from Stanmore Station car park and who ever these people were their stupidity had cost them dearly, so the Police could only go on the information they had, no one had thought to mention that they were on their way to Paris so the Police didn't have any other information to follow.

Tom and Sara were completely gob smacked, Tom informed the police that Christine had told them they were in Paris; the English-speaking police officer just shrugged his shoulders

"That Mr Gardener, is something you will have to take up with the English police we can't comment".

Tom and Sara decided to cut their losses and go home, only this was also a problem they would have no car so they would have to make the whole journey by Train,

"What the hell am I going to say to my insurer's two new cars in one year they're not going to believe this" laughed Tom.

Tom and Sara booked out of their Hotel and made their way to the Station but before they handed their room key in, Sara insisted on making one last use of the bed, almost tearing Toms clothes in her haste to get him back in bed, their session didn't last long, just a very quick quickie.

They put their now somewhat creased clothes back on and made their way. Their journey took them back through the Tunnel and on to Waterloo then catching a train to Peterborough.

At Peterborough Sara rang Christine, Christine was so pleased to here Sara's voice, Sara said they would call and see them later that day. Tom suggested they had a bite to eat before catching the train back to Spalding, Sara agreed and they made their way to the city centre to find a café. They soon found a café set back in a side street Tom ordered two cream teas and they sat and chatted about the past events, Tom although involved in the conversation Sara couldn't help but notice she hadn't got Tom's full attention,

"What's on your mind Tom (Tom didn't answer he just stared at the door, Sara nudged him) what's bothering you Tom" Sara asked,

"Sorry Sara love I was just thinking we've been in here for about twenty minutes and during that time this café has seen a complete change in customers so I'm wondering how many people actually walk in and out that door each day and how much money changes hands"

"What are you getting at Tom?"

"Fast food Sara, people will always buy food and lets face it what we've just eaten cost us near enough a fiver and it's the same stuff that you would get for a pound possibly pound fifty in a supermarket, so even with their overheads there must be a substantial profit, honestly Sara I think it's the sort of direction we should look too".

Sara advised Tom not to be too hasty and to weigh the whole situation up before rushing into things, Tom agreed. Time was getting on and they made their way back to the station to catch the train back to Spalding.

The train arrived at Spalding at just on six and once they were off the train they made their way back to Sara's flat for a wash and change of clothes, before they headed for Christine and Sam's place and of course due to the fact Tom was yet again without a car they needed to pick up Sara's car.

Chapter Six

Tom and Sara arrived at Christine and Sam's house about seven and to say Christine and Sam were pleased to see them was an understatement, Christine was very tearful, Sam insisted they had some tea with them, they agreed and Tom said he would nip to the pub up the road and get a couple of bottles of wine

Sam insisted on making the tea and told Sara and Christine to go into the lounge while she put something together. Tom wasn't gone long and soon he returned with three bottles of wine and eight cans of beer commenting on how much the pub had charged him compared to what it costs at the supermarket, they all laughed, Sara said

"It just shows how out of touch you are with Pub prices Tom",

Tom agreed and without further comment asked Sam for four glasses and a corkscrew to open the wine and poured out three gasses of wine and Tom had a glass of Beer. It wasn't long before Sam brought the food out she had made them a tossed Salad, oven chips and a Pizza, this went down great with all of them and it wasn't long before they, between them polished the lot off and also it would be fair to say the wine and the beer was also disappearing rather quickly so by the time the clock struck eleven neither Tom or Sara were in a fit state to leave Christine and Sam's flat, so both of them slept on the sofa. To say the least none of them looked that healthy. The following day being a Tuesday meant someone would have to open the office so reluctantly Christine volunteered saying it was just as well they lived within walking distance as she was in no fit state to drive and she would still be over the legal limit for alcohol, Tom told her they would join her soon but he fell back to sleep only to be woken an hour later by the phone ringing, it was Christine wanting to know when they were coming in, Tom woke Sara and Sam they quickly washed and dressed and walked to the office where Christine was in a total panic,

"That bloody phone hasn't stopped ringing from the moment I walked in the door, when I answered one phone the other phone rang" complained Christine,

She was so relieved when the others walked in she told them the local Press had been on the phone wanting to come round to the office and interview them all. The press told Christine they would ring in a couple of hours when the other three arrived. This was the sort of thing they could all well do without, so they all decided they would not give the press a story, so when the press did finally ring Tom took the call and told the lass on the other end of the phone they weren't interested in letting them do a story but Tom being Tom when the lass pleaded with him he hadn't got the heart to tell her where to get off, so he gave her permission to come round to the office after work and do a story.

The Press arrived about five thirty and after taking a couple of photo's, Tracey the girl from the press took their story when it came to talking to Christine (although the others couldn't understand why) there appeared to be friction between them, it was quite obvious they knew each other as when Tracey had finished her business, she went over to Christine and said something to her that put an expression on her face that what ever Tracey had said as she was leaving she hadn't wanted the others to hear. None of them made any comment to Christine but when Sam and Christine got home, Sam asked her if she had known the girl from the Press,

"I've never seen her before Sam"

"I don't believe you Christine",

Sam persisted on the issue until Christine admitted she had known Tracey but Sam wanted to know the full story, Sam could tell there was a lot more to Christine and Tracey than just a past meeting so reluctantly Christine told Sam all, she Said

"When I was fourteen and had just been into Hospital to have my appendix out Tracey was at the Hospital to we formed a friendship and we kept in touch and we remained friends for years after and that was it".

"And what else Christine?" Sam said

"That's all there is to it" Christine replied,

"Bull shit Chris, why don't you just tell me the whole bloody story and cut the crap out or I might form my own thoughts on this Tracey",

After a lot of shouting and screaming Christine gave in to Sam's pleading for the whole story so Christine told her how yes they had met in hospital but their friendship over the next few months had become more than just friends they ran away together only to be picked up by the Police,

"I'll bet that pleased your parents" said Sam interrupting

"I don't think at that point they twigged on I was gay"

"So what happened next Chris?"

"We were then separated but we finally arranged to meet in York where I kept Tracey hidden in my room for about a year Tracey posed as another student and somehow we managed to get away with it".

Sam was so intrigued Christine had never talked about her past relationships before in fact Sam thought she had been Christine's first and only love after all Christine was her first girl friend, although in fairness neither of them had ever discussed previous loves and lovers, Sam thought perhaps it was time they told each other the whole story of their past's. Christine went on to tell Sam how every thing went pear shape when she caught Tracey in bed with two girls from the school one of them only two days earlier had been teasing Christine calling her the Lincolnshire lezzy and threatening to beat her up and now there was this same girl in bed with Tracey and another girl who Christine didn't recognise. Within minutes of Christine entering the room things got rather nasty they were now insisting on Christine joining them, but Christine decided it was time she took control Christine grabbed one of the two girls by the hair dragged her out of the bed across the floor of the flat opened the door and dragged her into the corridor where she let go of her hair the girl still naked and very embarrassed, the other girl seeing what had happened to her friend decided it was a good idea to make a quick exit so when she returned to her room there was just her and Tracey who was now in tears and begging for forgiveness.

"What did you do Christine?"

"Sam I was besotted by her and she knew it, so I never mentioned it again, and then Tracey suggested we involved other people in our relationship including men, I agreed" Christine said

"I had never slept with a man, but I would have done anything for her and then things became more weird she started smoking the wacky backy and then she went on to the hard stuff, money went missing she was always with different men and woman I couldn't cope with all that and I threw her out".

"Did you miss her Christine?" Sam asked

"Yes Sam at that time I did and I would be lying to you if I said I didn't. I tried to take my mind off her by ploughing my heart into school work she kept trying to ring me I did agree once to meet her but backed out at the last minute and then I met you and you Sam are every thing she isn't so that is well in my past and when I saw her Today I was shocked to see she had a wedding ring on and was very pregnant. She has obviously settled down"

"She isn't a threat to me Chris is she?" Sam asked

"No Sam I love you, that's my past in every sordid detail and now you're my future a future I intend to enjoy with you Sam and only you, so what about you Sam, do you have a skeleton or two hiding in any of them cupboards"

"I wish" replied Sam

"You know all there is to know Chris like you I was bullied at school about my sexuality, never slept with a man although I did once have a boyfriend we did every thing else apart from going the whole way",

"Why?" Christine interrupted

"I was scared of getting pregnant and it didn't seem right so thankfully he dumped me but thinking back now I only let him go as far as he did so he would tell his friends and they would think I was straight and stop teasing me, it didn't work because after he dumped me I had a one stand with his sister although she never admitted it at the time. She told every one at school that I had tried to touch her up in the showers at the school and she had slapped my face for doing it the truth was she came into the showers and asked me to have sex with her and she would stop the others bullying and teasing me, so I did as she asked but things got worse, she even told my step parents and they threw me out calling me a freak"

"But I thought you said I was your first"

"Well in a round about sort of way you were, with others it was more like heavy petting as with you—well you know what I mean"

"So your step parents threw you out and that explains why you were in the children's home then" Christine said,

"Yes"-replied Sam,

"Why didn't you ever tell me?" Asked Christine,

"You've never asked and it's no longer important" replied Sam.

With all this talk of both of their past's both of them asking more and more questions, Christine asked Sam what happened to her real parents although Christine could see this upset Sam Christine persisted Christine had no idea Sam had been adopted, so were her parents still alive and if they were then why hadn't they tried to contact her and why hadn't she them. Perhaps they were dead, was her mother single? Maybe her new partner didn't know about Sam, but before she had time to put these questions to Sam the door bell rang, Sam answered it, it was Simon and Paul, Sam invited them in,

"Do you fancy going for a drink?" Simon asked them

"Where to?" enquired Christine

"Well we thought we could walk over to Low Fulney There's a pub come Restaurant over there we'll have a drink and get a Taxi back" said Paul.

"I don't think much to that word walk can't we get a Taxi both ways" said Christine

"You lazy bitch come on lets get ready and we'll walk, it'll do you good" said Sam and without further ado they got changed and made their way by foot.

The Pub at Low Fulney was about an hours walk from Christine and Sam's flat so this gave them plenty of time to tell the boys about the past events. They told them about how they thought Sara and Tom had been killed only to find out someone had stolen their car and how the Press had called to do a story on what had happened and take some Photo's of all four of them and Sam took this opportunity to get a bit of a dig in about Tracey, teasing Christine about her, Christine laughed her jokes off although it definitely hit a very sensitive spot. After the boys had listened to what Sam and Christine had to say Paul said

"Well our last few days seem to have been a damn site better than you ladies have had"

"Why's that?" asked Sam

"Well we've finally sold the house" said Simon,

The look on Christine and Sam's faces told Simon and Paul this did not please them Paul asked them whether there was a problem, Christine explained

"After we saw your house the other day and you told us you were selling it we fell in love with it and Sam and I decided to see about making you an offer but other things as we explained took the front seat of our minds so we lost out, never mind life's a shit"

"Sorry girls" Paul said

"But if the other buyers back out we'll let you know straight away".

They arrived at the pub at around eight and all bought a round of drinks each, Christine said she felt rather hungry, Simon commented he could eat a Horse, quick-witted Sam said,

"Looks like we'll have a Chinese then they do a good Horse".

Paul rang for a Taxi asking for it to collect them at quarter to eleven and drop them at the Chinese take away in the town.

They arrived at the Chinese just before Eleven, sat in a corner waiting for her order was Tracey, Christine ignored her but Sam insisted on speaking to her after all Sam wasn't too bothered whether she upset Tracey or not after the way she had treated Christine also she had just had four beers which gave her a bit more courage than usual so she thought what the heck and walked straight over to her put her face close up to hers looked her in the eyes.

"So sweetheart tell me what made you chose Spalding as a place to live"

"If you must know I don't live in Spalding although it's none of your business I live in Holbeach" Tracey replied sarcastically, Christine tried to pull Sam away but Sam wasn't finished,

"I've never met you before today, Christine hasn't spoke to you in years, you knew Christine lived in Spalding and we see you twice in one day I might be wrong but I don't call it a coincidence, I think you used your job to get into our lives, well let me tell you, you little slut if you come near us again I'll fucking floor you, do I make myself clear"

"If you think I'm here because of her, you are wrong" Tracey said

"I suggest you collect your food from the counter and go"

Tracey not bothering to answer Sam took her food and left. They all looked at Sam gob smacked

"You definitely told her" commented Paul

"Yes, she worries me" Sam said and she burst into tears, Christine put her arm around Sam

"Sam you're being silly, there was no need for any of that. You silly bitch I love you, she's what I said to you earlier, she's in my past. You played right into her hands doing what you did just then, having a go at her like that, she now knows she bothers you and Tracey being Tracey won't leave it at that you would have been better just to have ignored her"

Paul agreed but Simon reminded him of a similar incident where Paul had had a go at one of Simon's previous partners no more was said and they decided to head back to Christine and Sam's flat to eat their Chinky.

Back at the flat Sam got the plates out and Christine emptied the trays of food onto the plates only to realise something wasn't quite right, they had two extra trays of food and no bag with the chips in, Sam burst into a fit of laughter realising what had happened then the others realised with the argument in the Chinese, Tracey hadn't noticed she had picked up their bag containing four small bags of chips by mistake and they had taken her meal, Sam said

"I'm going to enjoy this knowing that bitch has paid for it and she has landed up with four bags of chips".

Chapter Seven

Over the next four or five weeks life settled down, their five minute claim to fame, came and went and the local paper with the picture of all four of them was now being used to wrap up fish and chips.

Tracey had not been seen again since the episode in the Chinese and unfortunately for Christine and Sam, Simon and Paul's house buyers had not backed out and they were just waiting on a moving date.

Tom and Sara seemed happy with their lives they were just about living together if Tom wasn't sleeping at Sara's, Sara would be sleeping at Tom's and they would always be seen holding hands if they were out together. Tom still wanted to sell the business but wasn't sure which way to go when he did, He needed a change but at the same time he was scared, the estate agent life was all Tom knew but he was getting to the state where he hated going to work in the mornings.

One Thursday afternoon just as Sara was on her way out of the office to nip to the bank who should walk through the door but Mr Green, Sara stopped and asked him if she could help him with anything, in his well known and abrupt manner he told her that he was quite capable of sorting out what he had come for himself and she should get on with her office duties, Sara called him a Pig and went off to the Bank. Mr Green then proceeded towards Tom's office knocked on the door and walked in shutting the door behind him. He didn't even look at Christine and Sam. After about ten minutes Sara came back, she didn't look too happy, Mr Green was still in the office with Tom, Tom rang through to Sara and asked her if she would bring two coffees through, while she was on the phone she told Tom how Mr Green had spoke to her on entering the shop and how he had ignored Christine and Sam, Tom didn't comment and asked her to come into his office and forget the coffees. Sara went into Tom's office and shut the door behind her; Tom introduced Sara to Mr Green,

"Sara this is Mr Green he's interested in buying the business, Mr Green this is Sara my fiancée, the girl who you was rude to, on your way in here and the other two girls, in case you're interested, that lass there with the dark hair is Christine, Sara's sister and the lass sat at the side of her with the blond hair is Sam, Christine's partner",

Tom then said to Sara

"Open the front door please Sara, Mr Green is leaving", without another word Mr Green walked out.

About three weeks later Tom told Sara that a company from Peterborough were paying them a visit and were interested in the business. The chap a Mr Roberts a well-spoken and very polite man arrived to see them on the Thursday morning and seemed very impressed, taking them all out for dinner before leaving to go back to Peterborough. When he had gone, Tom called Sara through to his office to put her in the picture. Apparently, Mr Roberts was interested in buying the whole business but he wanted Sara, Sam and Christine to stay on and run the shop and Tom to would be required to stay on for three months after completion of sale. Tom was now in a bit of a predicament and asked Sara what he should do, Sara suggested he asked Christine and Sam what they thought, so after work he asked Christine and Sam to hang on and Tom put it to them, Tom told them that within six months of him leaving he hoped to have something else on the go and hoped they would join him, obviously that was totally up to them, but he would promise he would see them right what ever they decided, Tom then said he didn't want them to decide anything now, to go away and talk about it with each other as he and Sara would be because even Tom wasn't sure this is what he really wanted.

Over the next few weeks Mr Roberts paid several visits to the shop always polite to the girls and they all seemed to like him but Tom still wasn't sure he was doing the right thing and decided to call all the girls together and discuss the whole situation in a more relaxed atmosphere so he asked Sara to book a table at a wine bar in town for that Friday.

Arriving at the wine bar, Tom ordered their meals from the set menu, Christine decided that before Tom had a chance to say anything, Christine being Christine decided she would tell him of her and Sam's intentions'

"Tom if you sell up, you needn't think we're stopping, we're a team. We all work well together and if we split as a team, Sam and I are moving on"

Tom wasn't quite expecting this sort of response, although he was happy that they thought this, Tom too didn't want to split them up he loved working with them, he agreed they should stay together, but Mr Roberts had laid down the terms of the sale and it was now up to Tom to give him his terms or withdraw from the sale after all nothing had been signed.

After they had decided they were staying together as a team no matter what, Tom insisted on no more shoptalk he ordered the drinks and told them he would sort things out the following morning with Mr Roberts.

After four or five rounds of drinks Tom order them a Taxi as none of them were in any fit state to drive and the fact it was absolutely pouring down outside it seemed the only option. When the Taxi arrived Tom suggested they all went back to his house and he would open a bottle or two, three, or maybe four if they were still standing, they all agreed.

Back at Toms, as he was a man of his word, he went to the fridge and took out a bottle of red and a bottle of white wine to which Sam pointed out in rather a pissed voice.

"Red wine should be served at room temperature not chilled" Tom laughed

"That shows how much I know about wine, come to think of it I've never tried red wine before Sara normally drinks it and she's never commented, have you Sara"

"No only because I hadn't got the heart to tell you, but if you noticed I always leave it standing in the glass for a while before I'd drink it, don't I my sugar plum" Sara replied,

"Yes well I'm not going to get out of the fact I'm definitely no connoisseur in wine am I" Tom said,

"No, but there are things that matter, that you do know your stuff on Tiger" Sara jested,

"Oh yes and what's that?" asked Tom,

"Well I think we'd better discuss this another time, when I can show you what I mean and not just tell you—" Sara said, and they all laughed

"Don't mind us, this is getting quite interesting" Sam said

Suddenly Christine in a loud slurred voice, said

"Look over there"

"Where?" asked Sam,

"There" said Christine,

"I must be blind because I can't see anything" replied Sam,

"That machine over there by the window" Christine said,

"I think she's on about the Karaoke machine" Tom said,

"Yes"-said Christine,

"That bloody Karaoke machine that's it, does it work Tom"

"Yes"-said Tom,

"Well—you'd better get it out and turn it on because me and Sam are a bit partial to Karaoke aren't we Sam" said Christine,

"Only when we're pissed" replied Sam,

So without further ado Tom did as the girls asked and switched the Karaoke machine on, asking Christine what songs she wanted on

"Anything, you choose" She said in a very pissed voice.

Tom picked out a couple of well known songs and put them on, the first, a Country and Western song and when Christine started singing it sounded like nothing on this earth and the fact she was drunk, didn't make it sound any better. Having heard Christine's attempt Tom suggested Sam had a go Sam choice was 'Missing' Sam was definitely a massive improvement on Christine. Sara's choice 'Think Twice' left the lot of them totally gob smacked, none of them had ever heard Sara sing before, she had a beautiful voice even though she had drank more than usual, then it came to Tom's attempt 'Hello Again' and if there had been a sober audience he would have received a standing ovation without doubt. This was definitely a talent Tom had never shared with anyone before. Christine said

"If it's the drink bringing this sound out then I suggest Tom—you should swim in it",

Sara was speechless, she insisted he sang another song but Tom was getting a bit embarrassed so he suggested Christine had another go but Sam quickly intervened and said she thought Sara should sing another reluctantly Sara agreed just to keep Christine away from the microphone. Sara had another go, the same beautiful voice, but with more confidence. Christine suggested Tom and Sara sang a song together Sam also thought this would be good, but Tom said he didn't think he could stand up long enough to do another and he was going to have to go bed before he fell and Sara agreed she to was tired so Tom showed Christine and Sam to the spare room while Sara got them some extra blankets and clean Towels for the morning.

The next morning Sam woke in a panic Christine had disappeared Sam rushed into Tom and Sara's room they went to investigate, after about five minutes and Sam still in utter panic they heard a moaning sound coming from under the bed Tom noticed a hand appearing from under the bed and Christine's voice in some state of panic, they realised what had happened, then her feet appeared,

"Grab her feet and pull her out" said Sara, Christine shouted

"No, no go away I'll be all right, I'm—"

But before she had chance to say another word Tom had pulled her from under the bed. It was hard to decide who was the most embarrassed Tom or Christine, Christine was totally naked and trying her hardiest to grab a blanket and get to her feet at the same time, Sara and Sam were in fits of hysterics so they couldn't help her and Tom now starting to see the funny side had also dropped into hysterics, Christine had got to the point where she thought sod it and stopped trying to cover herself up and was now seeing the funny side of the whole situation, her panic lapsed and turned to laughter.

Tom and Sara left the room so that Sam could help Christine sort herself out. Sara had a shower and Tom made a start on the breakfast and Sara set the table Sam suggesting that seeing that the rain had stopped from last night and it was a lovely sunny morning that they should have Breakfast on the Patio, Tom agreed. Tom soon had the food cooked up and Christine and Sam joined them outside in the garden

"Good god it's Christine I didn't recognise you with your clothes on" said Tom laughing

"Shut it Gardener" replied Christine smiling and sat down to Breakfast.

After breakfast, they all helped to clear away and Tom put the kettle on making them all a drink returning outside where they all sat and chatted. Tom was interested to how Christine had come to be under the bed. Christine said

"I don't really know, I can remember getting up in the night for a wee and when I came back to the room I think I must have lay on the floor instead of the bed and I must have rolled over a couple of times and landed up under the bed,

"Yes I can see what you've done, at home we sleep on a mattress on the floor, being pissed and not realising you lay on the floor you silly Bitch" said Sam laughing,

"I thought it was hard" added Christine

"And I remember thinking, that bloody Tart she's nicked all the blanket's and when I woke up and all I could see was—well I don't know what I could see and that's when I panicked and you lot came in",

"Don't you wear anything in bed?" Tom asked,

"You nosey bugger" Sara joked,

"No inquisitive, it sounds better", Tom said,

"Well if you must know, we don't, neither Sam nor I have ever worn a thing in bed have we Sam?" Christine said.

"No and if you're really interested we find it very exciting and I mean sexually exciting, don't we Chris" Sam added.

All this banter Tom was starting to get rather embarrassed and wishing he hadn't asked the question and kept his mouth shut. Christine then added

"I always find two nakcd bodies laying together especially of the same sex very exciting don't you Tom (not allowing him to answer she continued while Sara and Sam sat there trying to hold a straight face) It's like when I'm lay in bed with Sam the thought of her just being naked sends shivers though my spine, and it almost brings me to an orgasm, I just can't help it Tom, so Tom what sexual fetish's do you have"

"It's a lovely day shall we all go out" said Tom changing the subject,

Sara, Sam and Christine burst into fits of uncontrollable laughter. After about five minutes things had calmed down and Tom suggested again that they all should go out for the day,

"Where Tom" asked Sara

"What about Cromer" Sam said

"I'm all for that, Cromer one place I've never been, what about you Christine" said Sam excitedly

"Yes I'm all for Cromer" Christine replied,

"So, I'll make a picnic" said Sara

"No Sara we'll get some fish and chips there. On the way there, it wouldn't be a bad idea to call at the garage and sort out about getting another car" said Tom

"Well if I were you I wouldn't bother cleaning it" laughed Sam

"I wonder how long you'll have this one for, I dread to think how much your insurance is going to be this year" commented Sara

"So do I Sara, so do I".

Chapter Eight

They decided to use Sara's car, being the only one that fitted four comfortably. On the way, they called at the garage and Tom placed an order on a new car; however, the one Tom had originally wanted in the colour he wanted, meant Tom would have to wait six weeks for delivery so he ordered his second choice. Tom joined the others who were waiting patiently in Sara's car and they continued on their way to Cromer. The drive to Cromer takes about two hours from Spalding, although they did get caught in a bit of standing traffic and while in the queue a couple of young lads in an open top car thought it clever to make an improper remark to Sam through her open window, the remark being that they wouldn't mind giving her one and when Sam ignored them they had to go a little further and then further still until Christine who had just about had enough of these two silly little boys got out of the car which was still in standing traffic taking with her a can of fizzy drink walked calmly up to the lad's car and said to them,

"I want you to apologise to my girlfriend"

The lads made the drastic mistake of laughing at her, Christine turned away from them shook the can of drink in her hand several times turned back towards them open the can and dropped it into their car. The panic on their face, was a picture, Tom, Sara and Sam were laughing as were other car drivers around them, who had witnessed the whole business the only ones who didn't laugh were the boys they were to busy trying to avoid the spray of fizzy drink shooting out the can all over the inside of their car and Christine still calm although she was finding it hard not to laugh returned back to the car.

They arrived in Cromer about eleven and decided to go for a walk round the town. Sam said she would like to buy some fresh Crab to take home, Sam had never tried fresh Crab before and neither had Christine. There was definitely no shortage of shops selling Crab almost every other shop advertised Crab for sale and all being around the same price, Tom suggested that she waited until they were about to leave, so that the crab didn't go off with the heat, Sam agreed. Tom said

"Why don't we go to the top of the church and have a look at Cromer from up there",

Sara and Sam they readily agreed, Christine said

"I think I'll—if you lot don't mind—I'll stay down here",

"You bloody coward" commented Sara

"Yes you're right, I am" replied Christine.

Tom, Sara and Sam made their way up the narrow stone stairs to the top of the tower. Once at the top they could see for miles leaving Christine viewing the church and its surroundings from the ground. Christine decided to sit outside the church in the shade from the Sun only to be disturbed by the sounds of two voices she recognised from earlier, it was the two lads in the open top car, Christine pretended not to see them, but the one who had had the most mouth recognised her and seeing she was on her own, thought he would have a go at her, he went over to her and started firing abuse at her. Christine told him to grow up and go away, this made his remarks more abusive and there was no way Christine was going to take this and just as she was about to give him what for Tom appeared from no where, grabbed the lad by the scuff of the neck, his friend decided to try to help his mate but Tom see him coming and grabbed him as well with his other hand shoving them both to the floor, his mate wasn't in a hurry to get back up but the other one was still in a rather brave mood and decided to try his luck at Tom, getting to his feet and taking a swing at Tom, Tom ducked and he lost his balance and fell. This time Tom picked him up by the back of his neck, put his arm behind his back and pinned him face up to the church wall, then said to the lad

"I suggest that you and your little friend go as far away from us as you can get in ten seconds or you could be chewing you're next meal through your arse, before you go, apologise to my friends for the way you spoke to them (Tom then still holding him by the back of the neck and his arm behind his back turned him to face Sam and said to the lad) Come on then what are going to say to my friend Sam for what you said when she was in the car totally ignoring you and you made those childish, schoolboy remarks"

The lad now petrified and shaking said

"Sorry lady",

Tom then turned him towards Christine and now in a sarcastic voice said to the lad

"Now this is Christine, what do you have to say to her?"

"Sorry miss" The lad replied.

Tom putting his mouth close to the lad's ear said in a very quiet voice so that onlookers couldn't hear

"Now fuck off out of my sight you, little bag of shit, if I see you again, I will rip your fucking head off and shit down your throat. Now go"

Without looking back, he went, catching up with his mate who was now viewing the situation from a distance, just as they had disappeared from sight the Police turned up asking Tom what had been going on, they had had reports of an incident, Tom played it down and the Police left. Tom was quite chuffed at the way he handled the whole situation and the girls to were quite impressed.

"Why don't we go and get some fish and chips for dinner and sit on the front and eat them" suggested Tom.

The others agreed. After dinner Sara suggested they drive along the coast road to Wells and then onto Hunstanton, Sam said she would love to go along the coast road as long as she could get some fresh crabs, Christine and Tom were more than happy to move on after what had happened earlier. So they walked back to the car and headed to Wells joining the coast road. Tom knowing there to be a florist just off the main road between Salthouse and Clay next to the Sea asked Sara to pull in so he could get some flowers to lie on the beach where he had spread his mother and fathers ashes.

At Wells, Tom left the girls to wander round the small town while he made his way to the beach walking along the bank path, where he and his father had often walked, in total silence making their way to place flowers on the spot where his mothers ashes were and now Tom was doing the same trek on his own. Reaching the beach Tom lay the flowers on the spot where their ashes had been spread then taking control of his thoughts, he made his way back to the town centre where the others were, they never mentioned his visit to the beach, they all knew this was private to Tom, Sara just hugged him on his return as she could tell he had shed a tear or two.

While Tom had been at the beach, the girls had been window shopping and Sara had seen a shop selling paintings of Wells Harbour that she wanted Tom to have a look at, so leading the way Sara took Tom to the shop showing him the paintings she asked him what he thought. Tom studied the paintings closely and then looking at Sara said

"Which one do you like Sara?"

"I'm not bothered, I quite like all them all" replied Sara

"Well why don't we choose one each and we'll keep them for our bottom draw".

Sara laughed

"Bottom draw" she said

"Are you bloody thick or something he's trying to tell you something Sara" Christine interrupted jokingly

"Yes I am and I won't take no for an answer" Tom said,

"Well" Sara said

"I must be bloody thick because I haven't a clue what you're on about Tom",

"Look, we've been together since December, Engaged since April, I know it isn't long, but Sara I know what I want us to do",

"For Gods sake some one tell me what the hell he's on about" Sara said.

"I want us to get married, or at least make a date," Tom announced.

"Well you stupid fool why didn't you say, of course I think that's a great idea but when" Sara inquired.

"What about next April the third, that's one year after our engagement and also making it a millennium wedding" Tom said.

"I'm gob smacked" Sara replied.

"Sod being gob smacked, what's your answer" Christine asked.

"Yes—" Sara shouted.

"I think that's a yes Tom" Sam laughed.

Sara was close to tears.

"Tom why did you wait until Christine and Sam were with us, to ask me, and why did you wait until we are at Wells, I would have given you the same answer" asked Sara

"I know it maybe sounds silly to you three, but—as you know both my mother and fathers ashes are here, my Dad asked my Mum to marry him down this same street and if there is a life after death and they can hear us and see us I want them to hear your answer, and Christine and Sam—well, they are our friends and I wanted them to witness this day".

Sara holding back the tears, said

"Tom Gardener, I love you—I want you to take me to the beach",

Looking at Christine and Sam Sara said,

"Would you mind waiting here, I have something very important to do I won't be long"

Christine looked at her sister with a massive smile

"You take all the time you need, Sam and I will be in that Café on the corner over there and Sara I am really happy for you and you're the best sister a sister could wish for and what's even better you're my best friend, I love you Sara"

"I love you to Chris, thanks. We won't be long".

Leaving Christine and Sam outside the shop looking at the paintings Sara had admired so much; they turned to watch Sara and Tom walk hand in hand towards the beach.

"Don't they look good together Chris?"

"Yes Sam they do, they are two very lucky people".

Once Tom and Sara reached the beach Sara turned to Tom kissed him on the lips and said

"Stay here sweetheart and wait for me, I'll be five minutes"

Sara removed her shoes and handed them to Tom, Tom never questioned Sara on her reasons, he did as she asked watching her as she walked off across the raised wooden foot path onto the sand almost treading in Toms foot prints passing the line of small raised wooden Victorian style changing huts, that lined up like a row of proud soldiers on her left, towards the bunch of flowers that lay in the same place on the sand where Tom had placed them about an hour earlier. When Sara reached, the flowers she knelt down beside them touched them and looking directly at them quietly said

"I never met you Mrs Gardener, Tom talks about you a lot and I'm sure if we had met we would have been good friends. Mr Gardener, I remember you well and I have a lot to thank you for, as you were the one who introduced me to Tom. As you probably know Tom has asked me to marry, him and I've agreed. I know that you both love your son as I do and I promise to take care of him and hope that you give us both your blessing"

Without moving the flowers, Sara lent over and kissed them, got up from her knees and walked back towards Tom who was waiting patiently watching her every move.

When Sara reached Tom, she kissed him, Tom took her hand and they walked back towards the town. Tom didn't question Sara's actions he knew that she would tell him when she was ready.

They found Christine and Sam in the café, Christine ordered Sara and Tom a coffee and they sat and chatted before deciding to stay with the coast road and go to Hunstanton before it got to late, just as they we're about to leave Tom turned to the others and said

"Bloody hell, I've just remembered something—if you lot go to the car I'll catch up with you, give me two minutes".

The girls headed to the car park and waited for Tom. He wasn't long and with him, he had three flat parcels in his arms one of which he handed to Christine telling her that it was for her and Sam and to open it when they got home she kissed Tom on the cheek and thanked him.

Sara back in the driving seat was now heading towards Hunstanton on the coast road, Tom asked the others if they wanted to stop on the way for a drink but Sara pointed out, if she had another drink she would be peeing for the rest of the week, Christine and Sam agreed saying they to couldn't manage anther drink as they had had enough fluid in them to last them a fortnight. When they reached Thornham, the traffic seemed to get rather busy and by the time, they reached Holme they were hardly moving, Sara put the air conditioning on the car was at almost roasting point inside. It took just under an hour to get from Holme to Old Hunstanton where Tom suggested turning right down light house lane and cut through Old Hunstanton and rejoin the main drag that way only to find out others had the same idea. Road works had caused the tail back or at least the temporary lights that had been put up, so when they did finally make it to Hunstanton it was teatime.

"I don't know about you lot but I'm getting rather hungry" said Tom,

"Yes so am I" added Sam

"Come on then we'll find somewhere" said Tom

"Only if we're paying" said Sam

"No Today is on me and I won't have any arguments over it and I know a lovely place that does a lovely fish platter, in fact Sam you'll be able to get some fresh crab from there"

"It's not right Tom that you should pay for us" protested Christine

"Apart from that, you'll be married soon with four or five kids to feed and no money" laughed Sam

"Well I'll give you a ring for a sub but until then today is on me- although (looking towards Sara) four or five kids sound good we had better get some practice in making them what do you think Sara?"

"Dream on Tom, two's enough for any pocket but as for practice well I'm all for that", the others laughed.

Tom led the way to the café. Sara and Sam went and sat down after looking at what meals they did and telling Tom what they wanted, while Tom and Christine queued up for the food. Tom and Christine asked for the fish platter, Sam and Sara went for the fresh crab salad and they all asked for Banofee pie for afters only Sam found that crab washed down with Banofee pie didn't go and had to leave hers and Christine polished that off to.

Once they had finished their tea, they decided with it still being warm they would take a walk along the beach and up to the Pleasure beach that by the time they got there had closed Sara suggested they looked round the town Christine joking said

"From what I've seen that'll take at least three minutes"

"That's a bit of an over estimation more like two minutes" replied Tom.

"Well I still haven't got any crabs" complained Sam

"Thank God for that, Crabs are one thing I could well do without catching" laughed Christine

"You bitch" replied Sam.

"Come on" said Tom

"I'd forgotten about the crabs we had better get back to that café and get some before they close"

Without further ado, they made their way back to the café where Sam purchased ten freshly dressed crabs.

Sara suggested they made their way home and the others agreed

"It would be nice for a change if we all went to my flat people will think I've moved out" said Sara

"That's OK by us isn't it Chris (Christine nodded) but I had better put these in your fridge when we get there" said Sam

"That's something I was going to ask you Sam, what the hell have you got ten dressed crab for?" asked Christine

"Are well—with the answer to your question my sweetheart—can I have time to answer?"

"In other words Sam you don't know" Christine said.

"Give me time to work on it and I'm sure I will come up with something"

"Yes Sam but by then, that so called fresh bloody crab will have gone off and we'll have ten crab shell ash trays and none of us smoke" Joked Christine.

Tom and Sara didn't say a word they were finding it hard enough to keep a straight face, as Sam trying to defend herself against Christine's teasing with little success, Sam realising defeat was on the horizon admitted she had over done it with the crabs, so she suggested they ought to have them for supper, Christine burst into laughter as did Tom and Sara but they agree it might be the best idea.

The roads were pretty clear on their journey home; it only took about an hour and an half to an hour to get back to Sara's flat. The night was still warm; Sara got four beers from the fridge along with four of the controversial crabs, making sure to mention the six remaining crabs in the fridge just for a dig at Sam.

Sara suggested with it being so warm they sat out on the veranda for the evening where they all tucked into their crabs.

Christine and Sam left around eleven, leaving Tom and Sara alone, Sara went to the kitchen to put the kettle on, Tom followed her he lent against the sink unit while Sara made the coffees.

"Well, have you enjoyed today?" asked Tom

"I have, and Tom Gardener, I think you're the sweetest man I've ever known"

"And how many men have you known?" (Tom joked)

"Oh plenty, but none like you"

She stopped making the coffee turned towards him and they embraced, Tom whispered in Sara's ear

"Why don't we forget the drinks and go to bed?"

Sara in a knowing voice said,

"You're not going to be rude with me are you?"

"If you're lucky I might".

88

Chapter Nine

The next morning Sara was first out of bed, leaving Tom to lie in. She had a shower and put the breakfast on. Placing it on two trays, she took it through to the bedroom where Tom was sat up with the phone in his hand.

"Who are you ringing?" Sara asked

"The bloody room service, but I see you're here now, so come on madam what's taken you so long?"

"Sod off you silly bugger just eat unless of course you wish to wear it as a hat?"

"I think I'll eat it after all, I must say it looks extremely good but then again my dear, so do you"

"You creep, anyway cut the bullshit when we've had breakfast we are going to discuss April" said Sara

"April—yes—my favourite time of the year, or at least next year will be"

"You silly bugger, laughing aside Tom, we have got to sort things out, I know it's nearly ten months away but that's not long and especially bearing in mind it's the millennium next year so we should get the church booked and who are we inviting we don't have many friends and only a few family, which is a point who's going to give me away and who will you be having for your Best man"

"Don't panic sweetheart, everything will come together, we'll find someone to give you away, I know you would like to have asked your father or what ever you would like to call him, well you will find someone even if we have to drag someone off the street (Sara hugged Tom) I know who I'm asking to be my best man"

"Who?"

"You'll find out later after I've eaten this nearly cold breakfast, so come on you had better eat yours to, then I'll have a quick shower and we'll go for a long walk, the other day I picked up some property details to look at"

"So yesterday was planned?"

"Oh yes I just hoped you wouldn't turn me down or want to delay things now lets eat our breakfast".

After breakfast, Tom showered and dressed while Sara washed the pots up from breakfast. Tom suggested

"If we walked along the river bank towards Little London call and get the Sunday paper down Hawthorn Bank cut through St. John's Road and we can call at Christine and Sam's cadge a coffee off them, I also need a word with Sam"

"We had better ring them first to make sure they're in" replied Sara,

Tom rang, asking Sam if they were going to be home, as he needed to see them, Sam said they would be in all day.

"Come and have dinner with us"

"Hang on Sam, Sara; Sam wants us to stop for dinner, is that alright?"

"Fine by me Tom, ask her what time"

"Bloody hell Tom, just tell her you can come round when you like dinner will be ready for one".

Tom and Sara set off hand in hand on their walk, they saw a couple of people they recognised also out for a walk, Sara realising they were not the only ones out for a walk turned to Tom and said

"What a relief Tom, I thought we were the only sad people who went out walking on a Sunday morning",

"I used to go out jogging most Sundays and two to three days in the week that was before I fell head over heels in love with you and to be honest I need to start exercising again I'm getting a bit of a belly" replied Tom,

"I'm not surprised the amount of food we are putting away, so when we get home tonight I'll help you, you can start with press ups, and I'll let you know when I've had enough"

"Why wait until tonight sweetheart, we'll nip back to your flat now and I'll see how many I can do" Replied Tom laughing.

"Changing the subject, what's so urgent about seeing Christine and Sam?"

"You'll just have to wait and see"

"Well I to want a word with Christine too",

"What about?" asked Tom, Touching the side of her nose Sara replied

"You'll have to wait"

"You bitch" Tom joked putting his arm around Sara's waist and pulling her closer to him as they walked, soon reaching the paper shop Tom bought a paper and two ice lollies, they then made their way towards Christine and Sam's, Sam met them at the door and let them in,

"Chris is in the kitchen getting dinner on" said Sam

"I'll give her a hand and I need a word with her" Sara said,

"Yes and while Sara's helping Chris I would like to ask you a very big favour Sam" said Tom.

Sara went into the kitchen to help Christine, Tom and Sam sat in the lounge,

"Come on then Tom, spit it out what's so important it can't wait?" Sam asked,

"Will you be my best man—or woman, oh—what ever?"

91

"Well Tom that's a question I never thought I would be asked, but there you have it, life's full of surprises and yes Tom nothing would give me more pleasure, yes thank you I would love to"

Sam gave Tom a massive hug and Sara and Christine came into the room

"Hello and what's going on in here?" asked Christine

"Tom's asked me to be his best man and I've accepted" replied Sam,

"Well Sam I've got some news Sara asked me to be her chief bridesmaid"

"Yes (interrupted Sara looking at Tom) I was going to ask Sam to be my other bridesmaid but you've beat me to it"

"Well Sara my dear, ain't life a shit" joked Tom.

Christine went back into the kitchen and finished off preparing the dinner and after about five minutes came into the lounge with four plates handed them to Sam and asked her if she could set the table, Sam suggested with it being such a lovely day they ate out on the patio in the small rear garden, which they shared with other tenants although only Christine and Sam had ever bothered to maintain this area, Christine agreed so Sam set out the table and Christine arrived with the food that consisted of tossed salad roast chicken and chips and a bottle of red wine to wash it down with although the food in it's self was quite basic Christine had a talent in dressing the most basic of food up to make it look spectacular, needless to say the food was soon consumed along with the contents of the wine bottle.

Once they had finished Sam said she quite fancied a walk over to the park and small Museum near to where Sara's flat was, they all agreed. They hadn't been out of the flat two minutes when Sam's mobile phone started to ring, it was Simon, he wanted to know if her and Christine were still interested in buying their house Sam said

"I thought the sale had gone through Simon"

"The buyers have had a fall out or something we don't really know what but the top and bottom of it, they backed out just before the contracts were exchanged"

"Well—yes we're still interested aren't we Chris?" (Christine looked bewildered)

"I've no idea what the hell you're on about Sam my ears aren't that good"

"Sorry Chris" Sam hastily replied

"It's Simon he wants to know if we're still interested in buying their house"

"Tell him yes we'll ring him later—no tell him we'll pop and see him and Paul later" Christine said.

Sam passed on the message and ended the call.

"That's a turn up for the books" Christine said,

"Yes"-said Sam

"What was all that about" asked Sara

"You know I told you about those two lads we met, Paul and Simon and how we wouldn't have minded buying their house, if it hadn't have already been sold, well it appears their sale has fallen through"

"You go for it (Tom interrupted) if you like you can arrange your mortgage from work and sort out the other bits as well, that way it will keep your cost down"

"That would be great Tom" said Sam

"Why don't you and Sara come with us tonight?" asked Christine

"No" said Sara

"You pair go on your own we don't want to intrude, apart from that Tom needs to do some exercising and I'm going to help him with the press ups" Christine and Sam laughed,

"I bet you'll be helping him" Sam said sarcastically.

After dinner, Christine suggested a walk to the park. Once there Sam went to the little brick built café that stands in the middle of the park she got four teas and they sat outside at the tables provided and chatted. Sam asked Sara who she would be having for her other bridesmaids and if she was having a church do,

"Both of us want a church wedding don't we Tom (Tom nodded) so it will definitely be a church, as for bridesmaids there are my two God children Alice and Thomas, so I thought I'd ask their mum if Alice could be bridesmaid and Thomas—I know he's only two but he would make a lovely Page boy, the thing is I don't know who I'm going to ask to give me away, I do know one thing for certain it won't be that bastard at Bourne"

"What are you going to do about asking them Sara?" Tom asked

"I just don't know, they won't come if we invite them and if we don't invite them they will use it to their own means, to be honest with you I don't want them there, he isn't my dad any way so why should he give me away"

"I agree" said Christine

"He would ruin the day for you and you don't want to give him that chance, if you send him an invite, there's always that chance that he could turn up, just to course trouble, and perhaps the old bastard will drop dead before next April"

"You never know our luck" said Sara

"For all we know he could be dead now we would be the last to know after all he was supposed to be very ill, although he didn't look that bad when we went down"

"He's still alive and hates us, I saw that Mrs Ingamells in the supermarket the other day and she said he was still very ill but still calling everyone and I think by the way she was talking she was referring to us"

"I just can't understand that woman after what happened at Christmas she still speaks".

"I wouldn't mind looking round the Museum," said Tom

"I never saw a Museum round here when we came in the park or a sign that pointed to one"

"Well Sam, if you turn your head and look at that post your chair is leaning on there is a sign with an arrow on and surprisingly it says To the Museum," said Christine in a sarcastic tone

"Oh yes I didn't see that there" said Sam, they all laughed.

"Shall we go to the museum then?" Tom asked,

Tom led the way down the side of a grand old hall under an old brick arch passing a massive Magnolia tree standing gracefully to their left with its branches hanging to the ground, they entered the front door, the door that was once the entrance to some ones home and was now the entrance to the Museum.

Tom had passed through these doors several times before. He loved these old buildings and the history that surrounded them. He would stand and imagine what the people were like who lived in such grand places. When he was at school he traced the history of his own home back to its first owners even visiting their graves at Pinchbeck cemetery Tom loved to touch things from the past always wishing he had studied archaeology as it was he didn't so he took an interest in local history. They wandered around the Museum for about an hour looking at things Tom's eyes had seen before. Tom knew the history of this grand old Hall the lady who had once lived there who had given so much to the town even the Hospital which bares her family name Tom could tell you word for word what the boards standing in the museum said on the history of the surrounding marshes, but to be honest although this was one of Toms passion, not including Sara, it was quite obvious to him that the others found it to be rather boring so he suggested they went for a walk over to Holland Market shopping precinct, he knew Sara needed to get a few things, Sam had mentioned she needed some milk, not realising the time had now reached three and being a Sunday the supermarket on Holland Market closed at four so they needed to make haste.

They made the supermarket in good time Sara and Sam purchased their supplies and said their goodbyes Sam and Christine made their way home promising to ring Tom and Sara later and that if they were back from Paul and Simon's early enough they would ring them at Tom's and let them know about the house.

Sara and Tom headed to Sara's flat to collect Sara's car and then to Tom's house to look at the property brochures Tom had collected from work and other Estate Agents. Sara put the kettle on and Tom got the brochures from his brief case, Sara looked at all of them, noticing several of them as houses she had visited to value, commenting to Tom about them as she read the over glossy descriptions some of which Sara herself had written, pointing out one particular property, where Sara had described the property as in need of slight modernisation Sara said

"I should have put this house and its surroundings are in need of a large Bull Dozer and this one Tom, I've put, rear garden laid to grass with very mature shrub border, the truth is the grass is knee high covered in dog shit with the shrubs almost suffocating the entire back garden the insides are not much better"

"Your not impressed then Sara"

"You could say that, especially the prices some of these are it's not a wonder we can't get rid of them, look at this hundred and fifty two thousand pounds I advised the clients when I valued this one to put it on the market for hundred and ten thousand they took the hump saying their neighbour had just sold theirs for hundred and fifty two months earlier, the thing was their neighbour's house which we had sold was lovely theirs was a bloody slum waiting to collapse"

"So I suppose I'd better chuck these brochures out and first thing tomorrow I'll get some more"

"No you won't Tom"

"Well Sara Jane we will have to look for something soon, we don't have long"

"Why do we, what's wrong with this house, it's big, it's not been long since it was decorated, alright I will admit not totally to my taste structurally it's sound, completely double glazed, six bedrooms one for six nights of the week and on Sunday's we'll have to use the lounge and look at that garden, Tom it's beautiful a credit to you. I also know you don't really want to sell it if you're totally honest, Tom you have too many memories here, this is just Tom being Tom trying to please me"

"No Sara"

"Yes Tom, you're too bloody kind for your own good I love you and you don't have to do things just to please me, in all the time I've known you ,you have never said no to anything I've asked you always put me first others second and yourself last. If you're not careful people will take advantage of you and I worry that if I'm not careful I'll do the same although I hope you will tell me—so let's do what Tom wants to do for a change"

"Well I don't know really what to say to that Sara love"

"Hang on a minute I just thought (Sara interrupted) what did you called me?"

"When?" asked Tom

"You bloody know" Persisted Sara

"I don't know what the hell you're on about"

"Yes you do, you called me Sara—Jane"

"Oh that" replied Tom

"Yes you bugger who told you my second name is Jane"

"Why does it matter?"

"No—I suppose not, it's just the fact it's a name I'm not that keen on"

"But why I think it's a pretty name and it suits you, so tell me, why don't you like it?"

"I tell you why because that old bastard at Bourne would call me it and he was the only one who ever used it" replied Sara

"No one told me your second name is Jane, I was just sorting through some files the other day and I came across your C.V and it was on there along with other misleading facts I dare to mention especially as you've told me your whole life story"

"Oh—shit" said Sara

"Yes Oh—shit" laughed Tom

"I think I need to punish you, so get up them stairs now and by the time I get up there I want you in bed—but not asleep"

"Yes boss, anything you say boss" and Sara did just as Tom ordered and more besides.

The next morning Tom was first to rise around seven waking Sara with a coffee and reminding her he had to be in the office by eight, as an engineer was calling to repair the faulty lighting so he made himself a couple of rounds of toast to eat on the way and left, Sara came down to wave him off.

Tom asked Sara if he could borrow her car and he would ask one of the others to pick her up at nine, this wasn't a problem Tom asked Sara for her car keys

"My keys Oh—yes they are in it"

"That's rather silly Sara" Tom opened the door and stopped,

"What's the matter Tom?"

"Where's your car?"

"In the drive—or it was last night"

"Well the bloody thing isn't now"

"Tell me you're joking" replied Sara

"Do I look as if I'm joking, I'd better ring the police they're not going to believe this and I had better ring Christine and ask her to meet that engineer at the office. Here we go again" Tom said trying to see the funny side.

The Police arrived and took some details telling Sara they would be in touch and leaving Tom and Sara totally car less.

Once they shut the door to the Police Tom looked at Sara and grind.

"I think our insurers might want to see us" said Tom

"You're possibly right" Sara replied

"Sara if you catch the bus into town I'll ring the garage and find out how quick they can get that car here for and in the mean time we'll have to make do, I'll walk with you to the bus stop".

No sooner had Tom waved Sara off than his mobile phone rang, it was Christine's in a slightly bewildered voice. Tom asked her what the problem was.

"It's the office and well—it's Sara's car"

"Which is it Chris, Sara's car or the office?" Tom demanded

"Well it's both"

"Both"

"Both what do you mean both?" said Tom,

The voice then changed it was now Sam

"Listen Tom, it's me Tom, Christine's in a bit of a state, when we got here the door at the back of the office was wide open and Sara's car was parked at the front with the engine still running"

"Don't touch a thing call the Police. I'll be there as soon as I can get a Taxi" replied Tom.

Before Sam had time to tell him that the Police were already there Tom had rang off. The Police had found the car running and when they realised it had been reported missing they had tried to contact Sara but she wasn't at home. Sara arrived shortly after Sam had finished talking to Tom completely oblivious to the whole situation and shocked at seeing her car parked neatly outside the office in it's usual spot,

"What the hell is going on and what's my bloody car doing there?" demanded Sara

"I thought you might be able to tell us" one of the Police officer's replied

"How the hell should I know, me and my boyfriend only reported the bloody thing missing an hour or so ago and now it's sat there, someone's taking the piss"

"I think we had all better go inside and talk about this more calmly," advised one of the policemen

"I'll put the kettle on," said Sam.

Just then Tom turned up in a taxi

"What's going on?" demanded Tom

"Well Mr Gardener, it appears from what we can make out, your rear office door was left open and the car your girl friend reported missing is fully intact outside, with its engine running" said the Policeman, Tom looked baffled just then a chap walked in the door

"Can I help you" asked Christine

"Yes I hope so; I've come about the electric"

"Ah just the man, I was expecting you at eight" interrupted Tom

"I thought that's what you said but the lass in the office told me to come back at ten in fact the way she spoke to me I nearly didn't come back at all" said the electrician,

Tom, Sara, Christine and Sam looked baffled

"What lass?" Tom asked

"The girl in that car"

"That's my car and I had reported it missing," said Sara

"I don't know, but I thought she seemed a bit weird she was in a hurry to get shut of me, she told me she was going to ring my boss for disturbing her working. I just left"

"The thing is the only people who work here are us and I'm the boss so who ever this woman is I don't know" Tom said shaking his head.

The Police asked Tom to look round and see if anything was missing and asked Sara to have a look at her car as they were, now finished Tom couldn't find any damage or anything missing and Sara's car was just as she left it when it had been parked on the drive. The Police asked the electrician to leave his details, so they could take a statement off him later.

Once the Police had gone, Tom asked if they would all check their desk's as he thought it might be one of the opposition and check to see if the files were all still intact while he rang the local locksmith and arrange for all the office locks to be changed. Sara came into Tom's office and shut the door and burst into tears, seeing Sara in such a distressed state quickly Tom finish his phone conversation and went over to Sara trying to comfort her

"Don't worry sweetheart the main thing is no one has been hurt and nothing has been taken"

"I know that Tom, but last night as I always do, I left the keys in the ignition of the car, and the office keys were with them along with flat keys"

"Oh—shit your door keys for your flat",

"Yes Tom like the office keys my flat keys are no longer with them on the key ring also both sets of burglar alarm numbers are missing"

"You're as bad as me with bloody keys"

Tom told Christine and Sam to look after the office, Tom then rang his neighbour asking them to watch the house. Tom and Sara got into Sara's car and went over to Sara's flat. Fortunately there had been no intruders but just as a matter of course Tom purchased a new lock and fitted it himself while Sara changed the code for her burglar alarm and once they had finished at Sara's they headed for Tom's house.

There had been no intruders, but when Tom inspected the door locks he realised he couldn't change them and would have to have a locksmith in to change them so Tom rang the office and ask Christine to ask the locksmith when he called to go to Tom's house as well. The locksmith wasn't long before he turned up at Tom's house changing first the front door and then the back leaving Tom with a bill for two hundred and fifty pounds, Tom nearly fell over, the lock for his rear door alone was seventy-five pounds Tom was gob smacked looking at Sara he said

"I think we had better make sure and take care of these keys".

Tom changed his alarm code then they locked up and returned to the office Tom asked his neighbours to keep a look out for any strangers. On the way Tom said to Sara, he thought it might be advisable to inform the police on the key situation, Sara was a bit worried about what they might say about her leaving her keys in the car, she said

"They wanted to know why I'd left the car unlocked with the keys in it as it was",

"Yes"-said Tom

"Perhaps it might be better to forget about it and put it down to experience, although I must say this is bloody well bugging me who the hell is this mystery woman, what the hell did she want?"

"I don't know Tom but I'll tell you what I bet you she's local and what ever she wanted she didn't find, I may be wrong ,but I think she will be back".

They were soon back at the office, four sets of keys lay on Toms desk splitting them up he handed one front door key between Christine and Sam and a set of both front and back for himself and Sara and put the other keys in his brief case, to take home to put in a safe place.

The mornings events and excitement had calmed and the afternoon was showing signs of normality with the usual sound of chit-chat among the girls Christine and Sam finally got round to telling Tom and Sara how their visit to Paul and Simon's had gone

"Good news" said Sam

"No Sam, good news and bad news" corrected Christine

"Which is it good or bad news?" laughed Tom

"Well I suppose Chris is right, the good news is, we can and want to buy the house and the bad news is bloody Greens are selling it which means we have to make our offer to Mr Shit Head himself", the others laughed at Sam's remarks

"I could have a word with him if you like" said Tom

"It's O.K. Tom, I'm only joking anyway he dare not be funny because if he is, Simon has said he will be straight in his office, Tom you know you said you would help us sort a mortgage out well"

"Consider it done and now I think you should get on the phone to our Mr Green and make him your offer"

"O.K" replied Sam and did as Tom advised

"Well?" said Christine

"What did the pig say?"

"He's got to ring his clients and put the offer to them, you should know that"

"I didn't mean that, I meant, when he realised it was you?"

"Not a lot, although his manner seemed to change, he made some comment about it being nice to help someone in the trade, but there was a slight hint of sarcasm about his voice".

Chapter Ten

The next few weeks passed as weeks with not a great deal of excitement, only Tom taking collection of his third new car this year.

Mystery was still surrounding the identity of the woman seen in the office in fact Sam was now calling her the ghost with a driving licence much to the others amusement.

September had arrived, autumn was almost here the leaves on the trees were changing colour, some had turned a lovely red others a shade of brown. September the time of year Tom loved and if he could, he would try and get away for a long weekend up North, only this year he had Sara to consider perhaps she might not find it very appealing, but much to his delight, when he mentioned the idea to Sara she thought it great. Tom made all the arrangements for them to stop at a caravan park in a small place called Birnam in Scotland, just North of Perth. Tom said that the journey should take about seven hours with a couple of stops so he said they should have the Thursday through to the Tuesday off work, leaving Christine and Sam to look after the office.

They set out just after seven reaching the A1 at Newark at about eight where Tom filled his car up with diesel and collected a few bites, for the long journey ahead. The traffic wasn't over busy only slowing a little in places, once past Doncaster it became plain sailing to Scotch Corner where Tom suggested they stop for a lay-by Breakfast,

"What the hells a lay-by Breakfast?" asked Sara

"You're telling me you've never heard of a lay-by breakfast?"

"Yes that's right I haven't"

"Well my sweetheart you must have led a sheltered life free from salmonella, (Sara laughed) a lay-by Breakfast is what it says, and there's a little cafe in the lay-by at Scotch Corner they do a Breakfast bap that's out off this world"

"Yes Tom, but how far out of this world"

"Here we are" said Tom

"But it's full of Lorries, you'll have a job to park (Sara now a bit unsure as to whether she liked the idea of stopping here) I can wait to eat, if we can't park Tom"

"We'll get in somewhere, there's a space, so what would you like?"

"What ever you're having Tom"

"O.K sweet heart I'll be back in a minute".

Tom left the car soon returning with two cups of tea and going back to the counter and collected their food, which consisted of two large bacon and egg baps and two rather large pieces of cherry sponge. Sara although she had never eaten from one of these places before was pleasantly surprised by the quality and quantity of food they had supplied. Sara asked Tom to get some more cherry sponge to take with them. Having stopped for about half an hour they, made their move taking the A1, bypassing Newcastle with its Lady of the North. Within three hours, they were joining the Edinburgh bypass heading for the Fourth Road Bridge. The beauty of the scenery she had never before ventured so far north fascinated Sara. Once over the Bridge Sara said she needed to use the Toilets, Tom assured her they were only a few miles from the services saying they could get some dinner there, so being on a Motor way and not having much choice the Services it was. At the Services they both used the toilets and stretched their legs, Sara collected a rather large heap of Tourist information leaflets and then they had something to eat, before continuing their now short journey to the Holiday Park.

The Park situated just off the main road consisted of around a hundred or so rather smart caravans set in wooded grounds of a rather large house on the side of the River Tay. Tom had visited this site on several occasions as a child and also with his father not long before his death, Tom loved the spot. Once they had booked in and collected their keys, they made their way to their caravan, this was another new experience for Sara, she had never been inside a caravan before let alone had a holiday in one, there was no reason for this it just never happened and how pleasantly surprised she was by the space, Sara was well impressed. Tom got the cases from the car and Sara emptied them Tom said he was going to have a shower and then if she wanted they could go for a walk to the village,

"Sounds good to me said Sara, I think I'll have a shower too first".

They both showered and put on a change of clothes before making their way down to the River Tay walking towards Birnam. As they walked Tom pointed out parts of the walk that still held in his memory from when he was younger he pointed out the spot where he and his dad went fishing, the big old Oak where he and his mother had had their photograph taken, the photo that still holds pride of place on his Mantel piece at home, he laughed about the time he had fallen into a bunch of nettles and when his mother bent down to pick him up she to slipped and fell into them he said he reckoned people who saw them together must of thought they had a hereditary skin disorder, Sara laughed.

Reaching Birnam Tom suggested they went and had a drink and light refreshments before walking back to the caravan. Taking a different route, they made their way back Sara pointing out to Tom that she was well and truly worn out saying it had been a long day, Tom said he to felt tired and if she wanted they could go to bed, Sara nodded.

The next morning having slept well Sara woke to the smell of bacon cooking,

"That smells good Tom"

"It sure does, I thought with all that snoring you might have built yourself up a bit of an appetite"

"Yes but not that sort of appetite"

"Well Sara my sweet that could create a bit of a problem"

"Oh, shut up Tom and come here"

"I will, but do you want your Bacon burnt"

"O.K spoilsport, I'll get up, but don't think you got away with it".

Tom and Sara ate their breakfast after which Sara showered and dressed. Tom suggested they visit a few of the local attractions. Tom asked Sara if she had seen anything in the leaflets that took her fancy,

"Yes in-fact I see, not far from here their is a mountain side where Queen Victoria used go and have picnics and from what it says it makes a nice walk"

"Yes I know where you mean, Queens View"

"That's it, Queens View"

"I know it well", Sara made a few sandwiches and off they went making their first port of call Queens View, they only stopped a short time, then headed for the Hermitage, Sara loved this spot taking many photographs of Tom near the water fall then following the wooded walk holding Toms hand almost all the time, she was totally mesmerised by the beauty of it all, the colours of the leaves, greens and reds the shapes of the trees the gushing sound of the water as it hit the rocks all this was enhanced by the beauty of the day not a cloud in the sky.

After the Hermitage Tom asked Sara if she wanted to visit a whisky distillery to which she agreed so referring back to the leaflets Tom pointed one out that didn't appear to be to far away at Glenturret near Crieff. The roads were not what one would describe as good but within an hour they arrived and fortunately just in time for the last guided tour so they quickly paid the price and joined the tour, which both of them thoroughly enjoyed although like many of the others on the tour, Sara commented on the very boring voice of the guide, but they quickly forgot this bad point once they had been offered free sampling of the whisky. Sara said she would like to get a nice Bottle of something for Christine and Sam she went to the counter and tried a few more, in the end she settled for the spicy whisky also getting one for herself and Tom. It was getting late in the afternoon they decided to make their way back to the camp and spend the evening at the camp club where they could get quietly pissed and be able to walk or at the very least stagger to their bed.

The next morning Tom was yet again first out of the bed leaving Sara to sleep in only to be woken by the sound of Tom dropping a cup to the floor while attempting to make a coffee.

"My head, my bloody head Tom it's throbbing, can you pass me a couple of Paracetamols?"

"O.K sweetheart I'll get them, my heads banging too, I think I'll have a couple, to be honest with you I think we well and truly over did it last night"

"I think you're right Tom, it got rather embarrassing when you asked that Piper if he wore anything under his kilt and then tried to look, I'm surprised he didn't hit you"

"Well that was the last thing I meant to do, embarrass you my love and to be bloody honest with you I thought he was, that's why I bought him a large drink and quickly apologised to him but I must admit it was one hell of a night, so what shall we do today, it's lovely out there so if you get dressed we'll go for a walk I don't think we should drive this morning, so I'll show you the other end of the camp, where I stopped with my parents, I also want you to meet a couple of friends"

"I didn't know you had any friends here, you kept that quiet"

"Well although I said friends they were my parent's friends and I haven't spoken to them since the funeral and they don't know I'm here, but if you don't mind I would love them to meet you and invite them to the wedding"

"Why should I mind who you invite, I would love to meet them". So once, they got dressed not having managed to eat their breakfast Tom led the way down to a wooden looking permanent caravan.

"Do they actually live here all the time?"

"Well I think they have to vacate the site for about two or three months a year I'm not really sure, anyway it looks like their home". Tom knocked on the door and a lady answered, realising it was Tom she threw her arms around him calling her husband to come quick dragging him in, the lady let go of Tom and took hold of Sara's hand and took her inside saying

"Tom kept you quiet my dear, come on in and tell me all about yourself" said the lady.

Introducing herself as Margaret saying her husband is George she asked Sara her name, then putting the kettle on she asked Sara about herself. After which she told Sara how they lived in Spalding until about four years ago when George suffered a heart attack and was advised to pack in work, and with them already owning this van on site they decided to rent out the house out and come up here for nine months of the year,

"So how did you know Toms Dad?" asked Sara

"Like I said, we came from Spalding and we had a shoe shop next door to Toms estate agents and after Toms Mum died I would look after Tom when he came out of Hospital, he went through a very bad time but I suppose you know all that, (Sara not wanting her to think any different nodded) yes he took it bad and his Mother she would be really proud of the way he has turned out, a fine handsome young man and now he has finally got himself a beautiful girlfriend, so come on tell me is it serious between you"

"I love Tom very much and I know he loves me in fact Tom needs a word with you (just as Sara said that Tom and George walked in) and here he is"

"I take it that you're talking about me?"

"Yes Tom my boy I understand you have something to tell me and George"

"Well not actually tell you, more like ask you"

"Go on then spit it out Tom" said Margaret

"Me and Sara are getting married and I would be very upset if you two weren't there, so don't say you can't make it"

"So would I" added Sara

"Well George there's not a lot we can say to that"

"Yes there is Margaret, get the whisky bottle out, this calls for a celebration"

"Not for me" said Tom

"I over did it a bit last night"

"You can say that again, but seeing as your driving I'll have one" said Sara

"That's what I like to see a girl who likes a good whisky" said George

"So are you going to tell us the date of the special day or do we have to guess?" asked Margaret

"Were hoping on next April third if we get it" said Sara,

"That's a Monday" said Margaret

"Yes" said Sara

"But that's the date we got engaged"

"That's nice and we are very happy for you both and now we can make plans (and she gave Sara a gentle hug)

"So why don't you pair meet me and Sara in the club tonight about seven"

"Dear me Tom we haven't been in there in ages" said Margaret

"Well it'll do you good then, so that's a date, anyway Sara we had better make a move".

They made their way back to their caravan to pick up the car, Sara said she wouldn't mind looking at Pitlochry, Tom agreed saying he would show her the salmon ladders.

"I didn't know fish could climb ladders" said Sara

"Well it's not quite like that they don't actually climb ladders"

"No they do don't they (Sara laughing at Tom)

"You bitch, you're taking the piss"

"Yes your right my love, I am taking the piss" and Tom hugged her.

They visited the salmon ladders then made their way back to the site to have a very enjoyable night out with George and Margaret.

The following morning Tom and Sara were woken by Sara's mobile, it was Sam she had just had a call from Mrs Ingamells, apparently their stepfather had died in the night and their mother was asking for them, Christine had gone over to see her, Tom told Sara the news.

"Well I shan't pretend I'm bothered because I'm not" said Sara

"But Sara I still think you should go and see her"

"I suppose you're right but it's bloody typical, the old bastard even after death has to create problems and let's face it, my mother's not a lot better, now all of a sudden she wants us to drop every thing and go there"

"Well I think you should, I wish I could speak to my mother"

"O.K Tom I suppose your right"

"We can always come back again next year as man and wife"

"I'll get the cases packed and you had better go and tell your friends"

"O.K sweetheart I'll be as quick as I can"

"You take your time Tom, I'm in no hurry".

When Tom returned, they loaded the car handed the caravan keys in and made their way home. It took them about eight hours to get home, making a couple of stops on the way for food and drink one of the stops being at Sara's request was Scotch Corner for a lay-by breakfast and to buy some more cherry cake, this amused Tom.

At home, they quickly unloaded the car then headed straight to Christine and Sam's. Christine had only just returned from Bourne

"Come on then Chris, how is she?"

"To be honest with you, I can't make a lot of it"

"What do you mean?"

"She was really pleased to see me she hardly mentioned him just asking whether I would help her with the funeral arrangements she asked after you and she even asked after Sam saying perhaps we could all get to know each other now, do you know what Sara I think she's pleased the old bastards dead, I told her you are courting, but I didn't tell her you are getting married, I thought you might want to tell her"

"Thanks Chris"

"Go on then Sara ring her and make arrangements to go and see her, there's no time like the present" insisted Tom.

Sara lifting the receiver from Christine and Sam's phone dialled her Mothers number, it took long a time before the phone was answered, but it wasn't her Mothers voice, it was Sara's Uncle Ray who spoke, Ray was Jacks younger brother, he like Jack wasn't particularly fond of either her or Christine. He asked Sara what she wanted,

"Is mum there?" asked Sara

"No. What do you want? But then again I suppose that's a stupid question because now he's dead I should."

And before he could say any more he had the phone snatched from him,

Sara could hear a bit of a fuss going on and could also hear her mothers voice getting closer, Sara wasn't sure whether or not to put the receiver down or not, but then things changed and her mother spoke apologising for Rays rudeness saying,

"Ray's now leaving, (adding in louder voice) aren't you Ray"

Sara then heard a door slam.

"I'm sorry to hear about Dad" said Sara

"No you're not Sara, I said to Christine deep down as callous as it may seem if we are all honest, none of us are sorry to see him go, especially not me, towards the end he made me a prisoner in my own home, I'm glad he's gone and he can rot in hell and perhaps now there may be a chance we can be friends and perhaps be a proper family, after all as he told you himself he wasn't your real dad"

"Yes mum he definitely made that clear but you could have been nicer to us"

"Please Sara dear not now, come over to the house and we can have a chat?"

"When Mum?"

"Now if you like, and bring that handsome chap of yours with you"

Ending the call Sara told the others what had been said. She told Tom he had been asked down with her

"What both of us?" asked Tom

"Yes both of us" replied Sara.

Without further ado, Tom and Sara said their goodbyes and made their way to Bourne.

Chapter Eleven

Tom had never seen Sara's childhood home before and had always imagined a large hall type building with a long drive with immaculate gardens and he was surprised when Sara directed them to a run down farm house with over grown gardens and rusting farm machinery in the undergrowth

"Well Sara love, this wasn't how I imagined your family home to look, it's a bit run down"

"If you ask me Tom it's a bloody mess, it never used to be like this in fact that mess over there where that old tractor is, was at one time beautiful lawns but for some reason they've let it go"

"Perhaps it got too much for them" said Tom

"I can't weigh it up, it's definitely not lack of money he was loaded and from what I can remember when me and Chris came to try and sort things out standing at that door the hallway looked as if it hadn't been touched since we were young, anyway the curtains are twitching she's seen we're here, we'd better go in".

Getting out of the car they walked across the grass covered gravel path to the partially rotten front door and before Sara's hand reached the once gleaming brass door knocker the door opened and there stood Sara's mother with her arms out stretched, waiting to embrace her

"Come in I'll put the kettle on, go in the lounge you must be cold, you must be Tom, go on Sara show him to the lounge I'll be with you in a minute".

Sara led Tom along the hallway to a large room that stunk of stale cigarette smoke the walls were almost yellow with nicotine stains and it could be said that the house was to put it mildly a fucking mess. .

Sara was astonished and slightly ashamed at the state of this, her childhood home. This wasn't the house of her childhood memories with its immaculate paintwork and décor. Tom and Sara never said a word they just sat and waited for Sara's mum to enter the room and finally after what seemed ages she entered the room carrying a tray with three coffees and a plate of biscuits on it, she placed it on the rather dusty coffee table and sat on a chair facing them,

"Thank you for coming, Sara. I wouldn't have blamed you if you had told me where to go, I'm sorry love for the way things have been between us all, now he's dead I just hope we can put the past behind us"

"I don't want an apology mum, neither me or Christine ever blamed you although you could have— (Sara paused) Oh lets just forget about the past, tell me what are your plans, or is it to early"

"Well Sara I said to Christine I know you didn't like him, but will you come to the funeral just for me you could even help me with the arrangements, his brother Ray has been round trying to take over he's also trying to find out what's in the Will, he doesn't realise, but he's in for one hell of a shock"

"Why's that mum?"

"I'm the only beneficiary. As soon as I was told just how bad he was, I checked to make sure I would get everything I know Tom you probably think what a nasty old woman, yes I maybe am, that's only what he's made me, we haven't got on for years but I was scared of him and he had a hold over me"

"I'm not judging you Mrs Gray"

"Don't call me Mrs Gray call me Eileen, anyway as I was saying and stop me if I'm boring you, Jack as Sara has probably told you, he hated the girls and insisted I distanced myself from them"

"Yes but you're our mother" said Sara

"I know that Sara, and I know I was wrong. He controlled me in every way, I never had a choice, where would I have gone?"

"You could have come to me or Christine"

"Sara I was frightened he would tell you he wasn't your real father as it was he did anyway"

"So why didn't you leave then mum, we would have willingly helped you"

"Sara dear, he was a sick man with a short time to live and as I said I am the only beneficiary and he is loaded so no way was I going to let him leave the lot to his brother Ray or his church"

"Someone told me he had gone into religion in a big way"

"You're not kidding, it freaked me out"

"Mum, what has happened to the house, it's so run down it use to be beautiful"

"Jack decided when he retired to sack the two gardeners and the handyman Dave with big ideas on doing all the work himself, he cut the grass once and that was it, then one Sunday morning we were woken by a knock on the front door, it was a load of Bible bashers and he invited them in, there was no time for the house he lived at the church insisting I went to. I hated it the rubbish they preached was unbelievable"

"So why did you put up with it?"

"What could I do he had distanced me from you and Christine, I had no one only the Ingamells and they were scared of him"

"What do you mean they were scared of him mum?"

"About eight years ago he lent the Ingamells fifteen thousand pounds and Jacks interest rates were that high they couldn't afford the repayments, I recently found out he had an arrangement with Mr Ingamells that Mrs Ingamells could help with the repayments if you get my drift. So you can see why I'm so pleased he's gone and now all that's left to do is to bury him"

"Well mum I knew he was a bastard and that confirms it, you're keeping quiet Tom what do you think?"

"To be honest with you, I'm not sure, I've only ever met him the once at the Christmas meal and I saw there what the man was capable of. I can't get it round my head why you put up with it for so long. I know it's easy for us to say but you must have had your reasons, I don't think Eileen it's my place to judge"

"I agree with Tom, It's not fair for us to be judgemental," added Sara.

"I think looking at the time Mrs Gray—sorry I mean Eileen we had better make a move, it's getting on for twelve thirty" said Tom looking at his watch

"Oh my lord, so it is, you two go, and promise me you'll ring in the morning".

Eileen saw Tom and Sara to the front door kissing them both and thanking them for calling.

Watching her as they drove away Sara could see her eyes were full of sadness for the lost years and yet at the same time a look of hope for them all. By the time, Sara and Tom had reached the end of the road Sara was in tears,

"I do hope she will be O.K, she's had a shit life, the house seems calm, I wasn't scared of being there, and he was an utter bastard"

"Yes Sara but as callous as it may seem she chose it, there was no reason why she couldn't have left years ago"

"I know that Tom, but perhaps she's not telling us something. She never mentioned the funeral arrangements, only that she wanted us to help her; I think that was just a ploy to get us there"

"I guessed that the moment we walked in, he definitely sounds like he had led her a right dance. I bet the Ingamells are pleased he's dead"

"I'll bet they are Tom, they must have hated him as much as we did or even more"

"So who do you think will go to the funeral lets face it he didn't have any friends"

"I don't know, but if I were your mum I'd have him cremated to make sure the old bastard has gone let's face it, it's a waste of time him having a grave no one will ever visit if"

"Well we're home and I don't know about you but I'm knackered and I'm off to bed"

"So am I Tom, Oh yes and by the way Tom"

"What?"

"I love you"

"I love you too".

The next morning they were woken by the phone, Sara answered it; it was Christine.

"How did it go last night?"

"We couldn't really make a lot of it, she's definitely not upset. Chris while I'm thinking about it did she mention to you about the Ingamells"

"What about the Ingamells?'

Sara told Christine all of what their mother had said.

"Holy shit Sara that's a turn up for the books and she's such a bloody snob"

"So Sara are we going to the funeral or not"

"To be honest with you Chris, I would sooner not go, but I can't see a way out of it, can you?"

"Not really, I suppose we'll have to grin and bear it"

"What's Sam say about it?'

"She's not commented"

"Well Chris I'm going to get dressed, I'll see you at work".

Sara got up got, dressed and made the breakfast for her and Tom and they left for work. They hadn't been there long before Sara decided to ring her mother who at the time was still in bed so it took a long time for her to answer and Sara sensed that she wasn't alone as she was very cagey about what she said and when she asked Sara if she was at work Sara jokingly said

"No mum I'm outside"

"You're not um—I shall be a minute" she panicked.

Sara asked her mum what arrangements had been made about the funeral. She said it was to take place at Peterborough Crematorium and back to the house for sandwiches after a few more pleasantries Sara put the phone down obviously realising her mother was in a hurry to get away and mentioned her concerns to Christine who jokingly said,

"I hope she doesn't make too many sandwiches there'll only be me you and mum," Sara laughed

"I'll tell you what Chris I've a good mind to take a ride over there after work and try and find out what is going on she was definitely hiding something last night"

"I think if it's O.K with you I'll come too, when I went I saw a man leaving in a hurry, I'd like to find out more, especially after what you've said about your 'phone conversation"

Straight after work Christine and Sara drove over to Bourne to their mothers house and just as they pulled into the drive the same man Christine had seen the day earlier was driving off with their mother stood at her door waving and when she realised Christine and Sam had arrived she had a look of shock on her at seeing them.

122

They got out of the car and walked up to their mother who was waiting on the doorstep and before they could speak, their mother said

"That's Pete, um—Jacks friend"

They could tell she was lying. They followed their mother into the house and into the kitchen and much to their surprise the kitchen was spotless and although almost the same as they remembered appeared to have been recently decorated. Christine and Sara sat round the old yet immaculate wooden table, the same table they sat round as children; only this time they had no worries of the man who they thought to be their father walking through the door and shouting at them to be quiet. Christine was first to talk

"So mum Sara tells me you're having him cremated"

"Yes I thought it best in the circumstances"

"What do you mean what circumstances?" asked Sara

"Well girls it has become quite obvious today that he had no friends at all"

Christine looked at Sara and trying not to let her mother hear, in a quiet voice said

"I could have told her that",

"Today I must have rung about forty or more so called friends of his telling them the funeral has been arranged for Friday morning and every one I spoke to apart from the Ingamells are said too busy, in fact a couple of them were very rude and put the phone down, I think the only reason the Ingamells are going is to make sure they burn him, (Christine was having a job not to laugh) then again I can't blame people he wasn't a very nice person"

"What about his friends from the church and this mysterious friend Pete?" asked Christine

"Well—Um Pete he's busy and yes one or two are coming to represent the church, I had forgot about them"

Christine noticing a hesitation at the mention of Pete

"So mum this Pete, I don't believe he is who you say he is"

"What do you mean love?"

"Well for one I don't think he was dads—I mean Jacks friend and two I don't believe his name is Pete"

"Alright he's my friend, but his name is Pete or Peter"

"Just a friend mum or more tell me to mind my own business if you want after all it's nothing to do with us"

"O.K, Pete's been a very good friend, he's been there for me, we are close I was going to leave your dad once"

"He's wasn't our dad and he confirmed that" interrupted Christine

"No mum he's not, so who is?" added Sara

"Girls listen when this is all over, I will tell you everything. Anyway you tell me about what you two have been up to"

"No mum you still haven't told us who this Pete is, is he our dad?"

"No! He's definitely not your dad, I promise you both I will tell you who your real dad is when I'm ready, now you asked me about Pete"

"Are you in love with him" asked Sara

"Yes I am very much in love with him and he loves me and as I said I was going to leave Jack once but then he became ill and I couldn't, then I was told by the Doctor he hadn't long to live and when Jack found out he was dying he treated me like a piece of dirt, I was his slave. The Ingamells appeared at the door most days I would tell them to go away on his request and they found out he was terminally ill and never called again. All this time Pete supported me; we would meet at the supermarket, when he was too ill to leave his bed, late at night round the back of the house and when Jack went into hospital things became much easier, we were like young lovers"

"So if you hated him so much why didn't you ever contact me and Sara?"

"I was always worried you would tell me to go and I couldn't cope with that, I know you had a rotten childhood, I can tell you one thing it hurt me to think of the way you were treated, I know you can't remember but when you were young he absolutely spoiled the pair of you, you were his little angels and me and him were very much in love, then it must have been about the time Sara was two Jack came home from a night out with some friends and heard it said that you two were not his, he asked me and I told him that it was all lies but he then found out I had been lying and I confessed to him. He didn't throw me out he used the situation to his own means he totally changed he had woman after woman and bragged to me about it, making me think it was my fault and I believed it, after all where could I go and Jack was a very wealthy man so I stayed. Then he started putting up the barriers between us the mental cruelty started and when he found out that you were gay Christine it made his day, he didn't shut up about it"

"What do you mean I'm no different from any one else"

"I know that Christine, it was just something else for him to have a go over. I blamed myself and he knew it, anyway he's dead now so lets get this funeral over with and we'll all sit down and I'll tell you the rest, but I have to get some information"

"Information what information?" asked Sara

"About your real father"

"Is he still alive?" Sara persisted

"I don't know, look, I've already promised you, I will tell you and I will, when I'm ready. Now have you two eaten? (They both said they hadn't) Well could one of you go to the chippy and get some fish, chips and peas I don't know about you two but I'm starving, do you know its about ten years since I bought fish and chips from a chip shop so its on me"

"I had better ring Tom first" said Sara

"Yes and I had better give Sam a ring she'll be worried" added Christine,

"Go on then girls give them a ring and tell them that on Sunday I want you all to come for tea and it's not a request"

"My god Chris, I can see where you get it from"

"What's that?" asked their mother

"The others are always saying that I'm good at giving the orders out" they all laughed.

Sara rang Tom and Christine ran Sam saying they wouldn't be long and they were going to have a bit of tea with their mother. Christine said she would go and fetch their tea. Soon returning with three large potions of fish, chips and peas, this was the first meal they had shared with their mother in years. Once they had eaten, their mother made them another hot drink before they headed back towards Spalding. Their mother stood at the door and waved them off.

On their journey home, Sara asked Christine what she made of the whole situation

"To be honest with you Sara I don't really know"

"Well Chris I'm watching her, I know she's our mother and me, like you Chris I'm pleased she's back in our lives, but just remember for the last seven years she has pretended we haven't existed, yes she gave us her reasons but. Well we will just have to wait and see"

"I know what you're saying Sis".

Sara dropped Christine at her door and told her that she and Tom would call later.

Tom was waiting in anticipation and met her at the door

"Come on then fill me in what did she have to say"

"Give me a chance to get in the door and put the kettle on then my sugar plum I shall reveal all"

"Reveal all that sounds good".

And Sara gave Tom a big kiss before going to the kitchen to put the kettle on. They sat in the kitchen, Sara told Tom every detail of what had been said between her Mother, Christine and she, Tom listened intensely not once commenting. When she had finished he asked her what she intended to do.

"I said to Christine, I don't trust her, yes she's our mother, neither me or Chris know her at all, she was never there when we needed her, she's lied to us, she's never once tried to contact us, now she wants us all to be 'lovely dovey' I've just got a funny feeling about the whole situation"

"What do you mean Sara?"

"I wish I knew what I was trying to say"

"Do you want to be friendly with her Sara?"

"Yes of course I do, I think what I'm trying to say is that I'm scared of getting to close to her, she's my Mother I love her I just don't trust her, not one bit but at the same time I need to give her the benefit of the doubt, I keep expecting the bastard to turn up"

"If he does, run. No joking aside Sara we'll just see how things go, but don't let her get too deep into your life until you're sure yourself. Have you told her much about us?"

"Not really, we mainly talked about him and what I had told you and Christine didn't really mention Sam come to think of it"

"Anyway Tom it's eight and I promised Chris we would call"

"Ah yes I meant to tell you Sam rang while you were out and I invited them round here telling her they could stop the night, I thought we could have a couple bottles of wine without worrying and she agreed providing they could get us all a takeaway and who am I to turn down a curry so they will be here about half eight"

"Me and Chris have already eaten"

"Oh yes so you have well that means more for me and Sam"

"That will please Sam, my god look at the time, shit I had better have a shower quick"

"Go on then make haste".

Sara quickly showered and Christine and Sam arrived about quarter to nine

"Sorry we're a bit late but Sam couldn't keep her hands off me"

"You lucky sod" laughed Tom,

"Where's little sis?" asked Christine

"Sara's in the shower, she won't be long"

"No I won't 'because I'm here you plonker" said Sara

She walked into the room. Tom got the glasses out and Sara opened the wine

"Come on then what do you pair make of it?" asked Sam

Sara told Sam and Christine what she had told Tom all her thoughts and fears, Christine said her and Sam had had an almost identical conversation.

"What shall we do about the funeral" asked Sara

"To be honest with you Chris I don't really want to go, I know I shall have to if only for mum's sake but I feel a bit of a hypocrite having hated the bastard so much"

"I know just what you mean Sara"

"To be honest with you all, I for one shall not be going" said Sam

"No and I shan't, I said to Sara earlier that I didn't even know the man" added Tom

"So it's definitely only going to be you, me, mum and whoever we can drag off the streets Sara" laughed Christine.

Chapter Twelve

The next morning Sara was first up and collected the post from Tom's doormat noticing a letter for Christine it had been hand delivered, finding this a bit strange she handed the letter directly to Christine who quickly opened it with her fingers, still in bed, and still not fully awake. As she opened it she felt the ends of her fingers go cold, and then wet and then the pain, Christine screamed. Realising something had been placed in the envelope to cause her such pain she came to her full consciousness waking Sam at the side of her in a state of total confusion.

Sara rushed back into the room followed by Tom, the sheets on the bed were covered in blood, Christine was still screaming hysterically, Tom rushed to the bathroom and got a towel taking it quickly back to Christine and Sam wrapped it around her hand.

Christine's screams had now turned to sobs; Sam and Sara quickly dressed Christine while Tom slipped on his clothes and got the car out of the garage noticing Christine and Sam's car in the drive with all four tyres flat. Sara and Sam brought Christine to the car and Tom rushed her off to hospital. Sara told Tom to ring them when he knew what was happening.

They arrived at the hospital in Spalding only to be patched up and sent to the main hospital in Boston. While Christine was, being seen by the doctors Tom rang Sara to tell her where they were and also warn her about Christine and Sam's car but Sara had seen

"Who the hell has done this Tom?"

"I asked Christine, she's no idea have you saved the envelope?"

"Sam's got it, we're waiting for the police to call and take it away".

Sara called out the garage and she and Sam drove over to Boston. They found Tom sitting in the waiting area of the accident and emergency department when they arrived

"Where is she?" asked Sam who was still crying

"She's in with the nurse"

At that, Sam walked up to one of the nurses

"Where's Christine Gray?"

"Who are you Miss?" asked the nurse

"I'm her partner Sam Taylor, I live with her".

The nurse went away and returned a few minutes later

"You can come through Miss Taylor; Miss Gray wants to see you"

Sam was led to a curtain-covered cubicle where Christine was sat having the ends of two of her fingers stitched up

"Who's done this Chris?" asked Sam starting to cry again

"I've no idea, but I'll kill the bastards when I do find out"

"She's been very lucky" said the nurse

"You call it what you want lady, but I don't call it luck"

"No Miss I didn't mean it like that"

"No I know you didn't, I'm sorry I'm just so—Oh I don't know what I am, I just I can't work out why" Sam said in a frustrated voice.

Christine came away from the hospital with four stitches to her index finger and two to her middle finger. Tom and Sara still baffled by the whole situation decided to head straight to the office in Tom's car and Sam took Christine home in theirs. Having spent the entire journey home trying their hardest to think who could have done such a thing, they were totally baffled. After about an hour of being home they received a knock on the door, Christine now being paranoid ran to the bedroom and locked herself in, Sam tried to stop her, but couldn't, she didn't come out until Sam convinced her it was only the police calling to see if she was O.K and take a statement. The police told them that there was too much blood on the envelope to get any prints off it and they were hoping the letter inside might give up some clues

"What letter?" asked Christine

"Of course you wouldn't know but when we got it back to the police station, forensics opened it up and found a typed letter inside"

"Well what did it say?" asked Christine

"I'm not sure about the full content, but the sender made a derogatory remark about you, have you upset anyone recently?"

"No why, what did the letter say?"

"If you must know, it says, I'll get you slut"

"And that's it?" asked Sam

"I don't know, but it appears someone has either mistaken you for someone else or you have upset someone in a big way. If that's the case, we need to know before whoever it is does anything else. A few months ago at the same house in Pinchbeck a car was stolen and later found running at Gardeners estate agents, which had been left unlocked, and some strange woman had been seen at the scene. Now this happens at the same house. The big question is who ever it is that knew you were at that house last night. In my opinion, someone has definitely got it in for you. Tell me for your own sake who you think it might it be. Is there anyone you can think of?"

"Honestly I don't know".

Just as she had said that there was a knock on the door Sam answered it, it was the florist with two massive bouquets of flowers both with cards, Christine asked Sam to open them while the police were there, thinking them to be some sort of sad joke, but as it turned out one bouquet was from Tom and Christine and the other was from Simon and Paul. Sam looked puzzled

"What's up Sam?" asked Christine

"Well that's strange have you spoke to Simon or Paul Chris?"

"No, they must have rang the office about the house"

"Excuse me but who are Simon and Paul?" asked the copper

"Oh they're two lads who we are friendly with; in fact we're buying their house"

"They are two very kind young men who wouldn't harm a fly"

"Anyway there's nothing more we can do here so if you can remember anything that might help let us know, we'll be in touch".

And the police left, leaving Christine and Sam to discuss the day's events. Christine said she should ring Tom and Sara to thank them for the flowers. Once she had rang them she rang Simon and Paul's house Simon answered telling her Paul was out visiting a client and said they would call later on.

All that day Christine kept thinking who she might have upset but couldn't come up with a single name, she didn't really know that many people she like Sam only knew past lovers and family and the only one who might hate her enough to hurt her now lay in the morgue at Peterborough so unless someone had made a serious mistake or perhaps this could have been meant for Sara, but why had they got Christine's name, could it be a man, but she hadn't had a fall out with a man, although she had that do with them two lads up town the night they met Simon and Paul. Christine's mind was in a whirl should she suggest to Sara that it might be her that whoever it was wanted, no she couldn't it would only worry her and she might after all be wrong. Then there was another knock on the door yet another bouquet of flowers to Christine, Sam took them off the lass at the door and took them to Christine, Christine stared at them, and then said

"Is there a card with them?"

"No" replied Sam

"Throw them away, go on throw them".

Sam took them into the kitchen and put them into the bin then went back into the lounge and sat next to Christine, Christine started crying hysterically Sam cradled her in her arms trying to calm her and find out why the flowers had upset her so much all she could get out of Christine was chrysanthemums,

"I might have guessed that bitch was involved, I'll kill her—I'll bloody kill her"

"Who are you on about Chris?"

"That bloody Tracey"

"What would she want to do this for?"

"I don't know Sam, but she's the only one outside this flat who knows I hate Chrysanths, so unless you or she has told anyone, it must be her, or have you took a sudden hate for me"

"No Chris that's not fair, you know I love you"

"I know I'm sorry, I love you too"

"Don't you think we should let the police know?"

"No, I want to sort this one out, anyway we're not 100% sure it is her, but I think me and Tracey should have a chat"

"Only if I'm there" insisted Sam.

Later that day as promised Simon and Paul called to visit them; Christine thanked them yet again for the flowers

"That's O.K, but what a horrible thing to happen" said Simon

"We couldn't believe it when Tracey told us" added Paul

"So Tracey told you, how did Tracey know come to think of it how do you know Tracey?" said Christine.

"Me and Simon met Tracey about a year ago. Tracey was at Garrets nightclub in town with her partner, she had been told we are gay and she approached us saying she was gay too and her and her partner wanted to have a baby. She asked if either of us could help them, we told her we weren't interested. She went away the next time we saw her she was very pregnant and today she came out of hospital with a nine pound baby girl"

"She came out today you said?" asked Sam

"Yes today that's when she saw you with your hand all bandaged up and apparently some friend of hers told her what had occurred"

"Well that puts a different light on things" said Christine

"Why what's going on?" asked Simon.

Sam explained to Simon and Paul what they thought telling them about the fact that Christine was once seeing Tracey and the problem at the office.

"Oh dear me, I think I may have a few answers for you, though not in full" said Paul

"What do you mean?" asked Christine

"About two or three months ago I think was on my own in the town centre, Simon, I think was at work but anyway, a girl came over and spoke to me saying she was your friend Christine. She had seen me and Simon with you and Sam. We stood talking for about fifteen minutes, and then she got on to the subject of you saying how pleased she was you had settled down with such a beautiful partner. She asked where you work, I pointed to the shop and your sister was waving to me, and this girl said, Oh yes, I can see her waving. Before I had got time to say that's not you that's your sister she had gone over to the shop I thought she had gone to see you but she just stared in the window and I had to make a move back home, but thinking about it I must have had one of my 'mind absent' days, because if she knew you so well, she would have known where you work. Also I never thought to ask her name"

"What did she look like?" asked Sam

"I don't really know, she was quite petite, very pretty and very well spoken"

"Well I'm totally baffled, I've no idea who she could be" said Christine

"I tell you what, I'm not sure, but I think I may have seen her at Garrets just before that, but I wouldn't swear on it"

"So what do we do now?" asked Sam

"I don't know but one thing is for sure I won't settle until I know who this bitch is" replied Christine

"I know what you're saying Chris, but we can't go around accusing people when we're not sure if it's them whose done this" "said Sam

"Why don't you let me and Simon check this girl out first before we make any accusations?"

"And how do you intend to do that?" asked Christine

"This girl whoever she is obviously is gay because the only time we go to Garrets is on Tuesday night when it's recognised as gay night, so it must have been a Tuesday night I saw her there and I'm not sure, but I think she was with another girl who I know by sight, but not to talk to, and I know she is definitely gay, so I shall use her like her little sweet friend used me to find out who she is and then we will let you know and if by any luck this mystery girl is at Garrets on Tuesday we will give you a ring" explained Paul

"Why don't me and Sam just go with you on Tuesday"

"Christine, if you did that I know very well what you would do, you'd rip her head off before we found out if she was involved"

"You are right she would and I would help her so perhaps that's the best way to approach this" said Sam

"The thing is this is my problem and to be honest with you, I know you're only trying to help, but I don't like getting you involved"

"Shut up Christine, we're your friends and if one of our friends gets hurt, we want to help them and apart from that we're already involved so leave it to me and Simon".

Simon agreed with Paul's statement reluctantly Christine agreed saying if they didn't mind then she would go along with it. Just as they finished talking there was a knock on the door, before answering the door they all agreed not to mention this to any one else not even Tom or Sara.

Sam answered the door it was Tom and Sara

"Come in don't stand there anyway you don't need to knock"

"Your door was locked" replied Sara

"Oh that's your sister she's gone a bit paranoid"

"Well that's hardly surprising after what she's been through" commented Tom

"Have you thought as to who might be doing this?" enquired Sara

"No, we were just on about it to Paul and Simon" said Sam

"Sorry we didn't realise you had company" said Tom

"That doesn't matter come on through they would love to meet you"

Tom and Sara followed Sam into the lounge where Christine, Paul and Simon sat chatting, Tom stopped in his tracks just as he caught sight of Paul.

"Bloody hell, if it isn't old Taffy"

Paul stood up holding his hand out to Tom.

"My God. Bloody Tom Gardener! How the devil are you?"

"Well that knackered that introduction up, I take it that you pair know each other?" enquired Sam

"Yes we do, I haven't seen Tom since school days" said Paul

"Were you good friends?" enquired Simon in a rather worried tone of voice

"No, don't look so worried Simon, Tom's not gay we were very good friends" said Paul and they all laughed

"To be honest with you I had no idea that Paul was gay" added Tom

"To be truthful I didn't know myself until I met Simon and that was after I left school. I just knew I was different"

"So how did you meet Simon?" asked Christine

"I moved up the road from Simon and we became friends and started going to clubs together, then I found out he was gay. I don't know we just clicked, we fell in love"

"Well I think it's time we got a bottle out" said Sam.

The ice had been broken. They all sat down to a very enjoyable evening with Tom and Paul telling the others about their school days. Paul and Simon decided to make a move about eleven and just as they stood up to leave there was one almighty bang. Tom, Paul and Simon rushed outside to see what they could find but there was nothing out there, so putting it down to some drunks Paul and Simon left only to return two minutes later in a bit of a panic asking for Tom to come and have a look at something outside, telling Sara, Sam and Christine to stay inside. Tom followed them to Christine's car which was parked out on the road about hundred yards from her and Sam's flat, all the side near the road had been smashed in, Tom rang the police from his mobile they arrived within fifteen minutes they said it was possibly a drunk driver and they would make inquiries, Tom thanked Paul and Simon and they made their way home.

Back at the flat Tom told the girls what had happened, Christine became hysterical with Sam and Sara trying to console her, she insisted on seeing the car, she knew in her own mind this was no accident someone was out to hurt her and Tom and Sara also knew they weren't getting the whole story Tom put the kettle on making four coffee's then taking them through to the lounge.

"Come on then, what the hell is going on? We're not getting the whole story here are we?" said Tom

"To be honest with you Tom we weren't going to say anything but"

Sam explained about the mystery girl and what they intended doing

"When you do find out who this girl is, what do you intend doing?" asked Sara

"We don't know" said Sam

"I do, I'm going to rip her fucking head off"

"It's alright you saying that Chris but she might be totally innocent"

"It seems one bloody big coincidence that this woman goes round asking my friends questions about me, pretending to be my friend and then within a day or so an electrician sees a woman answering the same description in the office, she not seen for a while and when she reappears within a few days this happens. Something tells me I have the right to suspect her don't you?"

"I think you could have a point, but both me and Tom are just worried about you, all I want is for you to be careful"

"Are the police aware of this girl?" asked Tom

"No we don't want them to know, this is something we want to sort out ourselves" replied Christine

"But is that wise?"

"Tom involving the police won't stop her, it will just make her think I'm scared of her, that's one thing I'm not, the only advantage she has at the moment is we don't know who she is or where she lives, but that's about to change then she's in for one all mighty shock" said Christine

"I know you want revenge, all me and Tom are saying is just be careful, we love you and we don't want you to get hurt, or get in any trouble" added Sara

"I know that Sara, I just want to know why, then I'll rip her fucking head off" they all laughed

"Anyway I think we had better get that car moved" said Tom

"Yes I wouldn't have left it there if it hadn't have been for that prick upstairs parking his car in front of the garage doors" said Sam

"Give me the keys I think I'm the only one who hasn't had too much to drink".

Tom put Christine's car in her garage. The off side doors were so badly damaged he had to get in through the near side and climb over trying to avoid the broken glass. When Tom was walking back to the flat he noticed someone standing further up the road in the Bourne direction watching him, Tom pretended not to take any notice and went back to the flat. On returning to the flat he told the others, Christine was all for going after her but Tom suggested that he and Sam walked casually by her to see if Sam recognized her while Sara stayed with Christine, reluctantly Christine agreed.

Tom and Sam made their way out of the flat on to the main road and in the distance they could see someone now on the other side of the road watching their every movement they started to walk towards this person then within a hundred yards of reaching what they now recognised to be a female of very slim build she ran to a car jumped in and drove off. They didn't even get chance to get the registration number but as it went under the first street light they saw it to be a green mini and by the sounds of it, it wasn't too healthy.

"I think by the look of the way she moved then she didn't want us to see her" said Tom

"I think you're right and that car didn't sound none to healthy" replied Sam

"Well Sam, I think I'm going to have a closer look at Chris's car".

Tom went back to the flat and fetched a torch, inspecting the car it became obvious that the damage had been done by a green car, he then went to where the car had been parked at the time of the accident and inspected the road, this confirmed what Tom had thought, there at the same point where the off side of Christine's car would have been laid the chrome remains of a mini door handle and part of a door trim plus several peaces of rust particles. Tom recognized them to be off a Mini because he had on passing his car test owned a Mini, now Tom was sure Christine was more than likely right and this accident was in fact no accident and this woman or young lady was obvious a very disturbed individual Sam still with Tom witnessed what Tom did and they returned to the flat. Tom told Christine and Sara what happened showing them the door handle asking Christine if she knows or knew anyone with a green Mini Christine didn't so they decided to wait on Simon and Paul to see if she turned up on Tuesday night. They all thought it best not to mention any of this to Christine and Sara's mother and Christine said she would tell her that she cut her fingers on a knife. Christine asked Tom and Sara if they would stop the night they agreed Tom went home and fetched some clothes.

Chapter Thirteen

The next morning Tom was first up. He went to get Christine's car from the garage and take it to the body shop up the road and returned back to the others who were having breakfast.

"I've done you some bacon and eggs" said Christine cheerfully

"My god Chris it's nice to see you so happy again"

"Yes Tom I thought about it a lot in the night, she got to me last night, and that's just what she wanted, why should I let her win the day?. I said to Sara and Sam there's no way she's getting the better of me ,yesterday she won a battle, but she's not won the war, so come on Tom get that lot down you. What did the garage say about my car?"

"It's not as bad as we thought, all that's damaged is the off side doors so that will have to be replaced, the rest like the front wing have scratches that can be filled and painted so they reckon you can have it back by the end of the week. If you need a car, you can use mine. You can go to the funeral with your sister"

"O.K. Tom, can I ask you a favour, can I take a couple of days off?"

"We weren't expecting you in for the rest of the week anyway were we Sara"

"No Sis. What do you intend doing with your self? Hang on a minute, Sam love can you get some milk we haven't any?"

"Alright Chris" (and Sam left the flat)

"Now Sam's out the way, I was going to tell you yesterday, but we were all sidetracked. I've arranged for our relationship to blessed on Sam's twenty-fifth birthday that's on a Friday so I thought I could arrange a surprise party to celebrate both occasions, that gives me about six weeks, hopefully by then we will be in our new house on

Winsover Road, which reminds me, Tom in case you're wondering what had happened to that lovely painting you bought me and Chris, we are saving it to put up in our new house"

"I was worried in case you hadn't liked it and didn't like to say" replied Tom

"No Tom far from it, we intend putting it above the fire place"

"This party, can me and Sara help in anyway, we'd love to, in fact we would like to pay for it"

"No Tom, thanks, you're far to kind. This is my treat, but I would appreciate help with the food"

"No problem said Tom"

"I'll help you with preparing it" said Sara

"Anyway Chris, me and Sara had better get off to work and I can hear Sam coming"

"Hi you two, could only get one pint. Better get ready, I shan't be long Tom" said Sam

"What for?" asked Tom

"Work" replied Sam

"Take the day off with Christine, at least then we'll know she's O.K. Go on take the day off on me and enjoy it"

"I will, thanks Tom".

Tom and Sara left for work just as the postman arrived. Sam picked up the post and taking no chances opened it with a letter knife she had been given by her Grandfather many years earlier. There was no need for her to worry, but Sam wasn't going to take any chances.

Among the post was the letter they had both been waiting for. A letter from the solicitors, giving them a date for the signing of contracts, they were both excited by this news.

Christine rang Simon and Paul and spoke to Simon

"That's good news at least things are finally moving. How are you both?"

"I'll let Sam update you on further events".

Christine handed the phone to Sam. She told him what they had told Tom and Sara and why.

"To be honest with you Sam, I said to Paul that you should have told them, he agreed with me so. You've done the right thing. After all Sam they're already involved"

She told him about the green Mini.

"Did you say green Mini?"

"Yes why?" asked Sam

"Tracey has or had a green Mini"

"Oh—shit—so she does, I knew, that I knew someone with a green mini and she came here to interview us over the incident over Tom and Sara and the bitch turned up in a green Mini"

"Hang on Sam it might just be a coincidence after all this lass doesn't look like Tracey"

"No Simon what I'm saying is that confirms the connection. Do you have any idea where that bitch lives now?"

"No Sam. Leave it with us until Tuesday. Just be very careful, the pair of you. Paul and I will speak to you later, now take care".

Sam put the phone down and told Christine what Simon had said and she too could remember seeing Tracey in a green mini. Before Christine's had time to answer, her mother rang to ask if she was alright.

"Yes I'm fine I've just cut the ends of two of my fingers"

"I've just rang the office and Sara told me, as long as you're O.K. that's all that matters and its still O.K for Friday?"

"Yes mum, Sam won't be going"

"Why's that's Christine?"

"Mum he didn't like me, he hated Sam apart from that he didn't even know her. To be honest with you mum, I'd feel a bloody hypocrite, I'm only going for you. I just do not want to be there"

"I know that Christine dear. Sara didn't put it quite like that, but her words meant the same. I'm not daft and I can't blame you. Christine I understand that you and Samantha have got the day off work, why don't you both come over and we'll all go out for dinner, on me, after all, he has left me a rather wealthy widow. It'll give me a chance to meet Sam. So what do you say?"

"Hang on a minute (Christine covered the phone with her hand and asked Sam she nodded) Yes mum O.K (then in a whispery voice she said to her mother) don't call Sam, Samantha, she hates it"

"Sorry Christine, thanks for warning me"

"O.K Mum, give us an hour or so to get ready and we'll be there after all I would be a fool to give up a meal that he has indirectly paid for"

Her Mother laughed and they put the phone down

"What about that thing we call 'car' Chris?"

"Shit! I had completely forgotten about that, we haven't a car, I know Tom said we could borrow his, I don't like to"

"Well we will take the bus or get a taxi" replied Sam.

Finding out that there was no bus, Sam phoned for a taxi. They arrived at Christine's mums for twelve; she was surprised to see them arrive in a taxi.

"Where's your car?"

"It's at the garage; I had someone run into it last night"

"Why didn't say I would have come and picked you up?"

"No, it doesn't matter; anyway this is my partner Sam"

"Hello Sam, call me Eileen it's nice to meet you, I've heard a lot about you. Now girls, I know a nice pub at a little village out of town where we can get a bite to eat, so let's make a move and you can tell me all about yourself Sam".

They all got into Christine's mothers car. They headed out of Bourne to the village of Folkingham, to the pub there. Eileen asked the girls what they wanted to eat. Eileen told them how she and Peter would secretly meet there in the early part of their relationship

"So what's he really like this Peter then mum?"

"Well Christine he's not at all like your Dad"

"Mum I don't mean to be rude, but please don't refer to him as my dad because he isn't"

"Sorry Christine, I meant to say Jack. I was saying Pete isn't at all like Jack was, he's very kind, caring and very romantic"

"Is he married?" asked Christine

"His wife died of cancer about ten years ago"

"So what about children does he have any"

"Yes, twin girls, but they don't live round here, I believe he said one lives near Edinburgh and the other girl lives somewhere near Worcester. You would all like Peter, I'm sure"

"So when do we get the pleasure of meeting this Peter?"

"In a few weeks time, when things have settled a bit, (a waiter came to their table carrying three plates) look here comes the food".

They all had a very enjoyable meal before retuning back to the house.

"Mum?" asked Christine

"Yes?"

"Would you mind if I show Sam my old room and around the house?"

"Be my guest, nothing's been touched since you left so it will be rather dusty, after next week I'm going right though this house and getting rid of everything that's no good ready for when I sell it so if you see anything that takes your fancy that you and Sam could make use of, feel free to take it. I'll put the kettle on; I must get some drinks in for when you all come. Jack didn't allow alcohol in the house; he believed only the evil drank alcohol"

"He must have been pissed all the time then" laughed Christine

"Go on then see what you can find, I'll bring the coffee up stairs".

Christine led Sam out of the lounge into the murky hall up the very wide stairway to the landing.

"My god Chris, how big is this place"

"It's got eight bedrooms although not all of them have been used as bed rooms. This door here goes into my old room".

Christine pushed open a door, a door like all the others that was in need of a coat of paint, the other side of the door was what could only be described as a time capsule. The room was exactly how Christine had left it the day she walked out swearing never to return. Her empty drawers still lay on the floor in the same place; the blankets on the bed were pulled back as if she had just climbed out of it.

Christine was sure that under the years of dust you would find her fingerprints on the furniture.

"So this is where the young virginal Christine lived"

"Well I don't know about virginal, but yes this is where I spent most of my childhood".

All of her dolls still sat on top of the wardrobe in the corner of the room, Sam walked over and opened the door, and inside still hanging on the coat hangers were loads of dresses

"They never kept you short of clothes"

"To be honest with you, we never went without, it was just love we lacked, I suppose you could call it mental cruelty"

"What was your mum really like?"

"Sara and I had this conversation on the way home the other day, she asked me what I remembered and—eh. We had better discuss this later; I can hear her coming up the stairs".

Christine's mum entered the room carrying a tray with three coffees on.

"My god Christine it is rather dusty in here, but it's like I said no one has been in here since you left, so it's going to be. You said you're moving soon into a new place, so if you now live in a flat you'll need some more furniture, why don't you and Sam have all this in this room it only needs cleaning, that mattress will be that full of dust that'll want throwing but the rest is like new"

"Well mum, we won't turn you down"

"Before I move I must go into the loft, although do you think Sara's young man will have a look to see just what's up there"

"From what I can remember mum there's stairs to the loft, it's only like another room"

"I know that Christine but Jack had a security door fitted to it and I think the key along with the alarm code is in the safe and he has taken the safe code with him to the grave"

"That sounds about right for him; even now the pigs causing problems, what about his money can you get access to that?"

"Yes, I made sure of that two months before he died unknown to him I got him to sign some bank forms giving me full control of the bank account I also got a copy of the wills from the solicitors and as I told you, I am the only benefactor. The bastard has left one very tidy some. I got the last laugh"

"So why has his brother Ray been hanging round?" asked Christine

"I wasn't going to say anything Christine, but seeing as you mention it that was another reason I never contacted you. About three years ago Jack went to see his other brother Maurice in

Worcester, while he was away Ray called under the pretence that Jack had asked him to do some work in the house and we went for a drink, then one thing led to another and you can guess the rest, but Ray wouldn't leave it at that he pestered and pestered me I told him I wasn't interested and he threatened to tell Jack so I gave in to him. Then I met Pete and Ray found out and went to tell Jack about me and Pete. Jack having become so ill I had control, so he couldn't get near Jack to tell him. He called the day Jack died threatening to tell everyone about me, I told him I wasn't bothered. Yesterday I got a phone call from him saying that unless he could have access to the safe he would tell you what a tramp I am. I put the phone down on him"

"So like that he must know the combination?"

"I don't know but I guess that would make sense"

"And if he knows the combination he must know what's inside?"

"I guess so Christine"

"Well mum I think he knows a damn sight more than you do about the contents of the safe and the attic. I think we ought to find out just what he does know"

"How do you intend doing that?"

"Leave it with us mum we know a couple of chaps who would be more than willing to help"

"Yes I think I know who you mean" said Sam

"Let's leave it until after the funeral" said Eileen.

They drank their coffees before Christine showed Sam round the rest of the house pointing out parts of it that remained in her memory from her childhood. Eileen got out some old photos most of which Christine didn't know existed. Among the photos, Christine found one of her and Sara together Christine must have been about three and that would have made Sara about a year, she asked her mother if she could borrow the photo so she could get it enlarged as a surprise, saying she didn't want Sara to know.

"Of course you can. If you intend enlarging, you might be better off with the negatives"

"Do you have them?"

"Yes, I've always kept negatives, there in that old tin over there".

She opened the tin and after about five minutes of looking, she found the right one and handed it to Christine. Sam said she would like to have a look at the gardens,

"Gardens— it's more like a jungle, in fact I rang a chap only this morning that does odd jobs, and he's coming on Monday to clear it all up. A collector has been after that old tractor for ages, he's calling next Wednesday to remove it, it's bloody monstrosity"

"What's it doing there mum?"

"Some farmer in Tongue End owed Jack some money and couldn't afford to pay it back so, he got Ray to do his collections and Ray returned with that thing, parked it there and that's where it's remained since. If you want to have a wander, feel free"

"I know it sounds silly Eileen, but I've always tried to picture Chris's childhood home and now I have the chance to see it"

"Come on then we'll all go, I haven't been in those old sheds in years in fact nearly all this house and its out buildings haven't been entered since Jack sacked the staff so I have no idea what's in them.

Eileen led the way out to the rear of the house.

"See what I mean Sam it's rather a jungle but at one time it was a garden to be proud of, it's too big for me, just like the house and it's going to cost a pretty penny to get that back to its former glory. All the windows are rotten I just want shut of it, it's not that I have any good memories of the place"

They walked over towards some old dilapidated out buildings then Christine said excitedly.

"I know what's in there"

And she pulled back the old half-hanging door.

"Oh my God look at that"

"What?" asked Sam

"That"

And Christine went to the corner of the shed and pulled on some old sacking.

"There, my old bike left where I put it or should I say hid it away from that old bastard"

"Why's that?" inquired Sam

"Can you remember mum?"

"Oh yes in fact Christine, I helped you hide it from him"

"Come on don't leave me in suspense" said Sam

"I wasn't very old at the time"

"You were fourteen" said Eileen

"Yes I must have been, mum bought me that bike I was so proud of it and then he heard a rumour that I had been seen kissing a girl in the village so to punish me he locked me in my room. He said he was going to smash the bike up, but when he went out mum unlocked the door and we hid the bike in here and that's where it has been ever since"

"Well Christine, I can add to that, he beat me black and blue that night, saying I had hidden the bike" said Eileen

"To be honest with you, me and Sara always suspected he knocked you about although we never saw it, you always told us you had fallen and who were we to question you"

"Well roll on Friday and we can get back to being a proper family, what about your family Sam?"

"I was adopted and they disowned me when they found out I was gay, in fact my father beat the shit out of me"

"I will admit that when I found out for sure that Christine was gay, I was so upset, but once I got used to it, it didn't bother me. I will add I knew long before she admitted it to me and before Jack came in that night laughing about it. I'm very proud of the way both my daughters have turned out"

"Look over there"

Christine pointed to loose brick just above a shelf, she walked over and removed it, behind it she removed a small rusty tin placing it on an old bench and opened it to reveal all of her private letters and a couple of diaries from her teens, she had completely forgot about them until now.

"Do you mind if I take these home I don't think these are for your eyes Mum (knowing there to be some rather sordid details of her childhood sexual experiences) from what I can remember"

"No I think you should" laughed Eileen

"Do I get to see them?" ask Sam hopefully

"I don't think I'll be able to get away without showing you them Sam"

"Anyway come on girls I don't know about you two but I'm rather peckish and I've made some cherry and almond cake"

"That's my favourite" said Sam

"I know that Christine told me".

They all went back to the house Christine carrying the tin, they all sat in the kitchen and Eileen made a coffee and cut the cake

"So mum, what are your plans for the rest of the week?"

"Well tonight Pete's calling and we're going out for a meal then tomorrow I'm not sure"

"Tomorrow is Thursday so why don't you come to ours for dinner, it'll only be fish and chips and we'll go for a walk afterwards. If not I will be on my own as Sam's back at work"

"That sounds fine by me, as long as you haven't got anything else planned and I'm not intruding?"

"Don't be silly, course you're not intruding"

"As long as you're sure, so now I think we should get you pair back to Spalding. If you get your things together and Sam you take the rest of that cake with you, Oh yes and Christine don't forget that tin. I don't want that leaving here. I'll drive you home"

"Its O.K mum we can get a taxi"

"No I insist"

"Alright, as long as you stop for a coffee with us"

"That's sounds good to me, come on lets make a move".

They all got into Eileen's car, Eileen parked the car outside their flat and they all went up, Sam checked the answer phone for messages, Sara had rang leaving message for Sam to ring her, someone else had left a message, but Sam stopped it before the others could hear it, she realised it to be rather insulting. Christine put the kettle on and Sam rang Sara to find out what she wanted. Sara asked her not to say anything to Christine, but when they checked the answer phone, a message had been left for Christine, from some rather hysterical woman, it was rather threatening, saying that Christine wasn't getting away with destroying this woman's life and she would pay for the hurt she had caused her, the caller said that Christine was to look on the other day as a minor scratch and the real pain would follow.

"I think this has gone far enough Sam don't you?"

"Yes I do" replied Sam

"Both me and Tom think you should tell the police, to be honest a lot can happen between now and next Tuesday"

"I agree totally with you Sara"

"Sam me and Tom aren't doing anything tonight so why don't you and Chris come for tea and stop the night"

"O.K we will and by the way Sara your mums here at the moment"

"I see—I thought you were finding it hard to talk, tell mum I'll ring her in the morning".

__Chapter Fourteen__

Once Eileen had gone Sam told Christine what Sara had said, but Christine still didn't want to call the police. Christine wanted to find out who this woman was; she agreed to go to Tom and Sara to see what they had to say.

Tom collected Christine and Sam about six, taking them straight to his house, Sara had set the table for tea

"Did you have a nice time then Sis?" asked Sara

"Yes thanks we had a great time".

Christine told them about the days events. Sam told them about the mysterious tin.

"What tin's this Chris?" asked Sara.

"It's years since I looked"

"So do we get to see these letters Chris?"

"No you don't. Until I've read them myself I don't know whether or not I shall show Sam them" laughed Christine

"You had better" said Sam, they all laughed

"Come on then shall we have tea?" asked Tom.

They all sat down to their meal. After tea, Tom went to the kitchen to wash up leaving the girls to talk.

"So Christine, what in your heart do you want to do about this woman?"

"I know you all think I should go to the police, but in all honesty what can they do we can't prove anything?"

"Chris you went to the hospital, the police have the envelope then there's your car and now Tom and Sara have the tape"

"I know what you're saying, but even if they do catch her and the police do their bit, she'll possibly go to court and some geriatric half sharp judge who will slap her wrist tell her to be a good girl and send her home"

"As much as I don't like to admit it Chris, I think you're right" said Sara

"So what are you going to do?" asked Sam

"I don't know, I'm just hoping that Simon and Paul come up with a name and a possible address"

"Then I shall pay her a little visit"

"Not on your own you won't" said Sam

"No you're not Chris because I'm coming too" added Sara

Just then, Tom walked in the room, hearing the conversation, he said

"Can I drive the get away car, if the bitch doesn't let my tyres down first" the room was filled with laughter

"Come on let's get out of this serious mode and enjoy ourselves" insisted Sara.

They spent the rest of the evening disusing their mother.

"How did you find her?" Tom asked Sam

"Well she's definitely a character. It's certainly true that Chris takes after her"

"You cheeky bitch" jested Christine

"One thing's for sure she likes to be in control and that's something that baffles me"

"Why's that?" asked Sara

"I know she's your mother, but I can't weigh her up"

"What are you saying?" asked Christine

"To me although I might be wrong, she doesn't come across as the type of person who would let a man control her and from what you've said Chris, that Jack wasn't the type to put up with a woman who was always having affairs" said Sam

"I know what you're saying, but I can remember when we were kids, if he wasn't there, she was totally different to us. One year she joined us in Cornwall for a couple of days. Can you remember Sara?"

"Yes"-replied Sara

"We had a great time, mum was relaxed, then we went home and he was there and the barriers went up. Don't get me wrong, I'm not trying to defend her, but it was as if he had some kind of grip on her. I don't think he knew about the other men, he may have suspected her, but he was no angel and from what mum said he was giving Mrs Ingamells one"

"What can you make of it Tom?" asked Sam

"I'm keeping an open mind. I suppose I feel like you Sam I'm pleased that their mums talking to them. I just hope that's the way it'll stay. I think they should give her a chance and we should encourage their friendship to grow"

"I'm sure you're right" replied Sam

"What time are you expecting her tomorrow Chris?" asked Sara

"About eleven"

"Why don't you bring her round to the office she can have a coffee with us then you, Sam and Sara can go up the Pub for lunch"

"That sounds good to me what do you two think".

They all agreed then spent the rest of the evening drinking wine before going to bed.

Sam was first up leaving Christine to lie in, as she hadn't had a very good night her fingers had been throbbing, due to the fact she hadn't taken any pain killers in case she had a drink, now she was regretting it. Sam put the breakfast on taking Tom and Sara's to their room banging on their bedroom door.

"Room service, pull the sheets over you, I don't want to be sick and she marched in the room tray in hand with two coffees and two very large fry ups"

"Holy shit Sam, how the hell are we supposed to eat that lot?" asked Sara

"Tom have you seen what Sam's made us?"

Tom still half a sleep trying to open his eyes to the morning light casting them over the tray.

"Bloody hell Sam, is the rest of Pinchbeck joining us for breakfast?"

"Shut up and eat it, you pair of bitches, let's face it you don't get service like this when the others make breakfast"

"What's up?" shouted Christine from the other room

"Come here Chris and look what the room service staff have done me and Tom for breakfast".

"I can well imagine"

Christine took one look at the tray and burst into laughter

"It's alright you taking the piss there's one on the way for you Chris"

"No thanks Sam you eat it I'm not hungry, or at least not that hungry"

"Well it looks like I might have to eat it then" said Sam

"Now can you see why I won't let her make breakfast at home if I did we would be like a pair of bloody Sumo Wrestlers within a month".

Tom and Christine ate what they could and Sam ate all of Christine's and then finished off Tom and Sara's bacon and sausage.

"Where the hell does she put it all?" asked Tom

"God knows she's like this at home"

"There's nothing on her, she's like a bloody whippet"

"Christine Gray, are you calling me a dog?" laughed Sam

"No Sam love, I didn't mean it like that. Mind you, you are a bit of a bitch"

"Yes, but you love me all the same"

"Yes Sam I definitely do"

Christine kissed Sam on the lips

"You'll have me blushing in a minute. I have to go to work,"

"I had better drop you off at home on the way Chris"

"No Tom I'll catch the bus"

"No you won't, I'll take you home and I'll come into the flat with you, I don't want you taking any unnecessary risks the way things are"

"O.K if you insist".

Tom took Sara and Sam to the office and then Christine to her flat on the way Christine asked Tom if he had thought anymore about selling the business.

"To be well and truly honest with you Chris, I've decided to leave things as they are for a while. The only one who made me an offer close to what I wanted, was Greens and I wouldn't sell to him on principle, so we're staying put"

"Well at least that's good news Tom"

"Anyway give me your keys Chris and I'll have a look around"

"No it's alright Tom"

"No give me them I've told you I'm not taking any risks".

Christine handed Tom the keys and Tom entered the flat and had a look around finding nothing he called to Christine to check the answer phone but there were no messages. Tom left Christine and went off to work. Eileen turned up around eleven and Christine told her what Tom had said about going to the office. Eileen thought it to be a wonderful idea and she told Christine how she was looking forward to the day. She hadn't been to Spalding in years. Christine suggested to that Eileen put her car in her garage rather than leave it parked on the road and they would walk to the office.

"This is nice Christine, I've always dreamed of the day I could visit my daughters and their partners now that dream has come true"

"Well mum I can assure you, Sara and I are just as happy to have you being back in our lives"

"What about Tom and Sam, what do they think?"

"Tom and Sam are two very kind people, obviously they are wary of you, but that's natural, give them time"

"I hadn't noticed, both Sam and Tom seemed to welcome me with open arms"

"Yes mum because that's the way they are. I didn't quite mean it the way I said it. Neither of them has ever passed comment, but they will watch the situation from the fence"

"I know what you're saying and I can understand their concerns, I would be the same. Did you say Tom's surname is Gardener?"

"That's right mum"

"Oh so that must be his shop over there"

"Yes, but I don't know what's happening, Oh my god mum there's an ambulance coming. Oh shit lets get over there".

As Christine ran across the road she could see a man lying on the pavement face down with blood pouring from his head, there was a car wedged in the shop window next to Tom's shop. Sam and Sara were knelt down at the side of the man on the pavement, but where was Tom. Christine had not realised her mother hadn't followed her.

"Is it Tom?"

But they didn't answer Sara was crying, then there was one all mighty bang, they all turned to look and the shop front next door had given way and collapsed on the car then Christine saw Tom come running across the road with Eileen.

"What the hells happened?"

"I don't really know Tom we all heard this bang and the entire building shook. We went out side that car was through their window and this man lay here".

I rang for an ambulance. The Police have turned up the ambulance are seeing to the man on the pavement. The fire brigade had to be called to free the driver from the car and when the car was pulled out Tom's shop front window and the brickwork round it all cracked

"I'm sorry but we're going to have to ask you to vacate the building I think this may have caused some structural damage" instructed the fireman

"Fucking great. Well at least I won't be paying for it" said Tom in a rather pissed off tone

"Come on girls get your things together and have a early and long lunch, I had better stay here to keep an eye on things until the building inspector arrives, I'm sure he won't be in any great rush, and Sara sweetheart bring me a couple of rolls back".

The police then told Tom they had to cordon off the area for the safety of the public

"So what about my shop, the bloody windows cracked and the wall that separates has fallen leaving a bloody great hole"

"Just lock it up and we'll keep an eye on it until whoever arrives" said the policeman

"I don't mean to be a pain, but I don't want anyone in my shop unless I'm there, and I need to inform my insurers and get my builders in" replied Tom

"O.K sir that's completely up to you, but we need to do our investigations so unless you have anything you can help us with, I'll get on with my job"

"Cocky sod" Tom murmured

"What was that?" asked the police man

"You heard" replied Tom.

Having locked the shop up, Tom decided to go and join the others for a bar meal at The Feathers.

Once there he soon found Sara and the others tucking into scampi and chips

"They look good; I think that's what I'll have"

"I didn't think you were coming Tom" said Sara

"I wasn't, I'm sorry Eileen I didn't mean to be rude are you O.K"

"That's alright Tom, I could see you were rather occupied"

"Well I suppose that's one way to describe it (Tom laughed) are they looking after you"

"Yes Tom they are".

Tom went to the bar and made his order and at the same time getting another round of drinks before returning to their table

"What's happening then Tom?" asked Sara

"I don't know love, I rang Steve and he's sending someone round this afternoon to secure the shop and make a note of what work needs doing and I'm waiting for the insurers to ring me back, by the look of Simmonds shop, that's going to have to have its front ripped out and rebuilt. So if you want cheap shoes I would get in there" they all laughed

"Look out here comes that Mr Green" Sam pointed out

"Tom, Ladies" said Mr Green acknowledging them all, Tom nodded

"A bit of bad luck a Tom?"

"You could put it like that"

"Any one hurt?"

"A couple appear to be" replied Tom

"It looks like you could be closed for a while Tom?"

"Does it, well I don't know where you heard that from" said Tom

"Well looking at the damage, I just presumed and if it was the case, then perhaps I could help you?"

"Like how?"

"Well you could send your clients to us. I only mean just until you're sorted?"

"That's very caring of you, but to be well and truly honest with you I wouldn't trust you as far as I could throw you. So if you don't mind would you leave us to eat our dinners in peace".

Mr Green went away mumbling

"Oh dear that man doesn't look very happy" commented Eileen

"If you knew our Mr Green as well as I do, you would realise why I was so rude to him"

"I take it he is not a nice man?" replied Eileen

"Yes—that's one way of putting it" added Sam

"To be truthful the man is an arrogant pig, he treats his staff like dirt and speaks to his customers with contempt, and then he has the cheek to ask me if I would like to send them over to him, well he can dream on"

"Sit down and unwind Tom" said Sara

"I'm sorry this is just one of those very bad days"

"Give us a cuddle and shut up moaning".

Tom lent over and gave Sara a cuddle.

"Come on drink up, I'll get another round in and he went up to the bar soon returning with a tray of drinks. Just as he sat down, his mobile phone rang.

"Take these off me Sam that must be Steve. I'm going to have to love you and leave you till later Steve's at the shop; do you have your mobile with you Sara? (Sara nodded) I'll ring you when I hear something but I wouldn't rush back".

Tom kissed her and left the four of them chatting.

"Well mum this wasn't the kind of day I had planned for us"

"It doesn't matter Christine in fact it's been rather exciting although I don't know whether that's the right word"

"Where did you go when I ran off mum?"

"I didn't go anywhere I stayed the other side of the road I can't stand the sight of blood, then I saw Tom and came across"

"To be truthful I honestly thought it was Tom lying on the floor" Said Christine

"So did me and Sam, Tom had just nipped to the post office and then we heard this bang looked up and saw someone laying on the pavement, my bloody heart stopped beating"

"I'll bet" said Eileen

"At least none of you lot have been hurt"

"You're right mum, any way that's enough of this morbid situation. What shall we do until Tom calls us back, mum have you made any plans for this evening?"

"No Sara, why?"

"Me and Tom thought it would be nice if we got a takeaway in and all five of us ate it round my flat"

"That would be lovely Sara, but I mustn't be too late home, it's the funeral tomorrow"

"No problem. So what's your plans for the rest of the day?"

"I said to Christine I would like to look around Spalding and perhaps ride out to Weston. I've been told there is a really nice garden centre there"

"Oh you will like that, there's no end to see me and Chris go regularly don't we Chris"

"Well mum if you want to look round there we will need plenty of time so we had better make a move and have a look round Spalding first"

"That should take all of five minutes" said Sam they all laughed

"I tell you what I do need to do Christine"

"What's that mum"

"I need to get one of those mobile phones; you know one of those that you buy a card for"

"Yes mum Sam's got one, aren't we becoming a bit modern?"

"After tomorrow Christine you will see a completely different Eileen Gray to the one you know today"

"Good for you mum" said Sara

"Well I've had enough of my old life I'm having my hair done professionally on Monday and I think I'm going to treat myself to a brand new wardrobe, then I might even have a holiday aboard, do you know what I've not had a holiday since before my mum died, I went down to Cornwall to see her"

"Do you know mum me and Sara didn't find out about them dying until two years ago and that was only because someone sent us an anonymous letter and that had gone to my old address in York three years earlier"

"That was from me Christine, I dare not say who had sent it Jack would have gone spare if he had known and York was the only address I had, I had no idea either of you were in this area until we saw you that Christmas in the pub, I tried to find out where you were living, but you weren't in the phone book"

"Come on that's in the past now and if you want to go to the garden centre, look round Spalding and get a mobile we had better make a move" said Sara

Sara's mobile rang, it was Tom telling her not to bother going back to work the building work would take a couple of days and he was transferring the phones to the house telling her he would see her later. Sara told him that her mother and the others would be coming for tea, Tom said he would order a Chinese for about seven thirty.

Sara told the others what Tom had said,

"That's great, we can all go to the garden centre" Said Christine

"I think we should get mum a phone first" said Sara

"Well its mobile this week, hair do next is it a lap top the following week?" joked Sam

"Who knows, I could surprise you all, I might become a lap-dancer" replied Eileen joining in on their wind up.

"What a thought" laughed Christine

"Come on empty your glasses or we'll never get off and the day will have gone" said Sara.

They decided to go to Holland Market shopping centre where Sam had said they were doing an offer on mobile phones. Eileen purchased her first piece of technology and proud of it too, but she had to wait to have it registered before she could use it. They then had a look round the other shops in the shopping mall before going for walk round the town. Eileen couldn't get over the way it had changed since she was last there and was more than surprised at the number of empty shops. They decided to visit the civic centre and use their coffee bar finding it closed; they all got in Sara's car and headed for the garden centre.

At the garden centre, they all decided to go to the restaurant and get a coffee before having a wander around. Sam queued up for the drinks while the others found a table in the rather packed restaurant, Sam's eyes wandered round the room and caught a glimpse of a very petite young girl at first she seemed to watching her, then her eyes were on the others. This girl fitted the description that they were looking for; Sam tried to attract the others attention but in doing so the girl saw what she was doing and left in rather a hurry not finishing her drink. Sara came over to see what Sam wanted

"It's too late Sara, she's gone and you'll not catch her"

"What are you on about Sam?"

"That girl, the one who's trying to hurt Chris she was in here watching you lot"

"Where?"

"She was sat at that table"

"Do you know what, I thought she was staring at us, but then I thought it must have been my imagination"

"No Sara she was watching you, and she fitted the description to the word"

"She'll be well gone by now, but at least we know what she looks like" said Sara

"Yes I won't forget that face now all we need is a name and address" added Sam

"In all honesty Sam we couldn't have done a lot in here not without a lot of fuss"

"No but the net is closing in, I shan't say anything to Chris until we're on our own so your mother can't hear"

"No I'd sooner you didn't, that would be all we needed I had better go back to the others" Sara retuned to the table

"What's up with Sam?" asked Christine

"She wanted to know if we wanted any food. I told her no we were fine"

"God mum she's always hungry isn't she Sara?"

"Yes I don't know where she puts it all"

"She's not pregnant is she?" asked Eileen.

Sara and Christine burst into laughter; Sam finally got served and returned to the table

"What the hell is up with you lot?"

"Are you going to tell her Chris or shall I?"

"I think you should I might wee myself"

"We were telling our mother about how much you eat and she said are you pregnant".

Sam was now in a fit of hysterical laughter at hearing what she had said

"I wish Eileen, if I thought your daughter could get me pregnant, we would have had eight kids by now, but I'm afraid that unless there is a big development in medical science we won't be having biological children between us"

"How embarrassing, I didn't think, I'm sorry"

"Don't worry Eileen you've got nothing to be embarrassed about we find it very amusing".

They sat chatting for a while before having a wander round the garden centre.

"I could spend a fortune here if I thought I was stopping in that house, but I think what I shall have to do is come back when I've moved"

"Yes mum Sam and I buy all our plants from here, now we are moving the other tenants won't look after them so we've wasted our money because most of them won't move"

"That's a shame" said Eileen

"Tom gets all his plants from here" added Sara

"Now Tom is what I call a keen gardener" said Sam

"Yes, it is his pride and joy" added Sara.

They continued their walk round the garden centre before returning to the car then they decided to head back to Sam and Christine's flat to pick up Eileen's car.

"I've just realised" said Sara

"When I spoke to Tom earlier, he said he was going to arrange the Chinese for seven thirty but he didn't say where. We originally planned to have it at my flat but I had better ring him I think he may have changed his plans".

Sara rang Tom, he had forgot and had arranged for it to be delivered to his house in Pinchbeck, Sara said that she wanted to call round her flat first, to show her mother where she lived, and have a coffee, before going to Tom's.

"Mum, now you will see what a mucky messy thing your youngest daughter is"

"It's alright Chris, Sara paid me to go round yesterday and clean it out"

"Do you think for one minute Sam, I would trust you in my flat, with my dirty underwear lying about, you must be joking?"

"You bitch" they all laughed. They soon arrived at Sara's flat.

"What a lovely setting for a flat" commented Eileen

"Yes" replied Sara they haven't been flats long, this building used to be a mill, I was very lucky to get it as soon as they came on the market they were snatched up"

"It's really nice, it's the sort of thing I could do with" said Eileen

"The only problem is that some of them are privately rented, there's a couple down stairs turned their flat into what could only be described as a slum and the chap who owns it doesn't seem to care"

"I know just what you mean Sara, there is an estate in Bourne 99% of the tenants keep their houses lovely the other 1% have turned them into slums. Anyway, I haven't come to discuses the politics of life. I'm here to look at your wonderful flat. Have you got a date yet for moving Christine?"

"We have, but to be honest with you we're not holding our breaths are we Sam?"

"No they told us a fortnight on Friday, that's if everyone else in the chain agrees and two weeks is a long time"

"Drink up, it's time we made a move, I know Tom said seven thirty it's now six and I must get a bottle of red wine from the off licence" said Sara.

Christine and Sam got in Eileen's car and Sara went in hers picking up a bottle of red before going to Tom's.

Tom had already set the table for the five of them when they got there Tom was in the shower. Sara led them into the lounge then she went to see Tom who was drying himself.

"Hello sugar have you had a good day?" said Tom leaning over to kiss her dropping the towel

"You had better put something over that body or I might have to drag you into there (Sara pointing to the bedroom) and we have three very hungry visitors downstairs"

"Let them eat cake and put the stereo on loud, then rush your body back up here, don't worry I'll be waiting"

"Somehow or other, I don't think that will work Tom there might be a slight chance they could suspect something and apart from that you forgot to buy some cake so Rambo get dressed"

"Rotter" replied Tom.

Sara went and joined the others; Tom appeared a few minutes later

"The food will be here in about half an hour or so, so Eileen I have time to show you round the estate"

"What Tom actually means is he'll show you the back garden" joked Sam

"Alright little Miss Correction, the back garden" said Tom returning the joke.

Tom led the way with Eileen holding his arm, leaving Sara and the other two to chat.

"Has she mentioned the funeral Chris?" asked Sara

"Not really, only what you heard"

"We had better get the full details off her later; I don't even know where the crematorium is in Peterborough, seeing as she wanted us to help her with it she hasn't told us a lot"

"I think Christine, that business over helping her was just a talking point, to break the ice"

"Yes that sounds about right, I must be losing it, in my old age, I hadn't thought about that"

"Did you say losing it? You never had it in the first place Chris" joked Sam

"Oh you bitch"

"Girls, girls put the nails away" said Sara laughing, just then Tom and Eileen entered the room

"Well mum what's the verdict?"

"It's absolutely gorgeous Sara you were right when you said he had a nice garden"

"Christine and I were telling Tom about how nice your garden use to be"

"Yes it was, but what a shame now it's just an eye sore, I don't need a big garden at my age, just a little back and front one will do me nice"

There was a knock on the door.

"That must be the Chinese, I never thought Eileen but do you like Chinese food?" said Tom as he answered the door.

"I don't know Tom, but I'm prepared to try anything once, what's in it?"

"Well what I've ordered you Eileen is what we normally eat and that's roast Dog done in a sweet and sour Hedge Hog sauce"

"Take no notice of him mum, he's winding you up, now tell her the truth Tom" said Sara smiling at Tom

"I know he's only joking Sara"

"Eileen what I've ordered is house special Chow Mein and egg fried rice and several other bits that to be well, and truly honest with you I can't remember but I'm sure you will enjoy, if you don't I'll make you something else"

"Don't worry Tom; I'll enjoy it I'm sure".

True to her word, Eileen did enjoy her meal.

After the meal they all retired to the lounge having placed the dirty pots in Tom's newly purchased dishwasher

"Eileen, Sara and I have something to tell you, haven't we Sara?"

"Have we?"

"Yes Sara, think!"

"I'm sorry Tom but I don't know what you're on about"

"Next April Sara, ring any bells"

"Oh shit, sorry Tom I didn't realise what you were on about. Mum next April third me and Tom are getting married"

"Oh Sara that's lovely, congratulations, I'm so pleased for you both and I'm sure you will be happy, you're both two very lucky people"

"Mum just promise one thing, you will be there"

"You try keeping me away, that's wonderful news. Give me a hug. I must leave you all now tomorrow's a big day and I still have a lot of things to do, so I had better go home and get an early night. Eileen got up and kissed them all goodbye and left.

Once she had gone, they all sat discussing the day's events Tom told them that they had got all of tomorrow off as the builders won't have the shop repaired until Saturday.

"I had better ring her first thing in the morning to see what time she wants us there, I don't even know if we're going in one of the funeral cars or not" said Christine

"You had better ring as soon as you know Chris. We can take my car" said Sara

"You better had Sara I don't think yours will be ready until late tomorrow or early Saturday Chris, I meant to tell you the garage ran earlier and left a message saying to ring them late tomorrow"

"We don't really have a lot of choice then" replied Christine.

"What did you think to mum Tom? You seemed to be out in the garden for a fair old time"

"I found her to be a very nice lady, she stressed to me, that she wanted more than anything for you all to grow close and promised that she was full of good intentions and said that she wanted me and Sam to be her friends, she did say she wanted to put the past behind her"

"What about you Sam, what did you reckon to her?" asked Sara

"I'm like Tom I found her a really nice lady, very lonely and she was trying her utmost to please, she is and after today I think we should make her as welcome as we can"

The next morning Christine rang her mother and arranged to meet her at the crematorium at ten o'clock, having got directions off her. She then rang Sara to tell her, saying that if Tom didn't mind Sam would like a word with him, Sara handed Tom the phone and Sam took the phone off Christine.

"Tom I've been thinking how would you like me to treat you to a fish and chip meal this dinner in town?"

"Do you know Sam as soon as Sara handed me the phone I thought to myself, I'll bet this has something to do with food, but saying that the answer to your request is yes, I would love to join you for a candle lit dinner at the chippy, I'll call for you around twelve".

Chapter Fifteen

With Sara behind the wheel and Christine at her side both dressed very smartly in dark grey suits, looking very much like sisters, they made their way to the crematorium arriving at quarter to ten. Their mother had just arrived in a funeral car following the hearse with Jacks brother Maurice at her side and Ray and his wife Dorothy sat behind them.

Christine and Sara went into the chapel type building and waited. The only other people in there were the Ingamells they nodded to Christine and Sam then the six bearers entered carrying Jack's coffin, followed by Eileen, Maurice, Ray and Dorothy.

The service was short and sweet with two hymns allegedly or so Eileen had told the Vicar Jacks favourites *'The Lord is my Shepherd'* and *'Onward Christian Soldiers'*. When the Vicar announced what they were to sing Sara and Christine looked at each other and smiled, he hated these two hymns. All through the service Ray kept staring over at Christine and Sara, it got so obvious to them that Christine waved to him with a sarcastic grin on her face.

Once the service had finished and his coffin had disappeared behind the curtains they all formed a very small crowed outside to look at the few flowers and chat to each other, Ray headed straight to Sara and Christine.

"What are you two hypocritical bastards doing here?" he asked in a rather nasty tone of voice

"Me and Sara thought we would come along to make sure they burn the old bastard, then we can see what he's left, I suppose you, you old git, that's what you're here for to, the pickings Isn't it?"

Christine said in a rather unusually quiet voice followed by Sara's comments.

"By the way can you tell that old bag with you that when you finally snuff it, we would like to know we could do with another celebration?"

"Like I said bastards" replied Ray and went and joined his wife

"I don't think that man is very keen on us Sam do you?"

"Not in the slightest Christine, I don't give a toss" and they smiled at each other.

Eileen came over to them.

"Thanks for coming girls. (Then talking very quietly) Now I know I'm free, I'm just waiting for that puff of smoke then it's back to my place for sandwiches. What did that pig Ray want Christine?"

"I'll tell you later mum"

"He hasn't been upsetting you has he?"

"He doesn't worry us, he's just like his brother he's a pig"

"So he did say something to you?"

"Leave it mum, he's not worth it" said Sara

"No I'm not when we get back to the house I'll sort him"

"Mum, you need that safe opening before you fall out with him, so don't say a word to him, not until we have a word with our friends"

"O.K Sara but I want him out of our lives and soon"

"Leave it with us mum, look up there a puff of smoke lets make a move.

On the journey to their mums house Christine said to Sara she was going to give Simon a ring and ask him if he and Paul could help them out with a problem over the safe. When she rang, it was Paul who answered.

"What's up Chris?" asked Paul,

Christine explained to Paul about the safe and their dead step dad's brother Ray. How they needed to get the safe open, then once they had it open throw Ray out of the house,

"We wouldn't bother you Paul if it wasn't important"

"When do you want this doing?" asked Paul

"As soon as you can"

"What about later on I'll have a word with Simon he should soon be back from visiting a client, but I can't see a problem, I'll ring you in a while".

By the time they had reached the village of Langtoft, Paul had rang them back.

"I've had a word with Simon and he is all for it, he said you are to make the plans and ring us."

They all arrived at Eileen's house Sara and Sam followed their mother into the kitchen telling her they needed a quiet word with her

"Mum if you get chance, get Ray on his own and get him into the subject of the safe"

"Why Sara?"

"Mum get him to arrange with you to come back tonight so he can get what he wants from the safe and we'll do the rest"

"O.K, what ever you are up to if you think it will work I'll go along with it".

They helped their mother carry the sandwiches into the lounge before going to the other side of the room to leave her to chat with the others. Eileen didn't need to make a move; it wasn't long before Ray came over.

"Eileen dear, I need a quiet word"

"Yes Ray?"

"I don't know if Jack mentioned it to you, but not long before he left us, I gave to him some very important papers to look after, I believe he put them in the safe, to which I have the combination number, I take it that it's O.K for me to retrieve them from the safe"

"What are they?"

"Nothing much just some old photo's and that sort of thing, Oh yes and while I'm thinking about it Eileen the key for the loft room is in there and I have some papers in there I need, I'm sure you won't mind"

"No Ray that's fine"

"I'll go now while you have a chat with Dorothy, she's over there"

"No Ray, have some respect, you can't do that now, you'll have to come back later"

"But When?"

"You'll have to come later on"

"I really need them now"

"Ray if they have been in there as long as you say they have, then another couple of hours are not going to hurt are they"

"What time then?"

"I don't know make it around seven"

"But I'm busy then"

Knowing how desperate he was to get his hands on whatever was in the safe Eileen said

"What about sometime next week?"

"No I'll make it dead on seven tonight".

And Ray wandered off to speak to his wife.

It wasn't long before the only ones left were Eileen Sara and Christine

"I'm going to ask Tom to bring Sam over here later and Tom can clear a space in the barn to get the cars in out of sight" said Christine

"To be honest with you Sara it wouldn't be a bad idea to ask him to pick up Simon and Paul"

"Yes you're right Chris I forgot they won't know where to come".

Sara rang Tom who was sat in the chippy with Sam. She asked him to ring her from home before he left and she would fill him in on what was to happen.

"Enjoy your meal Tom. Loves yah" she said ending the call

"Do you know what Chris; I now know what it feels like for one of them detectives off the telly, when they are setting a trap to catch a criminal"

"Those programs on telly Sara, has no one ever told you they're not real".

"Well that took the shine off telly detectives for me, I'll just have to listen to the Archers at least that's real" they all laughed

"That's what I like to hear a sense of humour, something this house hasn't seen in years".

Tom rang Sara and she put him in the picture he told her to use some care in how they did this, or it could have some repercussions on their mother. He took Sam with him picking up Simon and Paul.

As they turned into Eileen's drive the drive, Paul shouted.

"Stop Tom, are we going down there?"

"Yes Why?"

"This Ray chap, he hasn't got a friend called Jack, who lives down there?"

"Jack, if it's the same man you're on about, he was cremated this morning and the chap we're setting up is his younger brother Ray" interrupted Sam

"Oh, shit. I know this Ray he was Jacks money collector and his muscle, but he must be an old man now"

"I think you had better wait until we get to the others and tell them what you know".

They continued down the drive to the house.

"Good god this has changed since I was last here. Look at it now, It's a bloody shit hole".

Sara met them at the door letting them all in.

"Have you got the kettle on?" asked Tom

"Yes"-replied Sara

"We had all better go into the lounge, Paul has something to tell us all" Eileen looked at Paul

"Don't I know you son?"

"You could. I think I knew your late husband, but I didn't know he was anything to do with Christine and Sara"

They all sat down. Sara brought through coffee and the remaining sandwiches from the funeral.

"Right Paul, fill us in, what do you know?" asked Tom

"About five years ago I got an envelope though the post, it was before I was seeing Simon they were photos of me in a rather compromising position with another man, the thing was my parents didn't know I was gay and were sending me a rather tidy allowance each week, but I knew, if they knew I was gay mum and dad would have stopped my allowance and they would have disowned me. With the photos there was a note telling me to go to a car park in Bourne where someone would discuses the photos with me. I did as the letter said and that's when I met this Ray. He said he knew how much allowance my parents were giving me and he wanted half so as to keep the negatives in a safe place where my parents couldn't find them, he told me if I didn't agree to his, demands, I said blackmail, he told me to call it what I wanted, but he wouldn't be able to stop them dropping through my parents door"

"Mum, do you have a photo of Ray?"

"Yes Sam I'll get you one. (Eileen went to the cupboard and got out a photo album and handed Paul a photo) is that him?"

"Yes and that's that Jack. I met him when I came here to make a late payment"

"How long did you pay him for?" asked Tom

"I don't know about two years then my parents got killed in car crash, I stopped paying and then they had no one to blackmail me with, I told everyone I'm gay",

"Did he tell you Simon?"

"Yes, A few years ago and when he told me about it, I wanted to come over here and beat shit out of them and get the money back but Paul wouldn't let me, so we put it down to a bad experience although I've always wanted revenge"

"It's a bit of a coincidence that a few years later we should bump into Christine and Sam" said Paul

"I'm going to enjoy meeting this Ray chap" said Simon

"Yes revenge is definitely going to be very sweet" said Paul

"Yes, I think Eileen I have a very good idea what is in that safe or at least what it has to do with and I think he intends continuing with Jacks very profitable business venture. I think we should see to it that as from today he ceases trading"

"Yes, Tom I think you're right, God I'm going to enjoy this" laughed Eileen.

"Well I think we should sort out what we are going to do. First just in case and knowing how eager he is to get into that safe, I suggest we move those cars off the drive"

"I said to mum and Chris, we could put them in the old barn round the back"

"No thanks Sara, that barn looks like it could give way at any time and I don't fancy ringing my insurers again this year, and I don't mean that as an insult to the state of your property Eileen. In fact, it might pay to park them well away from the house. Me and Sara will move them now" instructed Tom.

Tom and Sara went and moved the cars and parked them just up the road on the way back to the house Sara asked Tom where he thought they should hide.

"I thought we could hide in one of the bedrooms, just me and you like, then if we get bored—we could pass the time away doing what comes naturally"

"I might have expected an answer like that off you"

"Well you did ask, but joking aside I suggest we have a look around and we all scatter about the house.

Once they were back at the house and Tom asked Eileen if it was O.K for him Simon and Paul to have a look around so they can find the best spots for them all to hide.

"Show me where the Safe is?" asked Tom

"Come with me I'll show you, it's under the stairs" said Eileen
Eileen led Tom into the hall and to a locked door.

"Watch her Tom, she might do rude things to you" shouted Sam

"That's it" pointed Eileen

"That's not the safe is it?"

"Yes"-replied Eileen

"But that's just a standard room door with a lock on it"

"No Tom you have to open that door outwards then behind that is a big steel door that leads into a small steel room"

"So who has the key for this door?"

"I guess there must be one in the office and Ray will have one but it has an alarm on it"

"Can you find the key?"

"To be truly honest with you Tom, I wouldn't know where to look"

"I tell you what Eileen Jack definitely trusted Ray"

"They were very close"

"How come he never emptied the Safe just before Jack died"

"As soon as I was told Jack was dying, I made sure Ray never got near the Safe, if he called I would say Jack was out and once when he did get in the house, I found him just opening this door and I threatened to tell Jack so he locked the door back up"

"I think its time we put a plan of action together. Eileen you couldn't make us all a coffee please?"

"Do you know what mum; he's as bad as you and Christine for giving orders?"

"I don't mind Sara, anyway how can I say no when a man asks like that?"

Tom, Simon and Paul checked the lower part of the house for possible hiding spots, Tom suggested he would hide just inside the Parlour, the room that was almost opposite the door to the Safe, Simon would wait in the walk through Pantry until Ray was at the Safe, then Eileen pretending to be working in the kitchen could let him out, Paul would hide in the hall broom cupboard and finally the three girls just in case he escaped would hide outside and as soon as he was inside the house let his tyres down and tie some string across the front door, so if he legged it he would trip. Their plan looked good, their intentions were to gain entrance to the Safe and remove Ray from the house empty handed and unhurt, then they could retrieve what was in there and also get the keys to the loft room.

Chapter Sixteen

Ray arrived at six thirty turning his car around before parking it facing up the drive. He got out pressed the remote control to engage his central locking and made his way up the half dozen or so steps to the front door, using the door knocker he knocked three times, Eileen took a couple of minutes to answer then opening the door

"Hello Ray you're early"

"Yes I need to get this sorted, there are some urgent papers in there I need"

"I hope you have a key for that door because I don't have one?"

"No, Jack kept it in the office"

"Where Ray, I'll get it for you?"

"It's O.K; I'm quite capable of getting it myself"

"Be my guest, I'll put the kettle on"

"Don't make me one; I'll just get the papers and leave".

Eileen went to the kitchen pretending to make herself a drink, but letting Simon out of the pantry so he could get in position, only when she let him out he had found himself a weapon, a rolling pin looking at Eileen he smiled and whispered

"Just in case"

And he got into position. Outside the girls had put their plan into action. They were determined Ray wasn't going to escape, although Sam did get rather carried away, she wasn't happy with just letting his tyres down she found an old pitch fork and pushed it into the tyre walls, while Christine and Sara set about putting bailing twine across both the door entrances and just to be sure across the main drive.

Back inside Eileen was getting rather concerned Ray still hadn't returned from the office, so she decided to go and see what he was up to. On entering the room, she found Ray looking through a load of papers

"What are you doing? They're private, now get what you have come for and leave"

"Shut up, I'll leave when I'm ready and I'll look at what I want. So unless you intend stopping me I suggest you get back in the kitchen after all, you don't deserve any of what's been left so I think I might just take a few extra items"

"Look Ray I don't want any trouble, just take what ever it is you came for and leave"

"Did you say trouble, that's fucking rich coming from you isn't it"

"What are you getting at Ray?"

"Lets face it you've been a fucking problem all the time, my brother, god bless his soul was married to you, a fucking whore"

"What are you getting at?"

"You and your two bastard daughters, you needn't look at me like that, Jack told me every thing he was going to change the Wills, but you stopped that"

"I'm not listening to this just get what you came for and go before I call the police"

"Call them they might be interested in these papers and what connections you have with them"

"I know nothing of them"

"Will they believe your word or the word of a Magistrate?"

"That's a laugh you a Magistrate"

"Yes that's something you didn't know"

"So go on call the police"

Ray smirked at Eileen, knowing she wouldn't dare involve the Police, but Ray was unaware of the real reason. Leaving the office with a violent slamming of the door. Eileen went back to the kitchen and put the kettle on, she made herself a cup of tea, also warning Simon to get back in the pantry just in case Ray came down stairs. She then went into the Parlour and made hand signals to Tom to let him know what was happening, warning him to keep out of sight she could hear Ray making his way down the stairs. He came into the hall carrying a box full of papers, placing them on the floor near the front door, Ray went back upstairs, and five minutes later, he returned with yet another box.

"I think I had better put these in my car first (turning towards the front door. Then stopping in his tracks) No I'm not that daft, you might lock me out"

You could almost hear Eileen's heart miss a beat then restart when he changed his mind. Then he placed the box on the floor next to the other one. Ray pulled open the door that covered the safe door, reaching in his pocket he pulled out a piece of paper, reading it, he then pressed the numbers on the alarm system deactivating it. Keeping hold of the piece of paper reached back into his pocket and pulled out a large bunch of keys, the same keys that Eileen had seen Jack with on many occasions.

Holding the keys in his right hand he found the correct one and removed the lock and released the door from its locked position revealing a large steel door with two round dials and a key hole on it, He turned to Eileen who had been watching all the time and said

"Go away; get in the kitchen out of the way you're not seeing this".

Eileen not saying a word in reply, returned to the kitchen, it's just as well, she had completely forgotten Simon was back in the pantry, the pantry door could only be open out from the outside. Once out Simon got quickly into position still holding the rolling pin. Tom also was ready and Paul could see through the gap in the door that Ray was now turning the dials on the door; Tom could feel the adrenalin pumping through his body as the time was closing in. Ray put the key in the hole, the largest one on the bunch and turned it, the click of the lock freeing itself echoed throughout the house. Ray pushed the steel door inwards causing a squealing noise coming from the very dry hinges, and then BANG!!!

As the heavy steel door reached its full opening position, hitting against the inner casing of the steel room, but Tom still didn't give the order to move on him. Ray then put the keys and piece of paper back in his pocket walked away from the safe towards a small stool bent down to pick it up,

"NOW" shouted Tom

Tom pounced on him, holding him over the stool. Paul came out of the cupboard and Simon rushed from the kitchen. Ray being a very powerful built man jumped up, forcing Tom off his back. They all jumped on him. Paul shouted he's going to his pocket and Simon realising he had a weapon on him, hit him on the arm with the rolling pin just as his hand connected with the item in his pocket and then there was a massive bang and Ray dropped down to the ground having removed his hand from his pocket and he was holding his leg, in some considerable pain. He then tried to reach his pocket

"Get him keep his hand away from his pocket he's got a gun in there Paul grabbed his arms and held him I'll get some string".

Tom was right, he had a gun and with Simon, hitting his arm the reaction had caused Ray to squeeze the trigger. The last few minutes seemed like hours. Now it was all over.

Tom went outside to get some string seeing Eileen who had gone out the back door to be with the girls, was worried having heard the bang.

"What's happened Tom?" asked Sara

"He's shot himself in the leg"

"Shall we call for an ambulance" asked Sam

"I don't know what to do, but I think I had better get some string first and get him tied up, he's in some pain, he's still giving Simon and Paul a hard time holding him down".

Tom took some string in the house and tied his arms up"

"Well what shall we do now?" asked Tom

"I think we should call the police and let them call an ambulance, but lets not rush we'll leave him to suffer first, just like that bastard and his brother made me suffer" said Paul

"No, please let me go. I promise you you'll never hear from me again" pleaded Ray

"Let you go, that's, really fucking funny, dream on shit head. I'm going to savour this, you can't remember me can you? (Paul grabbed hold of his hair) look at me you bastard, I'm that—how did you put it—I think the words were arse stabber, and what about the money you took off me?"

"I'll pay you it all back"

Paul letting go of his hair pushed him to the floor and turned away from him.

"Call the police Tom. I want this bastard behind bars"

"Where's his gun?" asked Sam

"It's still in his pocket do you have any rubber gloves in the house Eileen?"

"I'll get you some Tom"

"We don't want any of our finger prints on it. (Eileen handed Tom some rubber gloves he put them on and reached in Ray's pocket and removed a small pistol that was now covered in blood from Ray's leg and placed it out of his sight in the lounge) Now we'll just have to watch him until the police arrive" said Tom

191

"Tom he's got the keys in his other pocket and the paper with the safe numbers on it" said Eileen.

Tom bent down put his hand in Rays other pocket and Paul got the bunch of keys out.

"We'll have these"

Ray was begging them to release him

"Come on boys, I'll pay you how much do you want. Name your price just let me go"

"Put the kettle on Eileen can you. The police will be here soon and I'm thirsty" said Simon

"I tell you what Tom; the bloody police are taking their time"

"Yes they are who rang them, did you Eileen?" asked Tom

"I was going to but something distracted me Tom, shit, I had better ring them"

"Yes he's making an awful mess of your hall carpet; in fact I think you had better ring for an ambulance"

"No just let me go" begged Jack

"It's lovely to see you squirm, this time you have really got your comeuppance you bastard" said Christine She spat in his face.

"Tom what are we doing with these boxes and we haven't looked in the Safe?"

"Well Sara as much as I would love to know what's in there we had better leave them for the police and not touch them"

Then they heard the sounds of sirens coming down the drive, Followed by the ambulance service. Sara opening the door letting them in, the police officer smiled

"Well if it isn't our number one pillar of society Mr Ray Gray".

The ambulance men got out of their vehicle opening the rear doors and pulling out a stretcher, bringing it with them to the hall where Ray was still laying they had untied his hands. His right trouser leg soaked in blood. The police officer in charge took the others into the lounge and told them to wait there while the ambulance man sorted Ray out. Within a few minutes, they heard the ambulance doors slam shut and then the ambulance drove away. The police officer entered the lounge

"Now what's been happening here? Although, I know I shouldn't say this, but knowing our Ray Gray it must be something really nasty (the police officer looked at Tom) don't I know you? (Tom shrugged his shoulders) Aren't you that estate agent from Spalding?"

"Yes"-replied Tom

"My god we do live an exciting life don't we" commented the police man,

Then a car drew up outside and two men dressed in suits got out walking towards the front door they walked past the police officer standing outside into the house and into the lounge.

"Hello, I'm detective Brian Davis and this is my partner D.C. Ralph Richards. Don't disappear I will need to question you all. Tom where is that the gun?"

"It's over here, I took it off him, I think he was about to use it on us" Tom replied

"There was no thinking about it Tom if you hadn't taken it, he would have used it on us" commented Paul

"We'll have that bagged up pleased Ralph".

D.C. Richards put some rubber gloves on then placing the safety catch in place put the gun in a plastic bag and sealed it.

"O.K is there anything else we should see before we go any further"

"Yes"-said Tom

"I think you should have a look in those boxes in the hall and also there was something in that Safe that he was interested in"

"And you're Mr?"

"Gardener, Tom Gardener"

"OK then Tom, it's all right if I call you Tom? (Tom nodded) O.K Tom, show me".

Tom led detective Davis into the hall and showed him the boxes still on the floor by the front door, then showed him the Safe under the stairs Davis walked in

"Dear me, that's more like a bank vault"

He called to his companion to come and have a look

"Ralph you had better get some help down here and remove all this money"

"Money what money?" inquired Tom.

Davis ignored Tom's question

"I need to speak to the lady of the house"

Davis took Eileen into the kitchen and asked her about the money and its origin.

"I have no idea, that's my late husbands Safe, I have never been in there"

"So tell me, how long has that Safe been there?" asked the detective

"Years I suppose, I can't remember"

"So what's your version of events?"

Eileen told him everything she knew and her suspicions of her late husbands and his brothers business the detectives never once disputed her words, it was as if what she was telling them they were already aware of.

After they had finished with Eileen, she returned to join the others back in the lounge, within a short while another car drew up on the drive and a couple more chaps in suits got out and entered the house. Davis let them in and led them to the Safe, then returning to the lounge he asked if he could now have a word with Tom, he followed him into the kitchen

"Sit down Tom, in your own words I want you to tell me exactly what happened".

Tom told them every thing that he knew. After he had finished Richards spoke.

"Didn't any of you think to call the police and let us sort it?"

Tom rather annoyed at Richards tone of voice looked him straight in the face.

"Tell me what the hell would you have done?"

"We had already got him under observation" answered Richards

"At the tax payer's expense, And tell me how did he get to become a magistrate?" added Tom

"Mr Gardener. How did he, that's a very good question" said Davis

"My name is Tom, and if you can't answer that, I'll tell you, bloody friends in very high places, that's how. Have you been watching him or not?"

"Alright Tom, yes we had been watching him for quite a time and in a round about sort of way you have helped us, but what you and your friends did was stupid, someone could have been seriously hurt and this could have been a different enquiry"

"Look I don't know where all this is leading, the only one that got hurt was Ray Gray, he's not dead, you lot have been watching him, we had no idea but now you've got him and a van full of evidence so what's the problem?"

"I don't think Tom you realise the seriousness of what you lot did, we can't just sit back and let people take the law into their own hands" said Davis

"No, other wise you will be out of a job" said Tom sarcastically

"I don't like your tone" said Richards angrily

Tom shrugged his shoulders at Richards's comments

"You asked me my version of events, you don't like what we did but the top and bottom of it is we got you results, now whether we are right or wrong you got your man. Tell me have I committed a crime?"

"Yes"-replied Richards

"We could start off with perverting the course of justice, and then there is the assault on Mr Gray and false imprisonment" Tom laughed at these threatened charges

"Look don't waste my time, if your going to charge me get on with it"

"Go back in the lounge Tom with the others and if we need you we'll call you. Ask Paul to come through".

Paul entered the kitchen and sat down he too gave a statement, telling them how he had been blackmailed by the brothers.

"So why didn't you come to us?" asked Davis

"Don't make me laugh, let me spell it out to you. You would have had to make it public and that would have destroyed my parents, and would you have believed me also at the time your ex—boss was his best friend, so what chance had I got"

"Who was that?" asked Davis

"I think his name was Williamson" replied Paul

"Oh yes that name rings a bell, he wasn't my boss, but yes I know who you mean, O.K. Paul you can go. Tell your friends to give their names and addresses to the policeman in the hall, and if we need them we will contact them".

Paul returned to the lounge and told them what Davis had said

"Me and Paul had better make a move now, it's getting late and I have a client to visit in the morning".

Paul and Simon said their goodbyes and left.

"The police never asked to see me and Sam" commented Sara

"They never asked to see Simon either" added Sam

"I think you'll find they have all the information they need. As arrogant as I found that Richards chap, not once did he question my version of events" said Tom whispering

"No they never questioned my version either" added Eileen

"You never mentioned the loft or the keys to the police did you?" asked Tom to Eileen

"No not after I heard them mention there was a lot of money in the Safe"

"That's what I thought, the thing is I'm not sure whether Ray knows about the loft?" said Tom

"He never mentioned it and thinking back I can remember when Jack had it altered, there was some reason why he didn't want Ray to know" replied Eileen

"Have they left the kitchen I'm bloody parched, I could do with a coffee and I think we should wait for them lot to go before we talk about this anymore. Eileen and Sara went to the kitchen leaving Sam and Tom in the lounge

"There's a lot going on here Tom that we don't know about and I'm sure Eileen's hiding something"

"I'm not sure Sam, I don't want to comment, but I will find out. I'm interested in what's up in that loft"

"Who has the keys Tom?"

"I do, Paul handed them to me and I'm keeping them in my pocket, I shall be first up in that loft soon as they've gone"

"Bloody hell Tom it's nearly ten and they are still taking papers out of that Safe"

"Yes Sam I did hear them saying they were nearly finished. I would have thought they will be off soon, I'm hanging around"

"So are me and Chris".

The Police left about ten thirty having totally emptied the Safe they gave Eileen a receipt for the money and items removed. They went on their way saying they would return.

"Thank god that's over" said Eileen

"I don't wish to worry you Eileen, but I think it's only just started, to be honest with you neither of them two detectives thought to ask about the office, or have a look in there"

"I've told them that Ray had already empted it"

"Eileen they should still have searched it"

"Anyway Tom are we going up in the loft".

Eileen led the way up the stairs along the landing to a closed door.

She turned the white marble handle pushing the door open to reveal another set of rather steep carpeted steps. Tom then took the lead being first to climb to reach a rather heavy looking door, retrieving the bunch of keys from his pocket, hoping that one of the keys would open this lock, he tried everyone of them but with no luck, they were the wrong keys.

"Let me try" instructed Christine

"You'll not open it" said Tom handing Christine the keys.

Tom was wrong. Christine found the right key and the lock clicked open. Christine pushed open the door and walked in, feeling for the light switch

"The light switch is just as you go in it's a pull cord near the left side of the wall" said Eileen

Waiting for the others to enter the room so she could join them Christine pulled the cord to reveal a red glow

"This is a bloody Dark room" said Sam

"Yes it is, did you know this was here Eileen" asked Tom"

"No I've never been up here before"

"So mum how did you know where the light switch was then?" asked Sara

"They're normally on the left as you walk in on the left"

"Yes mum, but unless it's a bathroom you would presume it's a switch so how did you know it was a cord" persisted Sara.

Eileen now embarrassed and realising the others were convinced she had been holding back on the truth.

"Mum, what's been going on here and we mean the truth?"

"O.K Tom, can I have the keys I'll show you something"

Tom handed Eileen the keys, taking them she walked to the far end of the loft, hanging on the wall was a black and white large oil painting. Eileen slid her hand down the left side and the painting opened like a door too reveal the panelled wall. Eileen pushed on the top half of one of the panelled sections and slid it to one side revealing a locked door, finding the correct key she opened the door.

Behind this door was what appeared to be the other half of the loft then Eileen turned the light on and they all stepped in.

"My god" said Sara

"Holy shit." said Christine

"I thought this loft seemed small for the size of this house" added Tom

"Mum cut the crap, what has been going on here and where has all this lot come from?" asked Sara

"I promise you all I was going to tell you, I was worried about the police finding out"

"So what did you really know about Jack's dealings?" asked Tom

"I swear I knew nothing of his dealings. I would be lying if I said I didn't know that he was into bad dealings, of course I knew he was corrupt. I kept out of it"

199

"So what about this lot here, some of these items must be worth a fortune" commented Tom

"About two years ago, Jack had this room put in and while he was out I would come up here. I was having an affair with the owner of the building company Pete. One weekend when Jack went to see his brother, Pete put this hidden door in and I had the key, so when Jack left the house, I would hide this lot up here, I didn't realise it was the same key that fitted the main lock, he didn't always lock the main door"

"Where did it all come from?" asked Sam

"Quite often if someone couldn't afford to pay Jack they would give him an item of around the same value, hence this lot"

"What did you tell him?"

"Sara, I knew he was a dying man, he didn't, and I had to look after my future"

"Mum your not answering the question, what did you tell him?" asked Christine

"I didn't"

"So as far as he was concerned they still owed him?" asked Sara

"Yes but who bothered about me. I know it was immoral. Don't judge me girls. You weren't in the situation I was in?"

"Alright Eileen, is there anything else we should know and I mean anything? Where do you think he may have kept all the photos and the negatives, to be a blackmailer he must have had some?" asked Tom

"I don't know. I think he must have had them in the Safe, although there might be some in that dark room, I don't think he told Ray of all his deals".

Tom went back into the dark room and opened the cupboards in all of them were a number of photos,

"We had better take these down stairs and have a good look through them, I hope none of you are in a hurry to go to bed" said Tom

"Tom look here" said Sam Pulling out one of the boxes

"It seems to be packed solid with ten and twenty pound notes"

"Well Eileen looks like suppers on you" laughed Tom

"Looking at that lot I think you're right Tom" replied Eileen.

They all took a box each and Tom returned for a second one shouting Sara up to give him a hand to carry it

"What the hells in that?" Asked Sara

"I think it's his wallet"

"Tom before you come down what are we going to do about all this lot, we can be done for withholding evidence"

"Sara I know what you're saying, I think we should keep this one away from the police, after all if we tell them they'll think your mothers involved in his blackmailing"

"Yes, but we are also helping her"

"I know Sara. What they don't know about, won't worry them, after all they've got what they want"

"Perhaps you're right Tom; it's just not like you to hold back information"

"I didn't like those detective's attitude. I am dammed if I am going to help them. This way at least your mother will come out with something, be it immoral"

"Tom I'm sure you're right, anyway we had better join the others before they send out a search party".

Sara helped Tom carry the heavy box down stairs and into the lounge where the others had started sorting through the mass of pictures while Eileen counted the tens and twenty pound notes. Tom opened the heavy box inside it. Tom found loads of negatives.

"This is great. I think we may have found the root to our Jacks evil system"

"What are we going to do with them Tom?" asked Sam

"Eileen if you don't mind I shall take these away and destroy them"

"Do what you like with them, but make sure you have all of them Tom and haven't left any".

"Shit—look here," shouted Sam.

Sam showed Christine a photo then she handed her a hand full.

"Holy Shit." said Christine

"What's up you pair?" asked Sara

"You have a look here at these".

Christine handed Sara the photos

"That's you and that Tracey Chris?"

"Yes Sara it is, I don't know what they are doing in here" said Christine

"Let me have a look. If there what I think they are, I might be able to shed some light" Sara handed them to Eileen

"I've not seen any of these photos before but I can remember him saying something about seeing you with some girl kissing, then he said he saw you a few days later with Sam"

"I'll bet he didn't put it like that" commented Sara

"No I don't think he did"

"But what the hell is he doing with these, who was he blackmailing—Oh no something tells me our other little friend has something to do with this, what do you reckon Sam?" asked Christine

"I think I know where you're coming from Chris and I think you could be right, we'll take these Tom" said Sam before she had a reply they were in her handbag

"Well I think we should put these in the cars now don't you and get them away from the house. We'll never get through this lot tonight"

"I think you're right. Tom we can get the cars while Sam, Chris and mum put this lot by the front door"

"What about the money?" asked Eileen

"Put it in a case and bring it with you" said Tom

"How much is there mum?" asked Christine

"£72780.00"

"I'll carry the case" laughed Christine

"Tom did you say bring it with me, where am I going?"

"Home with us, you're not staying here, you can stop with me and Sara tonight. I think it would be a good idea if you and Sam stop too Chris. Tomorrow you four can sort though these boxes and I'll burn them, come on then Sara we'll get the cars back".

Tom and Sara went and got the cars Eileen and Christine locked up the loft rooms having checked them for any missed photos.

They all helped to load the cars up having to walk round Ray's car still parked in the drive with its flat tyres. Just as Eileen was about to lock the front door up she heard her phone ring,

"Ignore it mum" said Christine

"It could be the police mum, you had better answer it" said Sara

"Oh it's you Dorothy, what do you want?"

"You bloody cow I've had the Police round here. You have destroyed my Ray, He's finished"

"What a shame Dorothy. It makes a change for someone to destroy him, after all, I wonder if it will ever be possible to count how many life's he and Jack have wrecked between them?"

"How dare you involve my Ray in Jacks Dealings?"

"Dorothy, sort it out with the police, they have enough evidence to put him away for life"

"You bloody old cow"

"Good night Dorothy and good bye. See you at the trial"

"That told her mum"

"Sara, she has had that coming a long time"

Eileen locked up the house and they all went off to Tom's house.

Chapter Seventeen

At Pinchbeck, Tom put the car in the garage, having carried the contents into the lounge while it was dark, the last thing Tom needed, was to be seen carrying boxes across the drive, from the boot of his car. Eileen and Sara made some drinks and Sam made some sandwiches. They all sat round the table in Tom's kitchen and started their search through the contents of the boxes.

"What shall I do with the money Tom" asked Eileen

"Leave it here Eileen, it will be safe, you can put it in dad's old Safe, I don't use it any more, you can keep the key and you can't be caught with it" said Tom

Tom showed her to the Safe upstairs in his father's bedroom, he opened a fitted wardrobe full of his fathers old clothes moved them back to reveal a three foot square Safe built into the wall, going to the bed he lifted the mattress and pulled a key from under it.

"Thanks Tom, for tonight"

"Think nothing of it, we're family anyway. There's the key I haven't opened this in ages, lets see what's in there, (Tom put the key in and unlocked it pulling back the steel door) Oh my god Eileen look at that lot, Sara come up here (Tom shouted and Sara rushed up to Tom and Eileen) look at that Sara",

"Oh shit—Tom, where did that lot come from there must be a couple of grand there" said Sara

"Before we put your money in there Eileen, can you count this Sara so we don't get it mixed up. I think dad just liked to keep cash handy, I had no idea that was there, it's definitely been an exciting night".

Sara counted the money in the safe. It added up to £3255.00 then Eileen put her money in the Safe

"I had better leave the key here Sara I might lose it"

"O.K mum I'll put it in mine and Tom's room. When you need the money just tell us. What are you going to do with it?"

"Sara I don't know, I want to help you with your wedding. Don't say anything to Christine and Sam; I want to help them with buying their house"

"Mum, that's lovely, we've not said anything to Chris and Sam, me and Tom have been worried about whether they have enough money what with them buying the house. Tom wanted to offer them some he was worried in case they felt insulted"

"Well Sara they won't need to worry soon"

"Anyway mum we had better join the others downstairs".

Sara locked the Safe up and put the key in a safe place in Tom's bedroom, before joining the others only to find Sam and Christine asleep on the settee

"Looks like they're comfortable" said Sara

"Yes I was chatting away to Christine, I went to the kitchen, when I came back she and Sam were flat out"

"Well Tom, it's been a long night. I think I'm off to bed, I'll just make a drink"

"I think to be honest with you Sara, I will too" added Eileen

"Tom what are you doing?"

"I'm going to keep looking through this lot, there's a lot to look through" replied Tom

"What are you looking for Tom, why don't we just burn the lot?" said Sara

"I want to see whether there is any more of Chris it might shed some more light on what's been going on"

"O.K Tom, what ever, I'll see you in the morning" said Sara bending down to kiss Tom.

Sara showed her mum to the guest room.

The next morning Sara woke around ten to find Tom had not been in bed all night she went downstairs to find him slumped on the table, Sam, and Christine still asleep on the settee

"Tom—Tom wake up love"

"What time is it?"

"It's ten Tom I'm going to put breakfast on and make coffee"

"God Sara I feel stiff"

"I wouldn't mind feeling a stiff Tom"

"I don't mean like that"

"It's just as well because me and Sam can do without watching you pair doing rude things this morning"

"Sorry Chris I didn't realise you were awake"

"I could see that"

"I was just saying to Tom. I'm putting some breakfast on so if you and Sam want to go and freshen up and I would before mum wakes up and wants the bathroom".

Christine and Sam went and had a wash and Christine went and woke her mother up. Sara got the breakfast ready and they all sat round the table eating and discussing the previous night's events.

"What time did you fall off to sleep Tom?"

"I couldn't tell you Sara"

"Did you find anything?"

"Oh yes, (Tom got up from the table and collected a hand full of photos from the French dresser and placed them between Christine and Sam) they're yours, the negatives are in there as well. Have a look at them and later. I am going to the office to see how the builders are getting on; I will bring the paper shredder back with me.

If you don't mind, you lot can run them through the shredder. That way they'll burn easier".

They finished their breakfast. While Sara and her mother washed up, Sam suggested she went back to the flat to get a change of clothes for her and Christine, she borrowed Sara's car.

"Christine, now Sam's gone I want you to show you something, Tom handed her another bundle of photos

"I found these in one of those boxes"

Christine looked closely at them.

"These were taken a few years ago before I moved in with Sam what the hell was he doing with them, he wasn't blackmailing me"

"I don't know Chris, he was definitely showing an interest in what you were doing and who you were with, I also think it may have some connection with the strange girl"

"Why do you say that Tom?"

"Because of these (Tom handed Christine some more photos) I found these in another box, they were just like that with an elastic band round them otherwise, I wouldn't have thought they had any connection with each other"

"That's me and Sam. It's when we first started seeing each other; I can't see what he wanted these for. Who is this, or need I not ask?"

"I'm not sure Chris but looking at her she fits the description of our little friend"

"So was she being blackmailed by him Tom?"

"I don't know Chris. Be honest are you sure you don't know her?"

"No Tom, I can honestly say with my hand on my heart, until lately, I'd never seen her before"

"O.K Chris. Paul and Simon know what she looks like, we had better show them this picture and see if it's the same girl"

"I'll give them a ring Tom"

"I'm off to the office now, if you come with me we can call at their house and show them to them".

Sam arrived back at Tom's with a change of clothes for her and Christine; Christine showed the photos to her. Sam agreed, the girl in the picture did match the description of her given by Simon and Paul.

"I'll bet Simon and Paul wish they had never met us" said Sam

"Well Sam, since I met you lot my life couldn't be called boring" joked Tom

"Up until a few months ago, I was just an every day run of the mill very attractive lesbian" laughed Sam

"Conceited bitch" added Christine

"I know that Chris, but you love me for it" replied Sam

"Anyway ladies, it's time we made a move. You're coming with me Chris aren't you?"

"Yes Tom"

"I'll come too if you don't mind?" asked Sam

"You be careful with those two raving nymphomaniacs in the car with you Tom" joked Sara

"I'm a damn sight safer than you would be with them, Sara my sweetheart" said Tom they all laughed and Sara kissed Tom as he left with Christine and Sam.

"Well mum, it's just me and you now, how are you feeling?"

"About what Sara?"

"About Jack dying?"

"I feel fine Sara dear"

"You must feel some deep down sadness after all those years of being with him"

"Sara, it's possibly hard for you to understand, but I feel free and a sense of relief. Sara I spent years dreaming of being friendly with you and Christine, meeting your partners having a normal relationship with you both. As the years went on I didn't think it possible, but you and Christine accepted me with open arms. Tom and Sam have not once judged me"

"Mum irrespective of what has happened and how that bastard treated me and Chris, it doesn't change the fact you're our mother and we love you"

"That's nice Sara, thank you and what ever you may think, I am very proud of the way both my daughters have turned out"

Sara gave her mother a hug.

"Well mum after I've made us both a coffee. What would you like to do today?"

"I had better ring Peter to tell him where I am, and thinking about it, it might be just as well to ring the police, if they go round the house they might think I've done a runner"

"I had forgotten all about that mum, yes you don't really want to go on a wanted list"

"I can see it now. News flash, have you seen this woman, if you do don't approach her, she's highly dangerous".

Sara laughed at her Mothers comments and handed her the phone then went into the kitchen to put the kettle on.

Eileen made her two phone calls then joined Sara in the kitchen.

"Everything O.K mum?"

"I think so. They say they want to see me"

"That's hardly surprising is it?"

"No, but they asked me if I would go down to the police station now"

"I'll ring Tom on his mobile. I'll take you. Did they say Bourne or Spalding?"

"Spalding"

"O.K don't worry, we'll go now"

Sara rang Tom and told him advising him to get rid of the boxes just in case the police called and then took her mother to the police station.

Once there, leaving Sara waited in the reception, a police officer took Eileen through to an interview room where they told her to wait for Davis to arrive.

After about ten minutes, the door opened and in walked Davis he sat down opposite her

"Mrs Gray we have some rather bad news, I'm afraid early this morning your late husbands Brother Ray died in hospital"

"How did he die?" asked Eileen showing no emotion

"We can't be sure, but we think it was a heart attack"

"And you have dragged me over here to tell me that, you could have told me that on the phone. Well I don't mean to sound rude, but I'm not really bothered"

"I'm sorry you feel like that but we do need to clear a few things up like the business over the £72780.00 and its origin and this piece of paper (Davis showed Eileen the piece of paper with the safe numbers on it) what is it?"

"I told you last night, that he had a piece of paper with the numbers on, now I don't where this is leading to, but I've told you all I know, am I under arrest?"

"No, we just need to sort a few things out and I'm asking you to help us" replied Davis

"But I've told you all I know, I don't know where the money came from, it's possible it's all kosher in which case that money belongs to me"

"Eileen, off the record, we know what Ray and Jack were up to. Their consistent bullying and blackmailing of the weaker members of our society"

"So why didn't you stop them?"

"We were having them watched but just as we were about to make our move Jack died, then you handed us Ray, now he's dead"

"It's not your day, my son is it?"

"You can go now"

"Thank you young man. Just remember you still have my money all £72780.00 of it"

"I'm sorry Mrs Gray, but that is still under investigation and we will let you know when we've finished our investigations".

Davis showed Eileen back to the reception where Sara was still waiting.

"No hand cuffs mum?"

"No Sara love it likes I'm a free woman again," laughed Eileen.

Eileen told Sara what Davis had said,

"So with Ray being dead does that mean that the money they removed will be returned to you?"

"I've no idea what they will do"

"Well if they do what with the other money, the stuff in the loft and the sale of the house you will be quite a wealthy lady?"

"Yes, looking at it like that, I think you're right Sara, we'll have to see".

Sara and Eileen went back to Tom's house. Tom and the others had not yet returned.

"If you put the kettle on mum, I'll give Tom a ring (Sara said picking up the phone) Tom! Where are you sweet?"

"We're still at Paul and Simon's and we could be a while yet"

"I've got some rather good news, Ray is dead, but I'll tell you the full story when you get back"

"Oh dear well I have some news for you, that's definitely the mystery girl, but I'll tell you about that when your mum isn't there,

Oh yes and I've got the shredder from the office. I'll see you in a while. Can you give the garage a ring to see if Chris's car is ready? Must go, loves you".

Sara went and joined her mother in the kitchen

"Are you hungry mum?"

"No I'm fine"

"Mum in a fortnight I'm going to look for a wedding dress with Chris and Sam will you come to?"

"Sara I would love to. Thank you for asking me"

"So what shall we do till the others get home"

"Well Sara I need to have a bit of a chat with you about you father".

"You mean my real father"

"Yes Sara, yours and Christine's real father"

"Who is he?"

"Sara I will tell you, but not just yet because I haven't traced him yet but I just want to tell you that I did get hold of his sister and he's still alive, but she wont tell me where he is living until she has spoken to him. I was going to say something when Christine was here, but I thought it best to tell you first, just letting you know I haven't forgot"

"So when will you know?"

"Hopefully this week"

"Mum does he know I exist?"

"I'm not sure"

"What do you mean?"

"Sara I will tell you the whole story soon, There is a lot more to this than meets the eye and I just need to find out something first"

"O.K mum but as long as you promise us as soon as you know you will tell us, anyway that sounds like them coming back".

The door opened and in walked Tom

"Where's Chris and Sam?" asked Sara

"Their coming later. I've dropped them off at the garage to collect Chris's car"

"Is it alright?"

"In a fashion"

"Why's that Tom?"

"It's going back the doors don't line up and the paint isn't right, but never mind that. What's been happening?"

Sara and Eileen told Tom what the police had said.

"That must mean that they have no more inquires to make, they will never really know how much money there was" said Tom

"I hope so Tom, but just in case they decide to make another visit, I had better go right through that house room by room" said Eileen

"That's probably best" replied Tom

"Shall I take you now mum?"

"I would think that would be a good idea Sara"

"When you have gone I'm going to shred this lot. (Tom pointing at the boxes of photos) I'll come over when I've done to help you" said Eileen

"On about photos Tom, you never finished off telling me what Simon and Paul said?" said Sara

"I'll tell you later love" replied Tom.

After Sara and her mother had gone, Tom set about shredding the boxes of photos then burning them in an old tin dustbin incinerator in his back garden. Just as he was about half way, he heard a car draw up on his drive, worried that it might be the police he walked round the side of the house to find Davis and Richards at his front door.

"Can I help you?" asked Tom

"Ah Tom, we didn't think you were in, we just need to clear a few things up. Can we come in and have a chat?"

"To be honest with you I'm rather busy" replied Tom trying to keep them out of the house

"We don't mind chatting while you carry on with what you're doing" replied Davis

"Having a bonfire are we Tom?" asked Richards

"What do you reckon?"

Sam and Christine arrived in Christine's car

"Family visit Tom, them pair live together as man and wife don't they" commented Richards in a very sarcastic voice

"Does that give you a problem; in fact I find your childish comment very insulting. I shall be contacting your superior and now I shall ask you to leave my property"

"Go and wait in the car Ralph. (Richards walked back to the car leaving Tom with Davis) Tom I'm sorry about Ralph's comments, that's just his way"

"That still doesn't alter what he said about my friends and further more I shall still be putting a complaint in. I suggest you get on with what you're here for then you can go"

"Tom we need some information on the money we removed from the Grays house"

"I told you last night I don't know a thing about its origin"

"We know he was a blackmailer, although we never found any photos"

"Look you have my statement. To be honest with you, now both Jack and Ray are dead, I think you are in Shit Street with your inquiries, don't you?"

"Tom, if you do come up with anything you can ring me on this number (Davis handed Tom a business card) and Tom I am sorry about Ralph's comments"

"Are you" replied Tom still very annoyed.

As Davis went to join Richards in their car Tom went up to the incinerator, lifted the lid and dropped the card Davis had given him in the fire.

All the time Christine and Sam had kept their distance waiting until Richards and Davis had driven out of the drive before joining Tom by the fire.

"What did they want Tom?" asked Sam.

Tom told them what they had come for but never mentioned Richard's comments about them.

"I'll tell you what Tom, I'm sure my heart missed a beat when I saw it was them pair, I was half expecting them to call today, but it would have to be just as I was burning this lot" said Tom

"Didn't they ask you what you were burning?" ask Sam

"No but he did say they were surprised at not finding any photos I pretended I never heard him"

"Much more to do Tom?" asked Christine

"No, but if you two want to shred them while I burn them, then we can get done and get over to Bourne to help your mum and Sara and while I'm there I want to have a look at something I saw in the garden"

"What's that Tom?" asked Christine

"Among the grass I'm sure I saw a Slop stone and it looked in immaculate condition" answered Tom

"A what?" asked Sam looking rather puzzled.

"A slop stone" replied Tom

"I don't mean to sound a bit thick but Tom what the hell is a slop stone—no Tom don't answer that show me when we get there we had better get them photos shredded come on Chris".

Leaving Tom in the garden, they went back into the house to complete their task taking them out to Tom.

Having put the last remains of the shredded photos in the fire, Tom waited until the last piece of shredded paper and plastic had turned to ash, stirring it so as to ensure there were no last remnants. When he was happy, they had gone he fetched a bucket of water and poured it into the incinerator so as to damp down the smouldering ash. Tom was happy that this evil mess had gone forever. Tom couldn't help but think of the hundred or so, poor victims that had had their lives destroyed by two men who they had probably never met, two evil bastards who made a lot of money out of other peoples private lives. Tom stood starring into the ashes.

"Tom—Tom, are you with us Tom?"

"Sorry Sam I was miles away"

"I could see that, what were you thinking about?"

"All those faces, all those people who lost money to two evil bastards, just because they did something in their lives that they thought others might look upon as wrong, so to save other peoples feelings they allowed them selves to be blackmailed by those two evil bastards"

"Well Tom I don't think they'll cause any more upset do you?"

"No Sam, I just wonder what would have happened if Ray had of got hold of these? Would he have carried on where Jack left off?"

"Possibly Tom, let's not think about what ifs, he's dead, so come on, forget about it, they aren't worth the bother, and they got their comeuppance. You let things upset you to much"

"You're to bloody kind Tom for your own good" added Christine

"Where the hell did you come from Chris?" asked Tom

"I was over there watching spiders eating a fly it had caught in its nest" replied Christine

"You sad git, anyway how long have spiders lived in nests Christine?" laughed Tom

"Oh yes sorry I meant webs" said Christine

"Silly sod, anyway it's time we made a move, Sara and Eileen will be wondering where we've been" added Sam.

They made their way to Bourne, calling at the chippy to collect some dinner for them all.

Chapter Eighteen

Sara and Eileen were busy searching Eileen's house for anything that they felt should really be destroyed. They had found another box of photos and negatives. This box had obviously been recent as the top ones had been taken on the newly opened Market Deeping bypass. They found some in the bottom draw of the office filing cabernet.

"I recognise this woman on here Sara"

"Who is she mum?"

"That was my friend. She was the one, I told that I was going to try to contact you and Christine, a good friend she turned out to be, she told Jack. She was telling Jack everything I was doing and saying"

"By the looks of these mum she to was being blackmailed by them, is this her husband she's kissing"

"Bloody hell no it isn't, I don't know who that is?"

"Does she live round here?"

"Yes, over by the outdoor swimming pool. Why Sara what are you going to do?"

"Nothing mum these belong to her so I shall just have to return them"

"No Sara, I've had enough trouble"

"Mum looking at these I'm pretty convinced she won't want any fuss. I just want to return them to her, after all mum they do belong to her" Sara laughed

"O.K Sara if you must, she has had it coming to her for a long time"

As they looked through the rest of the photos, the phone rang

"I'll bet that's Tom I'll get it. (Sara picked up the receiver) Hello"

"Who's that?" asked the caller

"It's Sara Gray"

"Put your mother on" ordered the caller

"Mum it's for you" Eileen took the phone

"Yes, who is it?" said Eileen to the caller

"You Cow"

"Oh Dorothy, what a pleasure I was wondering how long it would be before you rang" said Eileen

"I suppose you're satisfied now?"

"I won't be satisfied until Ray has been cremated like his brother"

"You are nothing but a Cow"

"Maybe I am, but at least I'm a rich Cow, how much money did Ray leave you from the blackmailing"

"My Ray wasn't involved in Jacks blackmailing, he was a magistrate"

"That show's how bent our British legal system has become, anyway if he wasn't involved, what did he want all those papers for last night, that the police now have?"

"You evil cow my Ray wouldn't harm a fly" Eileen laughed at Dorothy's statement then saying

"When you take that pig to the Crematorium, there should be a box with some ashes in it, it will be labelled up pig, can you collect them for me Dorothy love, and put them in the rubbish bin—Oh dear Sara the phones gone dead" they laughed

"I don't think she'll be inviting you to the funeral"

"There's a good chance you're right Sara dear. That sounds like Tom and the girls are here"

"Looks like they've brought some chips with them, if Sam hasn't eaten them" Sara went outside to meet them

"I see that bloody things still there?" Tom said to Sara pointing at Ray's car

"You've just reminded me Tom, I saw some keys on the hall table earlier I wonder if he dropped them in the struggle last night and they're the keys for that thing" said Sara

She went back into the house returning with the keys she pressed the demobilising pad and the car made a bleeping sound and Sara opened the doors.

"O.K Sara what are you going to do with that now?"

"Park it at the end of the drive and tell his wife to fetch it"

"You can't do that Sara the tyres are flat," said Tom.

Sara ignored Tom's comments she just grinned, got into the car, drove it out of the drive, and parked it on the main road leaving the keys in the ignition. When she got back to the house she asked her mother for Dorothy's phone number, Sara rang her putting on a posh voice.

"Hello I'm sorry to bother you, but do you own a silver motor car (reading the registration number out) with four flat tyres?"

"That's my husbands car where is it, how come the tyres are flat?"

"Firstly your husbands (Then Sara used her usual voice) car is at the top of my mothers drive with the keys in the ignition, it's a shame about the tyres, I don't know how they got like that, just get it moved you bloody old bag"

Sara put the phone down before she had chance to answer.

"There wasn't any need for that Sara?" said Tom

"So it's alright for her to ring up here and insult mum, are you saying I should be polite to her, well you can forget it"

"Sara calm down, I'm sorry, I didn't mean it to sound like that I was just saying we shouldn't bring ourselves down to her level"

"Yes Tom you're right, I'm sorry, let's finish our chips"

"Anyway Sara, I want to show you something"

Tom led Sara up the drive (leaving Christine and Sam chatting to Eileen) stopping about half way and pointed to on old beige sink like thing lying in the grass.

"What the hell is that?"

"That Sara dear, is a slop stone" replied Tom

"I shan't ask what a Slop stone is because looking at it I can see it's some kind of sink. Tom tell me what have you dragged me up here to show me this for?"

"Sara you know you said you always fancied a old style kitchen, well that's what I'm going to give you"

"So I take it that you are going to take that thing home and put it in the kitchen Tom I didn't quite mean that type of old kitchen"

"Sara I tell you what, if you don't like it I'll take it out"

"Go on then Tom, do what you must. I'm going to help mum otherwise we will never get done and I don't want the police poking around while that lot is still in the loft"

"O.K sweetheart, I'll give you a hand but come here, give us a big hug; you're going all serious what's up?"

"I'm sorry Tom, I just wonder where it all will end, it just seems everything that could go wrong, has, and even you said nothing ever happened in your life until you met me. I just wonder how much more you will take."

"Sara don't be silly, I love you and yes I will admit there's been a lot of strange things happen recently, that's what makes life exciting, it's not your fault. Sara I love you and always will, so stop being silly, anyway at least life's not boring so come on lets join the others" said Tom, Sara smiled

"I love you to Tom; on the way home I'll give you a hand to lift that old sink in the boot of the car". Sara kissed Tom

They walked hand in hand back up the drive to join the others.

Eileen was going through the cupboards in the lounge. Sam and Christine were upstairs checking the office.

"Where would you like us to check, mum?" asked Sara

"Do you want to go through to the Parlour" said Eileen

"There are some nice pieces of furniture in here Sara" said Tom

"It's looks as if it's not been shown a duster in years. This room was the pride of the house, we were never allowed in it as children now look at it, it's a mess"

"I'll tell you what Sara this place is going to take some selling, it needs too much money spending on it"

"Tom are you going to offer to try and sell it for her?"

"What do you think Sara?"

"I don't really know Tom; like you said it needs a lot spending on it The market is very good at the moment What do you reckon it'll make?"

"I don't know I suppose £200,000 maybe more"

"That much, my god Tom, I thought a lot less than that"

"There's a lot of land round it and it could be brought back to its former glory"

"Why don't you put it to mum, I'm sure she would love you to sell it for her?"

"Not now Sara, I'll bring it up tomorrow, we're here for tea, anyway have you found anything?"

"Not a thing Tom and I don't think we will, not in here anyway".

They went back into the lounge where Eileen was trying to open a bureau.

"Having problems Eileen?"

"Yes Tom for some reason this won't unlock"

"Have you got the right key?"

"It's the one he always used"

"Let's have a look",

Tom took the key off Eileen and put it in the lock

"There you are Eileen it just needed a mans touch"

"I've been messing around with that for ages; now let's see what he's been hiding in here".

Eileen pulled out the two-leaf support arms then pulled down the leaf.

"What a lovely bureau?" commented Tom

"Yes he spent weeks looking for one of these I do believe it's worth a few bob" said Eileen

"Anything of interest in there mum?"

"I'll tell what I'm looking for Sara, a little brown leather book. I thought about it earlier and when I found this key among that bunch that reminded me now…"

"Is that it Eileen?"

"Yes Tom that's it".

Eileen remove the leather bound pocket diary sized book from the bureau and opened it.

"Addresses, lots of addresses," said Eileen

"Any we know?" asked Tom

"I think they are possibly some of the people in the photos, I don't know" replied Eileen

"Can I have a look? (Eileen handed Tom the book) I think you could be right Eileen. Sara is this Christine's old address?"

"Yes Tom, that is and that's the one she shared with Sam in Selby" replied Sara

"He definitely showed interest in Chris's whereabouts, can I take this Eileen?" asked Tom

"Yes Tom take it. He absolutely hated the pair of you, I think he thought by getting at you two he was getting at me"

"I think mum both me and Chris had long since worked that out"

"Mum why did you never have any children with him?"

"That Sara was the same reason his anger with me got worse. He resented you and Christine. He was infertile"

"So did any of his so called friends know he wasn't our father?"

"Not as far as I'm aware. I'm sure after what Ray said he definitely told him, I'm not sure if he told the Ingamells, but as I told you he was sleeping with her anyway"

"How did they take his death?" asked Tom

"To be truthful Tom, they were as relieved as we were"

"He was definitely a control freak" added Tom.

Christine and Sam entered the room,

"Found anything?" asked Christine

"Only this" said Sara holding up the book.

"Me and Sam have, haven't we Sam?" Sam nodded

"Well Chris come on don't leave us in suspense" said Sara

"Do you remember this sis?" and Christine held up a rather bedraggled brown teddy

"Oh my god I often wondered what ever happened to him" said Sara holding out her hand to take the teddy off Christine

"Can you remember what you called it Sara?" asked Eileen

"Yes. What's-His-Name" replied Sara

"Can't you remember Sara?" asked Tom

"Yes Tom, that's what Sara called the bloody thing" said Christine

"What?" said Tom

"What's-his-name" repeated Sara

"That's what you called it (Sara nodded laughing embarrassingly) you sad kid" said Tom shaking his head in disbelief.

"There you are Tom, do you believe me now when I tell you she has always been a bit strange" laughed Christine

"You cheeky bitch" said Sara

"So now we have seen what Christine has found. I think that was the only remaining secret these walls hold, so we'll have a drink, and then we can bring all that stuff out of the loft and put it in one of the back rooms until you move Eileen. Then we're done" said Tom

"That's a point Tom I was going to say something earlier, but I didn't want too appear too pushy" said Eileen

"What's that?" asked Tom

"I don't know the first thing about selling a house, so you being in that line of work, I was wondering whether you could sort it out for me. Of course I'll pay you?" said Eileen

"Eileen you leave it to me and my fully trained staff, in fact I will send one of my more intelligent team members down on Monday to take some photos, Sam you can do that can't you?" asked Tom

"You swine"

Before Sara could finish Tom had left the room to help Eileen with the coffees.

After they had all had their coffees, they all went up into the dark room through into the hidden half of loft roof space.

"Do you know what is up here Eileen?"

"Not really Tom, I just put it up as quickly as I could before Jack heard me or saw me"

"Mum there's one thing that baffles me, you told us you couldn't get that main door open then you show us this lot saying you had a key, so what did you want the key out of the bunch for if you already have a key?"

"Because like I said to you Sara I didn't realise that my key also fitted that first door and Jack for some reason started locking it and I then gave the rest of the stuff to Pete to look after".

Sara let the subject of the key go; although she could tell, her mother wasn't being totally honest, she could see that the others had picked up on it. They set about clearing the items into Christine's old bedroom.

"Is there much at Pete's house?" asked Tom

"About a quarter of what's here" replied Eileen

"What the hell are you going to do with it all mum?" asked Sara

"Now we have got it down here we can see what there is we can split it all take what you want"

"Me and Tom don't want any of it, to be honest with you mum we haven't the room"

"Well Christine, Sam take what you want?"

"No thanks mum we couldn't put any of that in our house knowing how it was acquired" said Christine

"I can understand that. What shall I do with it!?" asked Eileen

"look Eileen I know a few dealers who might be interested in this lot, you could get quite a few bob out of it, so I suggest what you don't want you put to one side and sell the rest" said Tom and Eileen agreed

"We are soon going to have to go mum. Tom has to go and make sure the builders have locked up properly" said Sara

"Eileen half way down your drive there's an old slop stone can I have it?" asked Tom

"Of course you can, take it, to be honest with you I didn't realise that was still there. Don't forget, you're all here for tea tomorrow, so don't be any later than three"

"We too had better go mum, me and Sam have got to go and measure up for curtains tonight at our new house, did you want to come with us?"

"No, but thanks Christine. Peter's coming round tonight and I think we're going out for a meal. Oh and while I'm thinking about it, you mentioned your new home that's just reminded me I have something for you. (Eileen went to her hand bag and pulled out a large envelope and handed it to Christine) Take this love, don't open it until you're home, that's for you and Sam. I hope it will help you a little".

Christine kissed her mother and thanked her for the mysterious package and they left.

On the way out of the drive, Christine seeing Tom and Sara struggling to lift what could only be described as a mucky brown sink into the back of Tom's car

"Want any help?" asked Christine having wound down her window

"If you don't mind Chris this bloody thing's heavier than I thought" commented Tom almost dropping it.

Both Christine and Sam got out of the car they all took a corner each and lifted into the boot of the car.

"I suppose Tom this is that thing you were on about earlier"

"It is Chris, so, what do you reckon?"

"I'm not commenting Tom"

"You all laugh now, but bit of spit and polish and it will look like new"

"We had better follow you home you'll need a hand to get that thing out of the boot" laughed Christine.

__Chapter Nineteen__

On their journey, home both Christine and Sam's curiosity was getting the better of them.

"Open that envelope Sam" said Christine

"No Chris your mum said to wait until we were home"

"Sod that Sam open it now, I know you want to know what's in it"

"O.K if you insist".

Christine was right Sam did really want to know of its secret contents,

"Holy shit, look at this lot Chris"

Christine stared in disbelief; there in Sam's lap lay a large bundle of fifty-pound notes, she had to quickly put her eyes back on the road before she lost control of the car

"What the hell has she given us that for, pass me my mobile"

"You can't use that while you're driving. Who do you want to ring?"

"Sara, I want to know what she knows about this lot"

"I'll do it".

Sam rang Sara asking her to tell Tom to pull over

"I take it you've opened the envelope"

"Yes Sara, you know about it, but what's it for"

"Sam, you and Chris deserve that money, now put it in your handbag and use it"

"But Sara we don't want your mums money she'll need that"

"She's got plenty, lets face it Sam it wasn't her money in the first place, its only what that dead pig has taken off others, in all honesty it was his. Just look at it this way there's nothing he would want less than to think you and Chris are having a good time at his expense, so my best advise to you and Chris is enjoy it" said Sara ending the call.

Sam told Christine what Sara had said.

"I suppose what she said makes sense, it'll feel great to furnish our new home on him, what do you say Sam and after all we could definitely to with a bit more cash"

Sam lent over and kissed Christine on the cheek.

Tom and Sara talked about the visit to Simon and Paul's. Tom told her about the girl in the photo

"Paul said he was sure it's the same girl as he spoke to that day and Simon reckons she's the one he had seen at Garrets night club" said Tom

"So what happens now?" asked Sara

"Nothing until Tuesday and then they are going to see if she's at Garrets and if she is they will get talking to her, and try to find out where she lives, but just in case she isn't there. I've given them a photo of her, and they will ask around to see if anyone knows where she lives. They will ring Sam and Chris, they will sort it out from there"

"I can very well imagine what Chris will do, I am very surprised Chris isn't ignoring our advise and just going to Garrets" said Sara

"I think Sam has well warned her, otherwise she would have done"

"I wonder Tom if life will ever get back to normality". Tom laughed at Sara's comments.

Arriving at Tom's, they unloaded the slop stone. Christine and Sam went back to their flat.

On opening the door, Sam bent down to pick the post up from the floor, taking it into the kitchen to open.

"Chris look we've finally got a date to move in black and white"

"When Sam?"

"According to this next Friday"

"That's the first of October" said Christine

"I wonder whether Simon and Paul have had a letter."

"They never said this morning and I'm sure they would have rang"

"You silly sod, I didn't turn your mobile on until we were in the car, I'll ring them" said Sam

"No, we're off round there later on and I'm curious as to how much money is in there".

Sam got the money out and counted it

"Bloody hell Chris there's ten and half grand here"

"We'll put that straight in the bank on Monday Sam"

"We won't Chris, don't you think we would be risking it putting that amount of money in the bank, they might ask some questions?"

"Shit, I never thought about that, what shall we do with it?"

"I think we should forget about our wages going into the bank and live off that lot and if we buy anything we pay cash"

"Sam I've just thought about something none of us have checked to make sure that none of the money found are forgeries"

"They look fine" said Sam holding one up to inspect it

"I'll borrow that light that Tom has in his office to check cash with on Monday and we'll check the lot just to be safe. Sam my love, it's time we made a move, we told them we would be there by seven and it's now half six"

"Chris I don't know about you, but I'm rather hungry"

"Sam I would be shocked if you weren't, come on we'll get a takeaway later and if you're really hungry grab a packet of biscuits out of the cupboard"

"There aren't any in there"

"Only because you've eaten them"

"Well I was hungry, I know I'll quickly make a cheese sandwich and eat it on the way there"

"O.K Sam if you must while you're doing that I had better hide this money and I know just the place"

"Where Chris?"

"I'll get that tin tool box from the kitchen and put it in there providing you haven't eaten that"

"You cheeky bitch"

"Sam nothing would surprise me of you with your appetite, anyway I'll put this in the bed drawers".

Christine put the money in the toolbox and placed it under the bed in the drawer out of sight. Sam made herself a sandwich and they walked to Simon and Paul's.

Chapter Twenty

They arrived at Simon and Paul's house just after seven. Paul let them in.

"Sorry we're late Paul" said Christine

"Don't worry about that, we have some good news for you. Go into the lounge"

"So do we Paul"

"Obviously you've had a letter as well"

"Yes we move on Friday" said Sam

"Me and Simon move on Thursday so if you like you can start moving your stuff in when you like?"

"That would be great Paul" said Christine

Simon came into the lounge carrying a bottle of wine

"Hello girls, great news. We haven't any Champagne, so I'm afraid it's a bottle of cheap and nasty"

They all laughed at Simons comments

"By the way we also have a bit of news concerning your mysterious woman" said Paul

Christine and Sam sat up in their chairs as Simon took over.

"The girl in the picture is called Patricia Coleman and from what we've been told, she is or was having a serious relationship with your ex-friend Tracey"

"I just knew that fucking Tracey would be involved somewhere along the line"

"O.K Chris we already know that, lets hear what Simon has to say"

"This Patricia lives somewhere in Bretton, from what we've also been told she was pregnant, but where the baby is now, no one knows, also I was warned she's a very, very nasty piece of work, so tread carefully the rumours are that she stabbed her ex-husband when she found out he was having an affair"

"But I thought she's gay" said Sam

"Oh yes that was the funny thing about it, she's been having several affairs with different woman. She teased him about it, also she wasn't sleeping with him, so she says, but as soon as he left her for another woman she went fucking ballistic, going round to this woman's house, her husband opened the door and she stabbed him, fortunately she only caught his arm"

"Who told you all this Simon?" asked Sam

"We didn't say anything this morning because until we had seen the photos we weren't too sure it was her, but a couple of lads we know from Peterborough, have often given her a lift when that old green mini she had broke down"

"Didn't the police do anything?" asked Sam

"Her ex-husband didn't want to inform the police he is absolutely petrified of her and so is his girlfriend" said Paul

"So what does she want with me?"

"We don't know Chris, it must have something to do with you and that Tracey" answered Paul

"I think I'll give this Tracey a call" said Sam

"No leave it until Tuesday we hope to find out more then. Graham and Richard are calling for her to see if she wants to go with them to Garrets, then we can hopefully get a few more details, with a bit of look straight from the horses mouth" said Simon

"O.K, if we must I'm just getting rather pissed off with the whole situation" said Sam

"I'm sure you are Sam, but not as much as Chris is so, let's just leave it till Tuesday".

"Alright we had better get these curtains sorted"

Sam and Christine went into the bedrooms with pen, paper and tape measure.

"Pass me the tape measure Sam"

"Yes Ma'am, what ever you say Ma'am"

"Shut up you bitch and just pass me it"

They worked their way through the house measuring each window

"Another glass of wine girls (said Paul, not requiring an answer, filling their glasses) when you've done I thought we could go up the road for drink"

"Sounds good to me Paul. What about you Sam?" said Christine, Sam agreed.

Once they had finished, Sam said she wouldn't mind trying the new wine bar that had opened in town.

"I've heard it's not bad there I wouldn't mind having a look," said Christine

"O.K that's settled let's hit the town kids" laughed Simon.

It took them about twenty minutes to reach the wine bar that was situated close to Sara's flat. Once inside its popularity was far too obvious.

"How the hell are we going to get in here?" said Paul

"Just follow me" said Christine pushing though the crowd

"Watch your bums boys the bandits are here"

Came a comment from a mouthy young lad in the crowed, Christine heard his comments and pushed her way towards him

"Did you say something?" asked Christine to the lad

"Leave it Christine he isn't worth it" insisted Paul

"No Paul he's insulted us all"

"No slag I was on about your friends them pair of shirt lifters" said the lad

"Look mate we have just come for a quiet drink"

"You'll not reach the bar" said the lad standing in front of them.

At this Christine kneed him straight between the legs and he fell to the floor holding his bollocks, two bouncers soon appeared on the scene asking them all to leave, Christine, Sam, Paul and Simon left without having to be thrown out, but the lad wouldn't leave and had to be helped out by a bit of force with Christine waiting for him. As he came out the door, Christine went up to him.

"Who are you going to show off to now?" and she hit him straight in the face

"Leave him Chris he isn't worth it" insisted Simon

"Yes piss off slag, its fuck all to do with you" said the lad.

Having heard the comments from the lad Paul decided enough was enough and went straight up to him.

"Now little boy, it's way past your bed time it's obvious your friends don't want any trouble and neither do we, so I suggest you keep that rather large mouth of yours shut and go",

The others started to walk away from the lad, crossing over the river bridge heading towards the town centre, but he followed them all the time making insulting comments to them. Paul was now getting rather fed up with this lad and in a whispery voice said.

"Just follow me"

Paul lead them all down a little passage and the lad still followed them, Paul stopped about half way turned round and walked up to the boy.

"O.K rent a gob, what did you just say?"

"You heard, shirt lifter"

Before the lad said another word Paul had him by the throat and was holding him against a fence Simon seeing him reaching for his pocket grabbed his arm, Sam put her hand in his pocket removing what turned out to be a flick knife, realising what the lads intended,

Paul went wild hitting the lad several times before he fell to the floor. Paul lifted him up by the scuff of his neck stared him straight in face.

"Perhaps scum you might be a bit wiser next time, to think who you want to pick a fight with. Before I remove your teeth I want you to apologise to my friends"

"Sorry" the lad said quietly

"They never heard you shit head" said Paul

"Sorry" The lad said louder

"That's better now fuck off", and Paul pointed him in the opposite direction to them and pushed him on his way

"So where shall we go now boys?" asked Christine

"I know" said Sam

"We could do without any more suggestions off you Sam thank you" said Christine and they all laughed

"I'm coming to the conclusion that this pair is jinxed"

"I think Paul you're possibly right" replied Simon

"Well boys you could never say life is boring when you're out with us, could they Sam?"

"No Chris when we say we're going to hit the town we mean it"

"You're not joking and my knuckles are witness to that" said Paul

"Did that lad know you?"

"No Chris, but he recognised you two, I think he realised we are gay too"

"I didn't know him" said Christine

"Think back Chris to when we first met you pair, those two lads you had trouble with on Winsover Road, that was one of them"

"Oh my god I never recognised him" said Christine

"I wasn't sure if I had seen him before" added Sam

"So the nights still young, what shall we do? We don't want any suggestions off you Sam" said Paul

"Lets go to that pub on Winsover Road it's alright in there" said Christine.

At the pub, they entered a much friendlier atmosphere, Simon and Sam went to the bar to get the drinks leaving Paul and Chris to chat

"Paul I'm arranging to have our relationship blessed on fifth November, that's Sam's birthday, keep that day free, and tell Simon I want you pair there"

"Does Sam know?"

"No it's a surprise so tell Simon not to say a word"

"O.K Chris we'll be there"

Paul and Sam came back with the drinks.

"Get these down you, and we'll go for a Chinky" said Sam

"Bloody typical, food she never stops thinking about food" said Christine and they all laughed.

They all finished their drinks and having collected a Chinese takeaway decided Christine and Sam's flat was the closest and would go there and eat their meal.

At the flat Sam warmed some plates up and emptied the trays onto the them, then taking them through to the others in the lounge

"So how much notice do you have to give on this place?" asked Paul

"According to the landlord two months, but we only got confirmation on the moving date today. We only gave our notice in a week ago" replied Christine

"So what will you do?" asked Simon

"To be honest with you the landlord's a complete pig, if you notice our windows are the only ones that have seen a paint brush outside in years and that's because me and Chris did them. The inside was a total shit house, he thinks he's having the keys back early he's got no chance, he'll get them back when we get our deposit back and that won't be for another seven weeks, so we will leave some of our furniture in here"

"How are you moving?" asked Paul and before Sam or Christine had chance to answer there was a loud bang and the sound of braking glass coming from the bedroom, Christine rushed quickly into the bedroom followed closely by the others.

"Holy fucking shit" shouted Chris

She ran back through the lounge and out the flat door, down the stairs and into the street followed by Paul trying to stop her, but Chris was flaming with anger.

"Christine, they'll be long gone, you'll never catch them now" shouted Paul

"Paul this is that fucking cow again. I don't give a toss how fucking hard she thinks she is, I've had as much as I can take from her".

Paul was right there was no sign of anyone. Christine just slumped on the pavement outside in tears.

"Come on Chris lets go back to the flat"

"What have I done to her for her to hate me so much?"

"I don't know Chris, but I think it's time this was sorted out. I'm calling the police before someone gets hurt"

"No Paul I want to ask her why. I don't want to fight her. I don't even know her"

"Chris you don't want to know her, which you are right on. Look if you won't let us call the police, let me and Simon see if we can sort it"

"Please Paul can you try, because if not I'm sure I'll crack up" said Christine still crying

"Now come on, let's get inside and clear up, I'll find something to put in that hole"

"I hope none of the neighbours heard you say that, you'll ruin my Image" laughed Christine

"That's better Chris, a smile; anyway you're not my type. Now come on lets get in I'm bloody cold and dressed like that with no coat on you'll catch your death" Sam and Paul came out

"Did you catch them?" asked Sam

"No come on let's go in". They returned to the flat.

"We had better clean that mess up" said Chris still upset

"It's all right sweetheart me and Simons done it"

"Thank you Sam, thanks Simon"

"Forget it Chris"

"Was it who we think it was?"

"I guess so Simon, although we never saw a soul out there, but I think it was, yes" replied Paul

"She's got to be stopped, and soon before someone is really hurt" added Simon.

"By the way Chris how's your fingers?" asked Paul changing the subject slightly

"Big and swollen" said Sam with a dirty smile on her face

"You dirty bitch I was asking Chris, not you" said Simon

"Ignore her she's just a horny sod. My fingers are doing fine although Sam knocked a bottle of vinegar over the other night and it soaked through the dressing"

"How the hell did she do that?" asked Paul

"As usual, she was feeding her face, she put some vinegar on her chips straight from the bottle, she didn't put the lid back on I had my hand near the bottle she knocked it over and it soaked straight through my dressing"

"Yes, I nearly had to peel her off the ceiling" said Sam bursting into laughter

"My god, I'll bet life's never boring in this pad" joked Simon

"It isn't Simon, I can assure you, although at this present time I would be quite happy with a more boring life" said Christine

"I'm sure you would" added Paul

"So what are we going to do with this food?" asked Sam

"I've lost my appetite, you can have mine Sam" said Christine

"You can have ours as well Sam" added Simon,

"Don't mind if I do" replied Sam

And without further ado Sam emptied the remaining contents of all the plates on hers and set about eating it

"Oh my god, where the hell does she put it all?" asked Paul

"I'm past trying to work it out" replied Christine shaking her head.

The lads stayed till the early hours of Sunday morning, between them, they consumed and four bottles of wine, needless to say come the morning there were four rather sore heads, on four very tired people.

At Tom's house, Tom and Sara completely unaware of events at Christine and Sam's, they had spent the night looking through wedding books and holiday brochures, planning their big day and their honeymoon. They decided that if it was O.K by the Vicar they should try and book the parish church in Spalding for the Saturday first of April and not Monday the third, as they had originally decided, because it wouldn't be fair to their guests, how ever, they couldn't decide on where to go on their honeymoon, Tom said he would call at the travel agent on Monday to collect some more brochures. They set about writing out a list of guests,

"Have you decided who you are having to give you away Sara?"

"This is really bothering me Tom, I just don't know who to ask"

"Something will turn up"

"When are you getting your wedding dress?"

"I thought if it's O.K with you me, Mum, Sam and Chris will go over to Peterborough next Saturday to have a look at a few things"

"Fine Sara, that's not a problem, between now and then you had better look through these (Tom handed her some brochures on fitted kitchens) and see if there's anything that takes your fancy, I've got the builder calling next Saturday, it was going to be a surprise"

"Tom you're one in a million when I said I would like a new kitchen I didn't mean right away"

"Sara, you just give me some ideas, then after the kitchen we will set about the rest of the house, we will do it to the way you want it. I've been meaning to ask you for a while why don't you move in, after all you spend all your time here?"

"I thought you would never ask me"

"Great first thing in the morning we shall go over to your flat and collect all your clothes, before you change your mind"

"I love you Tom Gardener and there is no way I would change my mind, the question is will you get fed up with me?"

"Never, and I love you too" replied Tom

Leaning over giving her a long lingering kiss,

"Come on Tom" said Sara

Taking Tom by the hand leading up the stairs into the bedroom standing at the bottom of the bed, undressing him, kissing him more passionate than before, she pushed him on the bed, caressing every inch of his body before making love to him. They fell to sleep in each others arms. The next morning Tom was first out of bed making Sara a coffee, then having a shower and returning to the bedroom, where Sara still lay in bed.

"Come on love we have a lot to do today"

"Oh just a little longer, in fact Tom you can always join me under the sheets if you want"

"Oh yes and for what may I ask?" replied Tom with a large grin on his face

"Well Tom if you like, we could always carry on were we left off last night and have a dawn raid"

"A what?" said Tom laughing and knowing what Sara meant

"A dawn raid"

"Come on get up we have a lot to do, like empty your flat and move you in here before you change your mind. Don't forget we are at your mothers tonight, while you get dressed I'm going to ring your sister"

"You spoil sport" commented Sara.

Tom left the room and went downstairs to ring Christine. It seemed to take for ages before anyone answered,

"Hello who's that?"

"Hi Sam you sound rough"

"Don't speak to loud Tom. My fucking head god I feel rough. It was two before Simon and Paul left, three before Chris let me get to sleep"

"Alright Sam, don't tell me, what you did between two and Three just send me the video"

"You cheeky sod, anyway what do you want at bloody eight o'clock on a Sunday morning when me and Chris are still half pissed"

"I'm sorry Sam; I didn't mean to wake you"

"Come on Tom just tell me what you want, then I can go back to bed?"

"No Sam, now you're up you may as well stay up I've something to tell you" and Tom told her about Sara moving in

"About bloody time to Tom, while I m thinking about it we had some more trouble last night"

Sam told Tom about their visit to the wine bar and the brick through the window,

"Oh no, how has Chris taken it?"

"At the time bad, after a few drinks she forgot all about it"

"Anyway, what I actually rang for was to ask if you and Chris could meet Sara and I round at Sara's flat around eleven to help us move Sara's stuff out, but I think it might be as well for us to pick you up after I've picked up the van if I can get one on a Sunday"

"No problem Tom, we'll be ready. I meant to ask you, Oh never mind Chris will ask you later. Must go, I can hear Chris shouting for my body, I will have to go and fulfil her sexual needs"

"Around eleven Sam" said Tom putting the phone down laughing.

"What are you laughing at Tom?" asked Sara Putting her arms around Tom's neck

Tom told her what Sam had told him about the night's rather upsetting events he could see this distressed Sara. He assured her everything would turn out fine.

"I would love to put some hidden cameras in that flat"

"Keep dreaming Tom" laughed Sara

"You know this dawn raid you were on about Sara"

"Yes Tom"

"Well is it still on offer"

"It's too late Tom; you'll have to wait until tonight"

"But then it won't be a dawn raid"

"Tough, now as you said Tom dearest, we have a lot to do"

"O.K, it was just a thought".

Sara, smiling, left the room to have a shower while Tom rang his friend to ask to borrow his van.

There wasn't a problem. Tom went and collected it promising to return it later that day, returning to the house where Sara was on the phone to her mother telling her about their plans. Telling her, they would be round at hers about three.

"O.K Sara, are you ready?"

"Yes Tom, Sam rang said they would walk round it sounds as if Chris needs to get a bit of fresh air, from what Sam said, she's a bit worse for wear"

"Oh dear, not too good then"

Tom and Sara got in the van and headed to Sara's flat. Outside on the pavement waiting stood Sam and Christine,

"What the hell have you got that big thing for?" asked Sam

"You dirty swine" replied Tom

"The van you silly bugger"

"Well Sam one can never tell with you. (Then Tom looked at Christine)

What the hells up with you Chris?"

And before Christine had chance to answer him she turned away from him and was sick on the side of the road.

"Dear me Sam she doesn't look too good?" said Sara

"She was O.K until I made her a fry up. (Sam pointing down to were Christine had been sick and laughing uncontrollably) In fact Chris that egg still looks alright"

"Shut up you silly bitch it's not funny" said Christine getting rather annoyed with Sam's mickey taking.

Tom, Sara and Sam went into the flat leaving Christine sat on the floor of the van between the two rear open doors, not being in any fit state to climb the steps. Sara showed them what she wanted to take, offering Sam the rest of her furniture for her and Christine.

"No thanks Sara, to be honest with you, we haven't the room, not even in the new house, which reminds me since Chris is in no fit state to ask you (Sam turned towards Tom) could me and Chris have Friday off Tom, we're moving"

"Of course you can Sam, that's great news, me and Sara will give you a hand when we've finished at the office, won't we love?"

"Of course we will Sam, I would say that after we'd finished here we could all go for a drink, but looking at Chris, I somehow don't think it would be a good idea" said Sara laughing.

Having sorted out what she was taking they started to load the van. Inside the van, they found Christine fast asleep on the floor.

"My god look at that, you'll have to wake her up," said Tom laughing.

Sam shook Christine, reluctantly she woke up and they started loading the van, until they had all that Sara wanted.

"So Sara what happens now, are you putting it on the market?" asked Sam

"Yes, I can't see the sense in paying a mortgage on a flat I'm never going to use"

"So when are you putting it on the market?"

"Tomorrow Sam, I think tomorrow"

When they arrived back at Toms, they unloaded Sara's stuff into the garage.

When they carried in the last item, Tom was carrying it with Sam, a pine chest of draws, half way into the garage. Tom lost grip of it, it slipped out of his hands. The draws fell out spilling their contents onto the garage floor. Tom and Sara set about picking the items of clothing, mainly underwear, from the floor. Sam felt an hard object among them, thinking it to be nothing she freed it and soon realised what it was, holding up for all of them to see.

"Sara is this one of them new types of tooth brushes" Sam said laughing uncontrollably

"Holy shit. What the hell have you got that for Sara?" asked Tom trying not to laugh but finding it hard to keep a straight face

"Well Tom one thing is for sure it wasn't for cleaning her toe nails out with" replied Sam laughing

Even Christine had returned to the land of the living and joined in with the laughter. Sara was laughing, but only out of embarrassment. Once the laughter had calmed Sara snatched it off Sam.

"I'll have that otherwise if you and Chris get hold of it I'll never see it again" said Sara trying to hide her embarrassment

"Do you want me to put it in the bedroom Sara and perhaps you can show me how you use that later?" said Tom

"Tom you had better get some new batteries for, I'll bet them ones are flat" laughed Chris

Sara took it inside then returned to the others knowing she would have a job to live this one down, preparing herself for all the comments, and as she walked into the garage, Sam said

"All together buzz" and they all joined in,

"You rotten bitch" Sara said looking at Sam

"I know Sara, joking aside can me and Chris borrow it later we'll put in our own batteries, wont we Chris"

"I bet Sam if the truth was known you already have one" said Sara

"Sam shut up, don't you dare answer that" said Christine quickly

"Well Sam yes or no?" asked Tom

"Sod off, I'm not answering you" said Sam

"I'll take that as a yes" said Tom

"I wouldn't mind a coffee" said Christine quickly changing the subject.

Tom laughed, they all went into the house and had a drink, then took the van back.

While Tom had gone, they talked about going to their mothers for tea.

"I hope her cooking has improved" said Sara

"So do I Chris, although from what I can remember she never did that much cooking when we were there"

"So are you two going to ask her who your real father is?" asked Sam

"Yes Sam",

Sara told Christine what her mother had said when she was on her own with her, telling her how she had said she had spoke to their real father's sister.

"Why didn't she tell me that as well? Asked Christine

"I don't know, promise me you wont let on you know Chris"

"I won't say a word Sara, although I can't see what the big secret is" said Christine

"Neither can I, but she must have her reasons Chris" said Sara

"Tell me Sara did she give any clues at all in this secret conversation between you and her" asked Christine sarcastically

"Chris, there's no need to be like that with Sara" said Sam infuriated by Christine's attack on Sara

"No Chris, I didn't ask her to tell me" said Sara trying to defend herself

"I'm sorry sis, I didn't mean to upset you, I'm out of order" said Christine leaning over to give Sara a hug

"It's alright Chris, I know you didn't mean anything by it, I'm like you I just wish she would just tell us who he is and stop beating about the bush, we're not kids and we have the right to know. Look who's back, it's the stud" said Sara

"Still here then girls, I thought you might be up the shop getting some more batteries for the new toy" said Tom

248

"Shut it Gardener, there's a coffee in the kitchen drink it and get yourself ready to go down mums" replied Sara

"That told you Tom" said Sam

"Yes Sam, but do you know what, I'm going to do?" said Tom

"What's that?" asked Sam

"Just what Sara said, I'm not under the thumb, I do as I'm told, and it sounds better"

Tom left the room leaving the others laughing. Once they had all finished their drinks and Tom had rejoined them Sara suggested they all made a move to Bourne.

"You had better drop us of at our flat first Sara" instructed Sam

"What for?" asked Tom

"To collect the car" replied Sam

"Not on your nelly Sam, neither of you two are driving today, if you two drank as much as you said you did last night, and from the way Chris was earlier I don't doubt it, then you'll still be over the alcohol limit, so we'll all go in our car".

As they approached the end of Eileen's drive Sara turned to Tom

"Stop Tom it's only half two and I've just remembered I have something very important to do"

Tom slightly bewildered pulled over to the side of the road.

"What are you up to Sara?"

"Do you still have that address book Tom mum gave you from the bureau?"

"It's in the glove box"

Sara opened the glove box and pulled out the leather bounded address book.

"Well Sara are you going to tell us what the big deal is?" asked Christine

"Hang on a minute I'm not sure (Sara turned the pages until she finally found the address she was looking for) O.K Tom go past the drive and turn right at the top and I'll explain everything on the way" said Sara

She pulled the photos of the man and woman on the Deeping bypass from her handbag showing them to the others and telling them what their mother had said.

"I'm coming with you Sara," insisted Christine

"That's fine by me, pull up just there Tom" instructed Sara

"No trouble Sara please. Just hand her the photos and come away" pleaded Tom.

Christine and Sara, watched by Tom and Sam, got out of the car and made their way down the short drive to the large and well-maintained house. As they were just about to press the doorbell, a woman's voice spoke to them from behind a hedge

"Can I help you two girls?" asked the woman

"You might be able to (Sara looked at the lady then pulled out one of the photos and compared her with the woman in it) Yes I think you can. I'm pretty sure this is you is it not" said Sara handing her one of the photos.

"Where did you get these from?" said the woman looking rather worried

"We found these among the belongings of Jack Gray, I'm sure that name rings a few bells?" said Sara

"Where did he get them from and who the hell are you two?"

"I'm Sara Gray and this is my sister Christine Gray"

"You seem to recognise our names" commented Christine sarcastically

"Yes Jack did mention you" said the woman rather nervously

"So you didn't know that the man, who was blackmailing you, was also your best friend. You bloody cow and you also pretended to be our mothers best friend, so you could spy on her for him, was he giving you one" said Sara getting rather angry

"It wasn't like that" protested the woman

"Oh I think it was, but never mind we'll be in touch" Said Sara

Christine quickly snatched the photos back from the woman and they left. The woman begged them to give her the photos, they just laughed at her and got back in the car and Sara asked Tom to drive off.

"Why didn't you give her the photos Sara?" asked Christine

"I want her to sweat,"

"So what do you intend doing with them Sara?" asked Tom

"Same as the rest, sister dear, destroy them" replied Sara

"Isn't revenge sweet" laughed Tom.

Chapter Twenty-One

"What the hell is mum doing up here?" asked Sara, Tom pulled over

"What's up Eileen?" asked Tom

"It's O.K Tom, Sunday ritual, every Saturday night the kids come down the drive and play among the long grass, for some reason they drag both dustbins and leave them at the end of the drive" replied Eileen

"Leave them there I'll fetch them up later. Get in the car and we'll take you to the house" insisted Tom.

At the house, Eileen led them into the kitchen and they all sat down round the table.

"Something smells good mum?" said Christine

"Yes, I thought with it being a Sunday, I would do a roast, we'll eat in about an hour or so"

"Do you need a hand mum?" asked Sara

"No dear, but I would like a word with you and Christine"

"Would you like me and Sam to go out for a while Eileen?" asked Tom

"Not at all Tom dear, you two will also be interested in what I have to say"

"Are you sure Eileen we don't mind?" added Sam

"Honestly Tom, I would prefer you to stay" replied Eileen

"So mum what's up?"

"Nothings up Christine, I have some good news for you both. It's about you real father."

"This morning his sister rang, you know Sara I told you I had spoken to her"

"Why didn't you tell me that too mum?" said Christine interrupting her mother

"I was going to Christine; I had my reason's, let me tell you what she said. I need to tell you the whole story, so you can understand why. Before I met Jack I was a student nurse in Liverpool"

"I didn't know that mum" said Sara

"No Sara neither of you did, in fact to be honest with you both I never told either of you of my past life, I was made to feel ashamed of it, by Jack. During my time as a student in Liverpool, I had many boyfriends and got myself somewhat of a name. After a while I settled down, I got friendly with a very handsome lad, James Pilcher"

"Is he our father?" interrupted Christine impatiently

"Be quiet Chris let your mum finish" insisted Sam

"Yes Chris he is your dad, as I was saying I met James and we fell in love and I mean love. He was every thing I ever dreamed of I saw him every day, I even took him to meet my parents in Cornwall, then he told me he had had a letter from one of his pals. James was a brilliant guitarist and his pal had set up a band and wanted James to join them. I didn't want him to go but my opinion didn't count he told me he was bored with me, anyway and he left. I was devastated. After that, I lost all interest in men. I started drinking that got worse and soon became a problem. I was thrown out of university, my parents were absolutely furious, they sent me to Worcester to live with mum's sister who owned a nursing home for the elderly they gave me job and that's where I met Jack"

"What the hell was Jack doing there?" asked Sara

"He wasn't at the home. What I meant was I met him in Worcester. Jack was at the time living with his younger brother Maurice and his wife Jenny, we fell in love he took me to meet his parents who at the time lived in this house. I took him to meet my parents, they hated him, they found him a pompous arrogant young man, well that's how dad described him, but I was in love and within a year, we were married. My mum and dad never came to the wedding (Eileen got up from her chair) hang on I had better check on the meat"

"You sit down Eileen, I'll do that and I'll make us all a coffee" said Sam

"Thanks Sam dear, now where was I, Oh yes well after the wedding we moved into that house at the bottom of the garden there (Eileen pointed out of the kitchen window to a rather dilapidated old ruin of a house that could just be seen over the overgrown hedge) it was quite a nice house at the time, but as you see, time has taken it's toll"

"Yes mum, Sara and I used to play in it when we were kids, but I had no idea you ever lived there"

"Oh yes, they were the good days two years we lived there, then Jacks father died, within a year his mother died and Jack took over the family firm, with his brothers, but Maurice wasn't interested in farming so Jack and Ray bought him out. Ray got himself into money problems and Jack bought Ray out. All this time I hadn't seen my parents although I wanted to, but I felt that Jack wouldn't want me to, with him knowing they hated him so much and I suppose I felt I owed him a bit of loyalty"

"Mum where is all this leading to, where does our dad come in to all this?"

"Christine love I need to tell you everything, what I'm telling you is relevant, I want you both to know everything, too much has been kept from you both over the years, so please hear me out, then we'll have tea and you can ask questions. Now at this time Jack was going over to see his brother in Worcester a lot, or at least that's what I thought. so I was left alone a lot and one night I was so lonely I picked up the phone and dialled my parents number, dad answered when he heard my voice he burst into tears, that wasn't like him, in all my life he had never once shown any emotion. I always thought him to be a hard man. He was so pleased to hear my voice. We had a chat and he gave the phone to my mother she invited me down. When Jack got home, I told him, he went spare throwing a cup at the wall saying he didn't want me there, I was in tears, but after I told him, I was going whether he liked it or not he gave into me.

Two weeks later, I was on the train to Penrhyn. Dad met me at the station; I had a great time. Then mum told me that the young man I had once took down there to meet them, had written to them asking them if they could let him have my address, they never replied so he paid them a visit, mum and dad wouldn't give him my address, but promised to forward his address to me. The young man that had called was James. Mum handed me the piece of paper that he had scribbled his address on. I put the piece of paper in my handbag.

I stayed at mum and dads for a couple of days and when I got home, Jack never asked how my visit had gone. He told me that he had to go to his brothers again the following weekend and I shouldn't try to contact him because he and his brother had a lot to sort out. As soon as he had gone I took the piece of paper from my hand bag, stared at it for what seemed ages, thinking of James and the times we had had together, then for some reason I picked up the phone and dialled the number, he answered the phone. To hear his voice sent butterflies through my stomach. We spoke for ages he told me he had been married but his wife couldn't cope with the demands of the band. I told him how I was married, what Jack did, he told me he lived in Newark and suggested we met up for a drink. I agreed although I had know idea what excuse I would use to Jack. When Jack came home he told me he had to go back to his brothers the following weekend, but it was now becoming obvious to me that he was seeing someone else"

"Why didn't you ring Maurice mum?"

"Because I knew he would have asked Maurice to cover for him. It would have been a total waste of time. I played the good wife, but that was about to change, Jack left the house at three on the Friday afternoon and I was on the phone to James at one minute past three, arranging to meet him on the Saturday morning. I got the early bus to Sleaford. James was waiting for me at the bus stop. He stood there, he hadn't changed a bit, I felt those same feelings in my stomach I always had with him. We chatted and chatted he told me he still loved me, I never commented, but I agreed to meet him again. Jack came back and told me he was out again the next weekend, so I met James again we went for a ride in his car and ended up doing it"

"Doing what mum?" asked Christine laughing

"Shut up Chris and let her finish cause I'm getting hungry" added Sam

"Surprise bloody surprise" laughed Sara

"Turn the tea down a bit, Sam love can you, I fell pregnant straight away with Christine the problem was I hadn't been sleeping with Jack, so I knew who the father was. I had to get Jack in bed so he would think the baby was his. After all I knew James couldn't give me any security and as soon as I told him he got scared and I didn't here from him until about a year after Christine was born"

"So mum did you get Jack in bed?" asked Sara

"Yes so he thought you were his. Just after you were born I had it confirmed that Jack had been seeing some woman from out Maxey way. As hypocritical as it may sound, I was fuming and threatened to leave him. He still believed you were his Christine and he idolised you. He started his weekends away again; I got lonely and needed someone to talk to. So I rang James, he asked how Christine was, I told him if he wanted he could see her, he said he would like to so we met at Sleaford. He made a hell of a fuss of you Christine. I didn't see him for a month or two after that then one Saturday morning, there was a knock on the front door and when I opened it, it was James pretending to be a sales man just in case Jack was in. I invited him in, Christine was in bed and after a drink and a chat we landed up making love and the outcome of that was you Sara"

"So how did Jack find out mum?" asked Sara

"When you were about two you had an accident and there was something mentioned about having to give you blood and Jack said the only blood you could have was his, I panicked and had to tell him"

"What did he say mum?"

"That was the first time he hit me. He grabbed me by the hair dragged me up the stairs and hit me several times. He only stopped when I told him I knew about his affair with Dorothy and I was going to tell his brother He didn't deny it and he never threw me out. I never set eyes on James again. I knew in my heart that one day I would have to contact him, so that brings us to today as I said I spoke to his sister and she said she spoke to James on Friday and he wants to see you"

"He does, when?" asked Christine excitedly

"Apparently he's in Spain for the next two weeks with his son and grand daughter" said Eileen

"So we're aunties and we have a brother or sister" said Christine

"Fancy that auntie Sara that's nice" said Sara and tears trickled down her face

"So you say he wants to see us so when"

"I've given Cathy that's James sister my phone number he's going to ring as soon as he returns"

"Does his wife know mum?" asked Sara

"If she didn't, she does now. Cathy never mentioned her, she only mentioned that his son and granddaughter lived with him" replied Eileen

"Where is he living Eileen?" asked Tom

"Apparently he's living in a place called (and Eileen reached on top of the French dresser picking up a piece of paper reading from it) Tow Law"

"Where the hell is Tow Law?" asked Christine

"I've been through there it's a small village in County Durham" said Tom

"It's no good telling her Tom she has a job finding the office" laughed Sam

"I had noticed"

"Anyway, I don't know about you lot, but I'm rather hungry and that meat must be well done by now so lets get it sorted. Tom can you pour the wine out while I sort the rest out" asked Eileen.

Chapter Twenty-Two

The following morning, pouring with rain, Tom and Sara arrived at the office to find the builders still working on the front of the shop

"Morning Mr Gardener, morning Sara. You look as gorgeous as ever" Said Steve

"Morning Steve, will you be finished today?" said Tom

"I'm saying yes Tom, but that's providing the double glazing company turn up, they said they would be here by now" replied Steve

Just then, a small lorry turned up with very a large window in the back. Two minutes later Christine and Sam came Running up the pavement,

"Sorry we're late Tom we got stuck behind the railway barriers" said Sam

"But your flat is this side of the railway line" replied Tom looking baffled

"Yes but the wind took my brolly the other side of the crossing as soon as I got out of the flat" said Sam

"What wind, forget it, I wish I hadn't asked, by the way if I were you two I would leave your coats on this morning" said Tom.

The builders had all the front of the shop finished by dinner time, all that was left to do was the inside painting. Tom decided they should have an extended dinner break so the builders could get on, this would give Tom and Sara chance to contact the vicar at the parish church. They had something to eat with Christine and Sam then made their way to the church. They had no problem in booking the first of April. With the church organised that was one less thing to worry about.

"Are you still going for your dress on Saturday?" asked Tom

"I don't know Tom, I really wanted Chris and Sam there too, apart from that I would have liked to have chosen some bridesmaid dresses" replied Sara

"Have you contacted your two god children's mother yet?"

"Yes Tom, I thought I told you I spoke to Denise last week and she was over the moon that I had asked her. That's not a problem. I know it sounds a bit premature, but now I know I have at least one niece I'm hoping that I can ask her to be a bridesmaid as well"

"One things for sure, your family is definitely growing by the day" laughed Tom

"Going back to the dresses Tom, I think I'll wait for a couple of weeks until Chris and Sam have settled into there new house"

"That wouldn't be a bad idea, Oh yes remind me that Sam has to go to your mums this afternoon. What are you doing about your flat?"

"I think Tom, we should put it on the market now while things are good, if I leave it, there might be a slump"

"Sara it's just a thought, but have you considered renting it out?"

"I don't know Tom"

"You could make a bit out of a flat doing that. You could do are through the company; we rent out other flats although none of them is as nice as yours. That furniture you were going to dump, you could use that to furnish it with, and that way we can advertise it as a furnished flat"

"You've got a point there Tom. If you think it's a good idea, I'll go along with it"

"Let's face it you have nothing to loose"

"No Tom we have nothing to loose" said Sara and Tom laughed.

Tom and Sara made their way back to the pub, where Christine and Sam were waiting.

"Sorted, it's all arranged for the first of April" said Sara looking at Christine and Sam

"Our deepest sympathy Tom" said Christine laughing.

Back at the office the decorators had almost finished painting the new plaster and were just about ready to leave, as into the shop walked detective Davis and Richards

"Can we help you gentlemen? Are you interested in buying a new police station?" said Tom sarcastically

"Very funny, you'll have me in stitches" commented Richards

"I'm pleased you thought it was funny" replied Tom

"I see you've had some work done," said Davis

"Yes and I'm sure you are aware that someone decided to park a car through the shop next door damaging our front as well, but I'm sure you haven't come to pass pleasantries so what do you want?" asked Tom

"Can we go into the office (Tom led the way and Davis and Richards followed) it's about the money we were wondering if you have managed to shed some light on it" said Davis

"Look, I have told you all I know, now it seems to me that you are completely stuck on this one, as for that money I think you will find it is now the property of Mrs Gray and the tax man. I'm rather a busy man. I've told you all I know so unless there's anything else—don't slam our new door on the way out". Davis and Richards left without another word.

Sam spent the remainder of the afternoon, trying to place a value on Eileen's house reaching a decision between herself and Eileen, that an asking prise of £250,000 would be a fair price, explaining to Eileen, that once the grass had been cut and the paintwork had been tidied up, Tom would come and take some photos. Sam stopped for a cup of tea with Eileen and downed a full packet of biscuits, she left for the office.

"Tom will come and put you a for sale board up sometime this week" said Sam on her way out.

Chapter Twenty-Three

Tuesday evening arrived and it was quite obvious to Sam that Christine was in a very nervous state

"Calm down Chris love" said Sam

"I can't, Simon and Paul will be at Garrets now and they said they would ring"

"And I'm sure they will?" replied Sam

"But what if they don't?" just then the phone rang Christine picked up the receiver it was Paul

"Christine, Simon and I have been talking to Graham and Richard, they told us that they asked 'her' about you and she reckons you are seeing Tracey, this Patricia says you have destroyed her and Tracey's relationship, she is going to destroy you"

"Paul I hadn't set eyes on her since I left York until she came round and did the story for the paper"

"Well Chris that's what she said"

"I think Sam and I had better come over and sort this out"

"No Chris, she'll kill you"

"We're coming"

Christine and Sam made their way to Garrets. On entering the hall they caught site of Paul, who obviously had been watching out for them and rushed over

"I told you not to come Chris"

"I told her not to as well Paul, but she wouldn't listen. I wasn't go to let her come on her own" added Sam

"I know what you're both saying, but I've had enough of looking over my shoulder anymore, wondering what stunt that slag is going to pull next, so now I'm here I'll get this sorted once and for all so where is she?"

"I don't know Chris, look if you cause any trouble you'll get us all thrown out"

"Don't you worry about that; the only person who will be thrown out is me. Where the fuck is she?"

"She's over there" said Paul pointing to the bar

"Where?" asked Christine

"Oh she must have gone to the ladies," added Paul and without another word, Christine headed for the toilets followed closely by Sam. As she walked in a woman was lent over the sink swilling her face with water

"Are you Patricia?" asked Christine in an unbelievably calm voice,

The girl stood up straight looking in the mirror. Seeing it was Christine, she quickly turned round

"What the fuck do you want?"

"You ask me what I want, you've got some cheek, you fucking slag, don't let anyone in that door Sam"

"Now slag, before I kick shit out of that pretty little head of yours, I think that you should get your facts right, I'm not fucking Tracey, I hadn't even set eyes on her from leaving York, until the other week"

"That's not what she told me" said Patricia now looking rather worried

"I don't give a toss what she has told you, I'm telling you, O.K do I make myself clear (Patricia made a move for the door trying to push Sam to one side but Christine caught her by the hair and threw her to the floor) I asked you a question do I make myself clear?"

"Yes,"

"I didn't hear that Sam did you?"

"No Chris"

"Yes I said yes, look please don't hurt me. I've got it all wrong" said Patricia now crying

"You're fucking right you've got it wrong, you don't know me from fucking Adam. So what gives you the right to try and terrorise me, sending me letters with razorblades in"

Sam saw that when Christine mentioned the razorblades, Patricia smiled, seeing this expression angered Sam so much, that she shot away from the door pushed Christine to one side, grabbed Patricia by the hair pushing her into the toilet cubical and pushed her head into the toilet pan flushing the handle, then she pulled her head back up banging her face on the toilet wall knocking her to the floor kicking her as she went.

"Now bitch, you listen to me, and listen to me good, if you come anywhere near us again, I promise you I'll fucking kill you"

Sam finished off, by kicking her in the stomach, and then Christine bent down to her, looked her straight into her much bruised face.

"Now you little bitch, have you now got the message or should we spell it out any more so do you understand, Oh yes, the police have a description of you when you took it upon yourself to steel my bosses car and break into the shop, I take it that was you. (Patricia got up looking a bit of a mess and) by the way I'm not interested what these are all about (Christine took the photos that they had found in Jack and her mums house and threw them at her) but if you have been led to believe they're recent, then you have been led wrong, If you wasn't so fucking thick you would see, these were taken when I was in York, a few years ago, you stupid slag"

"But I was told they were recent" replied Patricia crying

"Just look at them, are you fucking blind as well as daft, I even look a lot younger"

"I thought you were supposed to be some hard case, well all you are is a piece of shit. Come on Chris lets go, you tell your friend Tracey I want a word with her" said Sam

"I don't see her any more. When I thought she was seeing Christine, I walked out on her" said Patricia

"You sad sick cow go on get out" she slid round Sam and ran out the door.

Christine and Sam went back into the dance hall.

"We were getting rather worried about you two, and there are a lot of ladies in this hall bursting for a wee, they were non to happy when the toilets were temporarily out of order" said Simon

"What the hell did you do to that Patricia she looked an awful mess" commented Paul

"You could say, we are pretty sure she has got the message and won't be bothering us again"

"She was crying when she left and I think she got in a taxi" said Simon

"Good, but I think we should have a word with that Tracey and put her right about a few things don't you Chris" added Sam

"Come and have a drink with us and we'll introduce you to some of our friends" insisted Simon.

The following day Christine and Sam arrived at the office before Tom and Sara

"My god this is a first" joked Tom

"Yes I feel like a new woman" replied Christine

"I thought you and Sam were happy together?" said Tom laughing,

"Not like that you silly sod, I love Sam very much," said Christine laughing.

Once they were all sat down, Christine told them of the previous night's events

"So do you think that's the end of it all" asked Sara

"Yes, but just to make sure we don't have any repercussions, tonight me and Sam are going over to see Tracey, just to let her know we know what she has been up to"

"You be careful Chris, she's just had a baby" added Sara

"Somehow sis I don't think we will have any trouble from her"

"I just don't want you to get into any trouble Chris"

"How do you know where she lives because didn't Paul say she had moved"

"According to Simon she still lives in Holbeach down Battles field Lane Sam has the number," said Christine.

They arrived at the address Simon had given them, only to find the number was wrong. The woman who lived there showed them the right house. It took sometime before she answered the door, and then she only opened it slightly, as a security chain had been attached from the inside

"Well, what a surprise I was wondering how long it would be before you pair turned up" said Tracey sarcastically

"Tracey, just open the door and we'll say what we have to say and go" said Sam leaning on the door

"Piss off slag" shouted Tracey

"What do you want with us?" asked Christine

"You know" added Tracey getting upset

"I'm sorry, but we don't, we have no idea what the hell you're on about" replied Christine

Tracey now crying, asked Sam to move from the door she released the chain and opened the door

"You had better come in"

They followed Tracey into her house as she led them into the lounge

"You had better sit down I'll put the kettle on" said Tracey

"Forget about that just tell us what's been going on" insisted Christine

Tracey went to a cupboard in the corner of her lounge and opened it removing a handful of pictures from it, and handed them to Christine

"Look Sam these are the same ones we found in mums house, where did you get these from Tracey?" asked Christine

"About a year ago they turned up on my doorstep. About a day or so later I received a phone call from some man saying that if I didn't want my partner to see them, then I had to pay an agreed amount. I had to tell Patricia, we had no money, we were looking to have a baby, I had found a gay friend who agreed to help me get pregnant, there was no way I was going to be blackmailed, the problem was because I didn't tell her until a few months later, she thought I was seeing you. A few months ago, I received another phone call from a different man telling us that you Chris had been behind the blackmailing. I loved Pat, I rang her and told her, pleading with her to come back to me, she asked me for your address, I didn't know it at the time although I did know where your sisters flat was. I told her and she followed her to Pinchbeck getting you mixed up because you look so similar and she took her or her partners car and decided to trash her office but was almost caught, and the rest is history"

"Tracey, we can assure you we had nothing to do with the blackmailing and didn't know about it until last week" said Sam

"So if it wasn't you who was it?" asked Tracey

"My Step father" said Christine

"I didn't know you had a step dad Christine" said Tracey

"Neither did I until a few months ago" said Christine

They told Tracey the story of the man she called dad turning out to be not her real dad.

"So why were you expecting us?" asked Sam

"I was woken at one this morning by a bang on the door, it was Patricia she was in one hell of a mess, you definitely made a good job of her she was screaming and shouting, calling me all the names under the sun, blaming me saying she never wanted to see me ever again and if she did she would knife me, the thing was her old man warned me she was a bit of a psychopath, I wouldn't have it, now I think he's right"

"I wouldn't call her very brave, from what I saw last night" added Sam

"Well you did surprise me, but she has had it coming to her" said Tracey

"Well Sam I think that's all we needed to know, we'll make a move" said Christine standing up

"O.K, if ever you're passing call in for a drink and Sam you are one very lucky girl, you take care of Chris, her type are few and far between" said Tracey showing them out.

"What did you make of what she had to say?" asked Christine

"I'm sure she was telling us the truth"

"That will be a first for her" replied Christine

"Well I found her very nice"

"Yes Sam dear but you have never lived with her, she's an evil manipulating little slag and if she could come between us two she would"

"So you don't like her?" laughed Sam

"I suppose you could say that" replied Christine

"Well I don't think we will get any more trouble from them pair.

Chris I love you" said Sam leaning over to give Christine a kiss on the cheek. Christine's mobile phone started to ring

"You had better get that Sam dear that's Sara's number"

"Hello Sara"

"Sam how did your visit go?"

"Not very well Sara the police turned up and your sister been arrested"

"What the hell for"

"A copper tried to stop her hitting that Tracey and Chris hit him on the nose"

"I bloody knew it, hit first, think later, well she's definitely got herself knee deep in shit this time, is she at Spalding police station Sam?"

"I think so Sara. I'm coming to yours now Sara. I'll tell you the full story then" said Sam

"Now don't you worry, we can get this sorted, we'll see you in a while and drive carefully" Sam ended the call

"You rotten bitch. I'll tell you what, I'll get out at the end of Tom and Sara's drive, you go in on your own and keep it going, I'll really wind her up".

Christine pulled up at the end of Tom and Sara's drive, letting Sam take the car the rest of the way alone. Sara and Tom hearing Sam pull up came out meet her.

"Come on in Sam love, we'll get this sorted"

They had just sat down when there was a bang on the door

"I'll get it Sara" said Tom it was Christine

"Quick Tom hide me" said Christine

"What the hell's going on Chris?"

"I did a runner from the police, when they got me out of their car"

"You bloody silly sod Chris, this is the first place they'll look, look Chris— (before Tom had finished his sentence he heard some laughter coming from the kitchen) this is a wind up Chris isn't it"

"Yes Tom" replied Christine now in a fit of hysterics

"You rotten bitch I hate you" said Tom,

"Come on lets get that kettle on and you can tell us what really did happen, without the bull shit—Christine and Sam set about telling Tom and Sara what had been said

"And is that the end of the whole rigmarole?"

"Yes thank god".

Chapter Twenty-Four

"Come on Chris get up" said Sam shaking her

"Bloody hell Sam what time is it?" replied Christine

Trying to focus her eyes towards the alarm clock

"Six and you should be up by now your mum will be here in an hour to help us move"

"Just another ten minutes"

"No Chris, come on, get up we've got a lot to do you have to box all those books up"

"What the hell for?"

"Chris I don't know if you have forgotten or not, but we are moving so come on out of bed" said Sam pulling back the sheets

"You rotten bitch"

"Up Chris, we have a lot to do before we pick the keys up. I've made you a coffee it's in the lounge"

"O.K Sam if I must" said Christine dragging herself from the bed

"Where's the bloody loo roll gone?" shouted Christine

"Oh—sorry Chris I'll get you it"

"What the hell have you took it out for?"

"I'm not leaving it"

"Did you not think we might need to use the loo today?"

"I said I'm sorry Chris. You have woken up in a right mood"

"I'm not in a mood. I just can't see why we need to get up so early, we don't get the keys until midday"

"God Chris you can be so bloody obstinate"

"I'm sorry Sam, come and give me a cuddle. I'll have a shower, and then I'll sort those books out"

"O.K, I had better put that money in a case, we'll put that in the boot of the car".

Eileen arrived just before seven just as Tom turned up to drop off a small lorry type van.

"Morning Tom, have they dragged you into help?"

"No, I'm just dropping this van off. I have too much to do at the office. I shall be round later with Sara"

Eileen and Tom went into the flat

"Morning you two, I hope you don't want to use the loo" said Christine sarcastically

"Shut it Chris" Sam said looking very annoyed at Christine

"Is someone going to tell me what Chris is on about?" asked Tom

"You don't want to know Tom".

Christine made them all a coffee. Tom and Sam carried the three-piece to the van, before Tom left to go to the office.

Christine, Sam and Eileen soon had the flat emptied and into the van by eleven. They decided to kill some time; they would walk to Greens estate agents to collect the keys. Mr Green told them that the keys wouldn't be ready until two

"You told us midday" Said Sam in a very annoyed voice

"Well I'm sorry and all that girls, but you should know better than most that, these things happen" commented Mr Green in his usual arrogant manner

"Pig" murmured Christine on her way out the door just low enough for him to here

"Come on girls lets go and see Tom and Sara" said Sam

"Oh they've soon got that put right," said Eileen referring to the front of the shop

"Can't you keep away from me for five minutes?"

"Don't flatter yourself Tom" replied Christine laughing

"So what brings you here then?" said Tom

"Because every one else was out and we're thirsty" laughed Sam

"I just knew there would have to be a drink in it somewhere, go and put the kettle on then Chris" said Tom.

Having told Tom and Sara the reason as to why they were there. Sam asked Tom if he could go and move the lorry out side their new house because none of them felt confident enough.

Making another visit to Greens at two o'clock, they were told to come back at four, when they finally were able to collect them.

"Thank god for that, never again will I comment when some one comes into the shop and moans about having to wait for their keys" said Christine

"Yes Chris, it's not that nice being on the receiving end" added Sam

"Just think I could have stayed in bed for another few hours after all" complained Christine

"Shut up bloody moaning and lets get moved" insisted Sam and Sam put the key in the front door lock and unlocked the door

"Hold on Sam before you go in I have something to do" said Christine walking up to the sold board and pulling it from the small front garden and laying it down the side of the house, she then walked up to Sam picked her up, asking Eileen to open the door she carried Sam over the door step,

"You silly sod" said Sam

"I know that, that's part of the reason you love me"

"Yes Chris I suppose it is, so let's get the lorry unloaded" replied Sam

"Look over there" said Eileen pointing to a large bouquet of flowers laying on the fire hearth

"Oh they're nice (said Sam bending over to pick them up and undoing the attached card then reading it) Hope you have as many happy times here as we have see you soon love from Simon and Paul"

"Isn't that a nice thought" said Eileen

"Yes it just shows there are still some nice people around, I'll ring them later to thank them" said Sam

"Come on then let's get this van unloaded while the weather holds. Sam you had better get that case out of the car" said Christine,

They soon had the van empty with no breakages, Tom and Sara arrived about five thirty.

"You've soon emptied that lot. Can you follow me Eileen, I'll take this van back to the rental company, I'll have a word with you about your house on the way back, you take my car" said Tom.

On the way back from the rental company, Tom drove the car handing Eileen the information on the sale of her house, telling her that the photographer had been today and taken some pictures.

"What do you reckon to that Eileen are you happy with the description"

"Yes Tom that's fine absolutely fine, do you think it'll take long to sell Tom, I shall need to start looking for another place"

"I couldn't tell you Eileen, but if you give me an idea on what sort of place you're looking for I'll keep an eye open and check with other agents, we can always find you somewhere to rent for a while, if need be, Sara is renting her flat out at the moment"

"To be honest with you Tom, I would like a bungalow, something with a not too large a garden and two or three bedrooms"

"I'll tell you what Eileen there are some new ones going up just off the Bourne Road, you may have seen them"

"No I can't say I have, can you get me the information on them"

"No problem Eileen leave it with me. Eileen tell me to mind my own business if you like, but we have all noticed that you haven't mentioned Peter lately"

"Oh—well Tom to be honest with you, he has distanced him self from me, I don't know why, I didn't say anything, but you know I was going to meet him on Saturday well he never turned up, that wasn't the first time, he has done it several times promising to see me and not turning up, leaving me waiting, I think he's just been using me and to be honest with you Tom if that's the kind of man he is I can well do without him".

Tom and Eileen arrived back at the house.

"Just the man, here hang this up there on that screw Tom" said Sam

She handed Tom a large picture that he recognised as being the one he had bought her and Christine on their day out to Wells.

"That looks nice there Tom" said Christine,

Tom never commented he was really pleased they had chosen to put this picture at the most prominent point of their lounge.

Sam decided, she didn't like Simon and Paul's choice of décor in the lounge so over the next few evenings, Sam set about stripping the walls down while Christine set about altering the garden laying down a patio, replacing old plants with new, she built a pond with a water fall that she designed herself, they decided they would use some of the money from Eileen to buy a new three-piece, carpet and curtains for the lounge. They asked Eileen and Sara if they would go with them to Peterborough and help them choose some new bits.

"Perhaps while we are here Sara you might like to look at some wedding dresses?" said Christine

"We can do that another time Chris"

"No sis, we have plenty of time and I'm sure you would love to if you're honest?"

"Well yes I wouldn't mind if it's O.K with the rest of you?" said Sara,

It didn't take long for Christine and Sam to agree on a choice of three-piece, and from the same shop, they ordered their curtains and carpets.

They decided to have some lunch in town and soon found a café.

"We'll have a look at some wedding dresses after this sis"

"I haven't decided what I'm wearing yet" added Sam

"I think Sam a nice grey trouser suit" said Sara

"I thought more like a top hat and tails" laughed Christine.

"So mum is Peter coming to the wedding?" asked Sara

"I don't think so Sara we haven't seen much of each other since Jack died" said Eileen almost in tears

"Oh—mum why what's up?" asked Christine

"It's just every time I ring him and ask him to come round there's always an excuse. I asked him for dinner last Sunday, but he had some gardening to do. I haven't spoken to him since. I take it that he doesn't want to see me any more" said Eileen obviously very upset

"I'm so sorry mum" said Sara trying to console her mother

"So mum what are you wearing for the big day?" asked Christine changing the subject

"I'm not sure Christine dear, I did think about a cream suit, but I shall wait until I've seen what's about, before making up my mind"

"Shall we make a move?" asked Sam getting up to pay the bill

"I'll pay that Sam" said Eileen pushing a twenty-pound note into Sam's hand.

They visited two bridal centres and not seeing anything that Sara could honestly say she liked, they decided to head for home.

"Call in at Market Deeping Sara dear can you there's a nice fresh fish shop there" asked Eileen.

While they all sat in the car, waiting for Eileen Sara noticed just across the road a bridal centre

"I wouldn't mind a look in there when mum comes back" said Sara pointing to the shop, Eileen retuned with her fish

"I never thought Sara but there's a bridal centre over there"

"Yes mum I was just saying to Chris and Sam I wouldn't mind a look" said Sara and they all went over to the shop

As soon as Sara walked through the shop door, she saw the dress of her dreams,

"Oh isn't that just gorgeous, I must try that on"

"Could I help you" asked the shop assistant

"Yes that dress could I try it on?" asked Sara

"Yes certainly you may" and the woman fetched a dress identical to the one on the mannequin.

"I like that one Sara" commented Sam pointing to a picture on the wall

"We do have our own designer who could help you design your own, we also make to order and hire out" said the shop assistant now helping to put the dress on Sara.

"Sara you look absolutely gorgeous" said Christine

"I'm so lucky to have two such pretty daughters you are going to be one very beautiful bride and I shall be so proud of you" said Eileen wiping the tears from her eyes

"Yes I must say Sara even I could fancy you" added Sam

"Could you Sam, well you never know" joked Sara and they all laughed

"Well Miss it's definitely you, although you need a slightly smaller size, may I ask what sort of price range you are looking for or are you looking to hire"

"I want to buy, how much is this one please?" asked Sara

"£900 that is one of our more expensive ones" said the woman

"Do you like that one Sara dear?"

"Yes mum I do"

"Well I'm paying for it, if that's what you want then you will have it"

"No mum" protested Sara

"Sara I'm paying and that's the end of it and what about the bridesmaids what are you having them in?" asked Eileen

"We do everything dress wise for a wedding and we can put you in touch with some very reputable caterers" added the shop assistant

"Mum you just bought me the dress"

"Sara I've dreamed of this day all my life, now I want to pay for it, let's look at some bridesmaids dresses do you know what colour you want?"

"I thought pink"

"Sara everyone has pink" said Christine

"Can we take some brochures with us?"

"Yes of cause you can, I'll get you some, now what are you doing about your dress Miss" said the assistant

"I'll have that one" said Sara

"Well we will take your measurements now and our dress makers will make you one, are you sure there's nothing you want changing?"

"No I want it just like that one," replied Sara.

Outside the shop, Sara gave her mother a hug

"Thank you mum"

"It's only what you deserve, I'm very proud of how you and Chris have turned out and very ashamed of the way I deserted you two when you needed me, yes very ashamed"

"Mum forget it we're just pleased to have you back in our lives and soon we will have our dad too" said Sara getting rather emotional

"Yes mum we are pleased to have you back and we both love you" added Christine

"Thank you girls, I love you too and what about my other daughter?"

They all looked bewildered

"What other daughter" asked Sara

"You Sam are you pleased I'm in your life?"

"Yes Eileen of cause I am" replied Sam reaching out to give Eileen a hug

"Good, let's get back to Spalding before we all get done for loitering" said Eileen.

Chapter Twenty-Five

A few days latter Eileen received a phone call from Tom saying someone would be calling to have a viewing on her property at around five o'clock; Sam would be present at the viewing.

"Will they turn up this time Tom?"

"I can only hope so, let's hope on third time lucky, keep smiling".

Eileen spent the whole day cleaning and tidying the house then checking to make sure the yard was tidy. About quarter to five the phone rang, Eileen thought it was Tom calling to cancel the appointment, when she heard the voice on the other end of the phone she nearly fell over

"Hello Eileen"

"Oh—my god its you—James"

"Yes Eileen it sure is, you are one very hard lady to get hold of. I must have rung you no end of times in the last week"

"I've been here, in fact the girls have rung me daily asking me if I'd heard from you, but saying that you could have rung while I was in the garden"

"So how is my daughter?"

"Daughters" corrected Eileen

"Eh—what?"

"You have two daughters" and Eileen explained to James about Sara

"Holy shit I promise you Eileen I never knew"

"But you did know about Christine why didn't ever try to contact her"

"Eileen I have been trying to trace you and her for the last ten years. The thing that baffles me is, I rang this same number about three years ago and some man said he had never heard of you. I called at your old address in Bourne about ten years ago and some very well spoken chap told me that you and husband had moved and he had no idea where"

"Old address James, I've never moved, I've always lived here I think the man you saw was Jack"

"Your husband"

"Yes James my husband"

"Eileen what do the girls know about me? When can I meet them?"

"As soon as you like"

"What about this weekend? I can travel down tomorrow. I would dearly love to see you to, if I can avoid bumping in to your husband"

"I'll tell you what James, if you bump into Jack, run, there's something drastically wrong, we cremated him six weeks ago"

"Oh I'm sorry"

"Don't be, I'm not. What about you, obviously there's a Mrs Pilcher?"

"Yes—I lost her twelve years ago she had a tumour on the brain, I still miss her" said James

"I am sorry to here that"

"You knew she was my second wife"

"Yes I did, if you remember, I have seen you since you split up from your first wife. Your sister told me you have a son and granddaughter?"

"Yes David and his daughter Jessica, she's lovely and he's a good lad and a great father"

"So what about Jessica's mother?"

"That's a bit of a mess, David and her got divorced about three years ago, she was into drugs in a big way. David got custody of Jessica and god knows where she is, some gutter some where I should imagine, she called about two years ago saw Jessica for two minutes.

286

Handed her to me and asked David for two hundred pounds, the bloody fool gave her it. Two weeks later she did the same trick but this time as he handed it to her; I took it off her and told her to go I'm not letting him feed her drug addition"

"I can't say as if I blame you. What does David think, to having two sisters?"

"Well he was shocked when I told him he had one sister, yes he's in for real surprise I don't think I shall tell him, we'll make that a surprise. Do you mind if I bring him?"

"Not at all the girls will be upset if you don't"

"When he found out you had rung my sister we were in Spain, he wanted to come home. When we got back home on Saturday he insisted I ring, but you must have been out"

"Yes we were out choosing some furniture for Chris and Sam's new house and looking for something for Sara that she will tell you about"

"Who is Sam?" asked James

"Are well this isn't really for me to say. So as far as you're concerned I haven't told you. Sam is Christine's gay partner and she's a really nice girl" said Eileen and there was a long pause

"So how long has Christine been gay?" asked James and Eileen laughed

"She's always been gay. It isn't an illness"

"No I didn't mean it like that"

"I can assure you when I first found out it came as a bit of a shock, but when you get to know her and Sam, you will see they're just the same as any other couple, possibly more in love than most. They are two very happy girls"

"So what about Sara is she gay?"

287

"No James Sara has a boyfriend Tom. You'll like him. You have two lovely daughters James, don't let Christine being gay put you off"

"No not at all Eileen I must admit it'll take some getting used to. I'm just pleased you told me I had better tell David"

"He won't be bothered will he?"

"No not at all, the biggest shock he's in for is when I tell him he has two sisters and not one. Today has definitely been full of surprises. So where shall we meet?" asked James and there was a knock on the door

"Hang on a minute James there's some one at the door"

Eileen answered the door it was Sam

"Is it O.K for us to look round Eileen we've done outside?"

"I'm so sorry Sam dear, I didn't realise you were here of course you can I'm on the phone help yourself" Eileen retuned to the phone

"Sorry about that James someone has come to look round the house I'm trying to sell it, now where were we?"

"I asked you where you think we should meet."

"Here if you like James. You know where I live so this is possibly the best place"

"Fine what I'll do when we get there I'll book into a hotel, we shouldn't have any problem getting a room this time of the year"

"If you get stuck, I can always put you up"

"No we'll find somewhere. I had better go now and ring David; I'll see you about ten in the morning so till then you take care"

Eileen hearing those last six words knew the phone would go dead as she could remember he always ended their phone calls with them six words 'so till then you take care'. Eileen smiled to herself as she placed down the receiver just as Sam entered the room.

"Would you like a drink?" asked Eileen to the couple looking round her house

"Yes that would be nice, teas please"

"And you Sam?"

"Yes pleased Eileen, we are just about finished".

Once the couple had, gone Eileen told Sam about her phone call then Sam rang Christine and told her. Christine was in tears. Sam got the same response from Sara, they all agreed to meet at Eileen's, at ten in the morning.

"I won't sleep tonight" said Sara

"That just what Christine said." Said Sam

While Sam was on the phone, Eileen put the kettle on and made another drink for her and Sam and she got a packet of biscuits from the pantry.

"So what did they think?" asked Eileen

"You never can tell, but it is what they are looking for, and they seemed very interested"

Just then, Sam's mobile rang.

"Hello, is that Miss Taylor?"

"Yes?"

"It's Simon Jarvis here. My wife and I have just left you, would your client be open to offers"

"I'm not sure Mr Jarvis; the asking price is as I explained is very reasonable. How much are you looking at?"

"We would like to make an offer of £240'000"

"Obviously Mr Jarvis I shall put your offer to our client and I will get back to you".

Sam told Eileen about the offer. Eileen was all for accepting their offer

"Let them sweat, they want this place I'm sure you'll get the asking price"

No sooner had she finished advising Eileen, her mobile rang

"Hello Sam Taylor," said Sam

"Hello its Simon Jarvis did you contact your client"

"Yes I was going to ring you"

"What did your client say?"

"No she says she wants the asking price of 250'000 and no less"

"O.K we'll have it. My solicitor will be in touch and I'll call round your office in the morning"

"O.K Mr Jarvis I'll tell Mrs Gray and we'll look forward to seeing you" said Sam

"Well, what did they say?"

"Give me a chance. They have offered you the asking price; obviously they saw it was a bargain"

"I wonder what they want a house this size for."

"To convert it into an old people's home they've bought several off us around this size, that's why I was so sure they would buy it"

"Well this calls for a celebration I'll put the kettle on" said Eileen

"Not for me Eileen, I must get home. I had better ring Tom and tell him the good news, by the way if I were you I would start looking for another place"

"Tom said he was going to find out about those new houses going up just as you go into Spalding"

"That's great Eileen; they look nice places, O.K I must go"

"Thank you dear, you've been great. I'll see you in the morning".

The following morning Christine picked up Sara at eight

"This will be the first time you've been early in your life Chris"

"Yes you're possibly right sis and it's the first time I've ever felt so nervous"

"Me to I feel sick with nerves. I hardly slept a wink last night"

"Let's go"

Arriving at their mums Eileen was in the kitchen making herself some breakfast

"Where are Tom and Sam?" Asked Eileen

"They both said they thought it would best, if we met him the first time on our own," said Sam

"Yes I think that's a good idea" said Eileen

"Mum does he know I'm gay?"

"Yes Christine, he does, I told him yesterday"

"What did he say?"

"Nothing Christine, why should he, do you think that would bother him, he's not like that. I'm sure you will like him. Come on you two join me in some breakfast, they won't be here for another hour or so"

"Is David and little Jessica coming to?" asked Sara excitedly

"Yes they're all coming and what's better there're stopping until tomorrow".

Just before ten, they heard the sound of a car coming down the drive Christine went to window and peered out

"It's them, Sara, mum it's them" said Christine excitedly,

Sara rushed to the door almost ripping it off its frame; they were all soon stood waiting impatiently for them.

"You're right mum, he's definitely a handsome chap" commented Sara in a whispering voice,

As he walked from the car and approached them, he held out his arms to them

"Hello girls" said James

They all shook hands and James kissed them on the cheek. David was standing at the side of the car, not really knowing how to react with his daughter in his arms clinging to his neck. Sara went over to him

"You must be David and you must be Jessica, I'm Auntie Sara and that lady is your Auntie Christine. Can I hold her David?" said Sara holding out her arms

"Are you going to give me a hug?" and Jessica let go of her dad and went to Sara.

Christine went over to David and kissed her brother on the cheek.

"Now then little brother tell me what's it like to go to bed and wake up to find out you have two older sisters and not one?" Said Christine

David never answered. His father had only told him of Sara as they pulled into the drive, he was still in shock but trying to hide it. He just held out his arms and they hugged each other.

"Shall we all go inside?" asked Eileen.

Inside the house, Eileen put the kettle on while the others tried to catch up with the past years.

"What do you do for a living dad, you don't mind me calling you dad do you?" asked Sara

"No Sara I would love you to. I work for myself, as an accountant and David works with me"

"So you're no longer a musician?" asked Christine

"No I packed that in, it doesn't make for a good marriage, as I soon found out, anyway tell me what do you two do for a living?" asked James

"We work for Sara's boyfriend Tom; he's an estate agent in Spalding. We live in Spalding, mum is looking to move over there too" answered Christine

"That's nice, so when do we get to meet Tom and Sam?"

"Tonight, we can all go out for a drink"

"O.K that suits me but we'll have to go some where that children can go" said James

"No problem we know just the place, it's in Spalding" said Christine.

"I'll ring Tom and tell him and you can stop round ours tonight mum" said Sara

"How will we know where you live?" asked David

"I'll tell you what; I'll come over to Spalding about seven with you and your Dad, that'll solve that problem".

They all met up at Tom and Sara's house where James, David and Jessica were introduced to Tom and Sam. They went to a pub at low Fulney. They talked and talked, had a bar meal, Sam spent most of the time playing with Jessica. Towards the end of the night, Tom suggested a nightcap at his house, but James said they had to go back to their hotel and get Jessica to bed. They arranged to meet in the morning. With long hugs, they all made their way home Jessica had fallen asleep in her dad's arms.

On the Sunday, Christine having hardly slept a wink, woke at seven waking Sam.

"Bloody typical when I want to sleep in you decide to wake me up"

"I'm sorry Sam I'm going to ring Sara" said Christine picking up the phone,

Sara too couldn't sleep and had been out of bed since six leaving Tom to sleep

"Sorry to bother you sis, but I've been thinking about yesterday it went so well"

"Yes Chris I've been thinking, tell me Chris do you think it's too early to ask him to give me away. Do you think I should ask David if Jessica can be a bridesmaid?"

"Yes sis, I think it's a great idea, I'm asking him David and Jessica to mine and Sam's blessing next month"

"I can see what mum saw in him" said Sara

"So can I, he's a definite stunner and so is David"

"I thought Chris, perhaps today, we could all go to yours and Sam's house and nip over the road to that pub, and they allow children in there"

"That sounds fine by me".

David rang Sara around nine, saying that they would meet them at eleven so Sara gave him directions to Christine and Sam's. After she put the phone down to David, Sara took coffees up to Tom and her mother who were now awake. She sat on the edge of her mother's bed.

"Do you wish things had been different and you had married dad?"

"Yes Sara dear, but if I had, then you wouldn't have met Tom, and Christine wouldn't have met Sam, everything in our life is for a reason. I'm a big believer that destiny decides our future."

"Yes mum your right" Sara said giving her mother a hug

"Thinking back, the thing that I should have changed, was giving you and Christine more hugs".

On their way to Christine and Sam's they passed James, David and Jessica going the other way

"Flash your lights Tom I think they're lost" said Sara and Tom pulled over

"Ring his mobile I've got his number here" said Eileen handing Sara one of James business cards he had handed her at the pub

"Dad, stop you're going the wrong way" said Sara

He turned round; catching up with them, he followed them to Christine's and Sam's.

Sam made them all a coffee leaving them to chat

"This is a nice place Christine it's very much like the one you had David at Castleside" commented James

"It is Dad only this place is in a lot nicer condition" added David

"Where's Castleside?" asked Christine

"It's just up the road from 'Tow Law' talking of which when are you all coming up to see us?" asked James

"Soon dad, we hope," said Sara

"Good. Now Sara, Tom told me last night that you and him are to marry in April, I was wondering what sort of things are you looking for as presents?" asked James

"Well dad there is only one thing you could do for me" "What's that?" asked James

"Give me away"

"Sara come here, there's nothing I would want more than to walk you down the aisle" said James holding out his arms to give her a hug

"David there's something I want to ask you, can Jessica be one of my bridesmaids?"

"Yes Sara of course she can. You would like to wear a pretty dress and be a bridesmaid for your Aunty Sara wouldn't you Jessica?" said David, Jessica nodded

"So shall we all go for a drink across the road?" Asked Sam

"Yes, shandy for me. I've got to drive home, how are getting home Eileen?" asked James

"I'll take her later, so I had better not drink," said Tom

"Look why don't we all go for a burger and chips, I'm sure Jessica would prefer that, and you get a toy, would you like that Jessica? (Jessica nodded) good that's settled, then if the rain holds off, I want to take some photographs of us all then I thought we could give you a guided tour of the grand city of Spalding" laughed Christine

"Yes that sounds great, I would like to see where you all work" said David

"Work, you mean where they spend their holidays" laughed Tom

"My god Tom Gardener you've got room to talk" added Sam

"Come on you lot, we have a little girl here who is absolutely starving" said Sara taking hold of Jessica's hand and going to the door.

James, David and Jessica left the others around six and headed home, exchanging phone numbers and addresses then kissing each other they promised to ring each other regularly.

Chapter Twenty-Six

Over the next week both Christine and Sara rang their father every day Christine invited him, David and Jessica to Sam's surprise birthday party and blessing of their relationship, he accepted but would ask David, David rang Christine back and said he and their dad would be going, but he was leaving Jessica with his aunty Cathy in Newcastle.

Although Sam knew, Christine was up to something, with her birthday only six days away, was sure it had something to do with that, but when she confronted Christine, she just laughed it off. She also knew Tom and Sara were in on the secret. Tom and Sara insisted that the pair of them took the Friday off; she also noticed an awful lot of whispering going on between them so when the Friday did arrive Sam was relieved.

Christine was out of bed by seven, leaving Sam so sleep until ten she would have slept longer, but the phone rang. Christine was in the shower

"It's your Dad Chris"

"Sam tell him I'll ring him back in a minute" shouted Christine from the shower quickly getting dressed.

She rang her father back while Sam had a shower

"Yes dad you rang, where are you?" asked Christine

"We're just at the services at Colsterworth we thought we would go to your mothers and stay there until two.

We will bring her over to the church for three. We're going to get something to eat now" said James

Sam walked into the room

"O.K dad send my love to David and Jessica, see you dad" said Christine ending the call

"What did he have to say?" asked Sam

"He was just saying he was going to try to get over within the next few weeks, I also told him it's your birthday and he apologised for not wishing you a happy birthday" said Christine

"Chris what do you reckon your dad and David make of us"

"I can't answer that Sam because, I don't know, but I know from what mum said, he seemed shocked at first, but when he met you he commented to her about how happy we looked"

"Christine—you are happy aren't you"

"Of course Sam, I'm very happy and very much in love with you and Sam my sweet I have something for you (going to the bedroom and returning with two beautifully wrapped presents) I know its something you wanted"

Sam carefully unwrapped the smaller of the two

"Oh—Chris that's lovely (Sam held up an aubergine pencil skirt and jacket to match then opening the other present) Christine come here I love you, thank you" said Sam holding up a Grey hand embroidered sleeveless sweater.

"So are you going to put them on?" asked Christine

"Yes I think I will, I now know why Tom and Sara got me those shoes and insisted I had them last night"

"You see there was a method in their madness, so go on Sam get dressed before I drag you back to bed, standing there like that naked is doing things to me" said Christine and Sam soon returned

"Well what do you think?"

"Sam you look gorgeous"

"So what shall we do today?"

"I thought Sam we could go out for the after noon perhaps Peterborough, Oh—Sam remind me about three O'clock I must call at the church up the road, I promised Sara I would call and get something off the vicar"

"If we are going to Peterborough I had better get changed".

At twenty to three, Sam reminded Christine they had to call at the church, before supposedly going to Peterborough. Parking their car outside the church,

"Looks as if something is going on here Chris you had better be quiet"

"You had better come with me Sam in case I need a hand"

So Sam walked with Christine to the church, just as they opened the door, Sam realised that things were not as they seemed. Her jaw dropped seeing and recognising all the faces inside the church, once inside, Christine turned and faced. Christine speaking so others in the church could hear her

"Sam you know we talked about having our relationship blessed (Sam nodded) Sam I love you and want to spend the rest of my life with you, I know we can't get married, so Sam Taylor will you do the next best thing?"

"Christine you are one in a million, I love you".

Holding hands, they walked down the aisle where the vicar waited to bless their relationship while all their family and friends watched on.

The service lasted about twenty minutes finishing with Tom handing the vicar two identical rings that he blessed and Sara placed one on Sam's finger and Tom placed the other on Christine's finger then they signed a non-legal contract and Christine and Sam kissed before they went outside to have their photos taken. The day had gone to plan; they all went from the church to the town centre for a reception.

Sam was completely taken back by the whole situation she knew something was going on, but she had never imagined anything like this and seeing the way the hall had been laid out she just threw her arms around Christine in tears

"I love you Chris, I really do"

"The nights not finished yet Sam tomorrow we catch a train to London to see a show and I've booked us into a hotel for a night"

"You're—I love you so much Chris," said Sam searching for words

"Hello daughter number three, you look terrific come and have a drink with me (Leading Sam to a table by the arm) do you know what Sam when I spoke to Eileen a few weeks ago on the phone and she told me about you and Christine, I must admit it knocked me for six, but do you know what as soon as I met you both and saw you together all my worries vanished, and I know I can speak for David too, you are just made for each other. You are both two extremely lucky people. David and I are very happy for you both"

"Thank you James and thank you for coming" said Sam and she kissed him on the cheek.

Sam then wandered back over to Christine who was sat with David, Sara and Tom

"So Sara, what part did you play in this?" asked Sam

"Not a thing, everything you see has been arranged by Chris and the service was totally designed by her," replied Sara.

Christine took Sam by the hand and led her up to a large table and standing behind it knocked three times to attract everyone's attention

"Thank you all for coming to help us all celebrate two special occasions, the blessing of mine and Sam's relationship and Sam reaching the age of twenty-five. (Then looking over at the caterers in the corner) Bring out the cakes now please. (Carrying two iced cakes one with twenty-five candles on and the other the shape of a heart and placed them on the table in front of them) There isn't enough candles on this cake (they all laughed) Sam blow out the candles"

She blew them out and they all sang 'Happy Birthday' to her. Sam gave a little speech thanking everyone for coming, thanking Christine for all she had done to make her birthday special and hoping that one day the law will be changed, so all gays can marry the same as heterosexuals.

After Sara's speech, everyone was asked to go outside, where Tom had arranged a surprise, telling Sam to go to the front of the crowd, Tom lit a fuse and within seconds, the sky was a mass of colour and then the words happy birthday Sam appeared on a wall

"Well Sam, we couldn't have a birthday party on November the fifth without fireworks"

"Thank you Tom" said Sam kissing him on the cheek.

The party went on until one in the morning needless to say they were rather tired when they got up in the morning at eight so they could catch the train to Peterborough and then on to London although once in the train they managed to get some sleep.

Once at London they got on the underground that took them within a few hundred yards of their hotel where they booked in before jumping back on the underground to do some sight seeing. Visiting a well-known department store and toyshop where Christine bought Jessica a doll for her sixth birthday.

Returning back to their hotel to have some tea, then a shower and change for the show. They both thoroughly enjoyed the show and had a takeaway supper to eat, while they looked at the colourful lights that lit up the capitals shops by night.

"I could live like this all the time Chris"

"If we had the money we would, so until then I'm afraid you have to have your dreams under the bright lights of Spalding"

"What bloody bright lights?"

"Well Sam dear there's that strect light outside our bedroom window"

"You silly sod"

"So Sam, I think we should head back to the hotel then tomorrow its back to reality"

"Oh Chris don't remind me, the last two days have been unforgettable" and Sam lent over and kissed Christine on the cheek.

They woke the next morning bright and early going down to the restaurant for a full English breakfast

"Fancy a walk Sam"

"Yes why not it looks nice out there".

So hand in hand, they took a stroll.

"I've loved this weekend Chris thank you"

They stopped and kissed in the middle of the park

"Well Sam that made people look"

"I couldn't give a toss Chris, I love you and I don't care if the whole world knows".

After their walk, they headed back to the hotel to collect their luggage and head home back to sunny Spalding.

Once home Christine rang Sara to tell her of the good time they had had, then her mother and then her father and brother.

"Bloody hell Chris we've only been home five minutes"

"I know Sam; I want every one to know what a good time we've had"

"O.K do what you must I'm having a shower".

Over the next few weeks, Sara spent most of her spare time arranging her wedding.

Eileen had put a deposit down, on one of the bungalows in the Holland Park in Spalding; she had also received some good news of the money the police had removed from her house, she had been told that due to lack of evidence on the origin of the money. They could not prove it to be stolen, or immorally received; they had decided to return it. Tom advised her to get herself an accountant so as to get things above board. Tom too was busy trying to get the kitchen finished, Tom had put the Slop stone in place removing the old sink and fitting two reproduction wooden drainers.

Sara was very pleasantly surprised and she had disregarded her earlier reservations.

Chapter Twenty-Seven

Christmas 1999 was only weeks away, the millennium celebrations were in the thoughts of everyone everywhere.

Tom had bought loads of fireworks and was hoping to have a bit of a party in the garden. Christmas arrived with little fuss Tom and Sara arranged to meet Christine, Sam and Eileen for a drink round the pub.

Tom and Sara had bought each other clothes; Christine and Sam had got each other eternity rings and had asked Eileen round for dinner. Tom and Sara had also been asked but declined the offer saying with it being their last Christmas before they got married they would be taking a visit over to Wells.

Tom and Sara not staying long at the pub made their way over to Wells, obviously with it being Christmas Day the roads were just about empty. They arrived there in good time they decided to drive down to the beach parking their car at the end of the narrow lane

"Come on Sara you'll need your coat"

"God Tom, it's rather cold"

Tom got a bunch of flowers from the boot.

"I thought you got two bunches Tom"

"I did they're for something else"

Tom and Sara walked hand in hand to the spot on the beach where Tom's mother and fathers' ashes had been spread.

"You still miss them Tom don't you?"

"Yes Sara, I do, I know I was fifteen when mum died, I remember the hurt and the feeling of loss. I often wondered what she would have looked like now"

"Be honest with me Tom what do you think she would have thought of you seeing me" "Dad once said to me, Son do what you must in life and we will support you as long as you're as happy as we

305

are and remember son we love you, so yes they would have been happy for us"

"That's nice, you were very lucky to have such caring parents (Tom made a hole in the sand and placed the flowers in it then patted the sand round the stems) they look as if they have grown there Tom"

"Yes Sara they do—I could live here Sara"

"I'll tell you what, we would need bloody thick coats and when that tide comes in you'll ruin your shoes"

"Silly sod, I didn't mean right here, I meant Wells"

"Yes it's nice" said Sara not wanting to take this conversation any further.

They went back to the car deciding to go home.

Just out of Wells Tom pulled over onto the side of the road

"What's up Tom?" asked Sara

"I just have to do something"

"No Tom don't" said Sara realising what Tom was up to.

He opened the boot and removed the other bunch of flowers

"I have to Sara"

"Well Tom don't expect me to agree with you. Those two bastards could have killed us"

Tom ignored Sara's remarks and placed the bunch of flowers along side several other bunches that had been laid obviously by the two lads family and friends and Tom got back in the car.

"I know you are still bitter, and yes those two boys were stupid and that stupidity cost them dearly, but at the end of the day those two boys were someone's children"

"Don't preach to me Tom"

"I'm not Sara I'm just telling you why"

"O.K Tom you've told me, I don't agree with you. I think they are scum, now lets forget it".

Tom could see this distressed Sara, and now wished he hadn't done it although he still felt he was right. Tom sensed an atmosphere between them all the way to kings Lynn.

"I'm sorry Sara I didn't want to upset you"

"Well you did"

"What's up this isn't like you?"

"You just can't grasp it Tom, can you. I will never forgive them two— I don't know what to call them, when I saw you being put into that ambulance last boxing day, I honestly thought I'd lost you, and those two wouldn't have given a toss, then you place flowers there I wouldn't even waste my spit on them"

"O.K Sara, I take your point, lets just agree to disagree,(Tom pulled into a lay-by)give us a kiss (Sara lent over and kissed Tom on the lips) is that the best you can do?"

"Tom pulled Sara towards him and kissed her passionately undoing her jeans as they embraced

"No Tom not here some one will see us"

"Sod them anyway its getting dark and they won't be able to see in"

Sara gave in to Tom, helping him remove her pants she then removed his trousers and boxer shorts they were both naked from the waist down

"Oh shit Tom there's a car pulled in behind us"

"Oh no you're right there is, just sit normal they can't see our lower half"

"They will if you don't do something with that"

"I'll tell you what Sara you wrap your hands round it and they won't see it (Just then the car pulled out from behind them and went) well I'm waiting"

"O.K but if the police turn up I'll let you do all the talking" laughed Sara

"Hopefully you won't be able to"

"Shut up and let your seat back before I change my mind, then you can return the favour" said Sara bursting into laughter

"What's up with you?"

"I was just thinking what a way to spend Christmas day and what do you think my mother would say if I told her"

"She would almost certainly be jealous and lets face it, all she has had is stuffed turkey at least you'll have something else stuffed, so go on have a meal of it because I'm getting hungry to"

"One things for sure Tom we'll never look at this lay-by the same again".

They stayed there for about an hour before heading back home they laughed about their lay-by passion all the way home.

"Oh Sara while I'm thinking about it Chris gave me something for us both and asked us to open it in bed"

"But she has already given us our presents, Oh no where is it?"

"In the dash board pocket, why?" (Sara reached inside the dash board pocket and removed a large cylinder shape present

"Are you daft or what Tom don't you know what it is?"

"Sara I don't know, I had hell of a job getting it in there" Sara removed the Christmas paper that covered it to reveal a cylinder shape tube

"Now Tom do you know what it is?"

"No I've no—oh shit it isn't?"

"Yes Tom, it is and look she's even written on the bloody tag 'batteries included have fun love Christine and Sam', the cheeky bitch, look what it says on the tube, put this with the other one' she's a silly sod"

"Well we had better make sure it works" needless to say they spent the rest of the night in bed not watching television.

The following morning Tom and Sara where woken by the phone
Sara answered it

"Hi sis, did you have a nice day yesterday?"

"Yes Chris what bloody time is it"

"God almighty Sara its ten o'clock"

"Holy shit it isn't, I've got the dinner to get ready anyway what do you want?"

"Dear me who's a grumpy then. I've just rang to see whether or not your new toy works and does it do the job?"

"I don't know we haven't tried it you silly sod, fancy buying us that"

"So Sara you never used it"

"No we didn't, so I don't know whether or not it works" replied Sara

"Sara it definitely works me and Sam tried it out before we wrapped it up and I was ringing you to make sure you washed it before you use it"

"No Chris you didn't, tell me you didn't" said Sara sounding worried

"No Sara we didn't, but at least I now know you and Tom had a good night little sister bye-bye"

"You bitch you bloody bitch" said Sara laughing trying to cover up her embarrassment of being caught out.

"I take it that was Chris, what's she want?" asked Tom waking up

"I fell for it hook line and sinker"

"You bloody fool, that'll teach you, come on we had better get up. I'll give you a hand getting dinner ready".

Christmas just about over, Sara started writing out wedding invitations while Tom, prepared the garden for the millennium. He asked Paul to give him a hand to put a clear plastic cover over the

309

patio. Paul helped him design a frame for the start of the firework display, when they came to attaching the fireworks Paul noticed they were all damp

"Oh shit. Paul there's over a hundred pounds worth there"

"I know, you shouldn't do this, but if I were you I would lay them out on the floor near one of the radiators"

"Yes that's a good idea, I'll do it later, but don't tell Sara she'll go ballistic"

"Yes, I should imagine she would, don't you tell her I told you to do it, I don't want a slapping" laughed Paul.

Tom waited until Sara had nipped to her mums, and then he took them up into the spare bedroom and as Paul suggested laid them out on the floor by the radiator.

"That should do it Sara doesn't go in there much any way, what we'll do is wait until tomorrow by then they should be dry so we'll try one".

The following day Paul turned up at Tom's to be met by Sara

"Did you know about those fireworks in the bedroom Paul?"

"Um— (Seeing Tom standing behind her shaking his head and making signal with his hands) No Sara"

"Well I've told him, I don't want those bloody things in the house, they're bloody dangerous they should be in a tin"

"O.K Sara you've made your point, Paul and I have a lot to do"

Sara stormed off into the lounge

"I take it that she found them then?"

"Did she! And she was non too happy"

"I could see that"

"I'll give her a while and nip in and see her, I'll do my usual grovelling"

"Well at least they're dry".

The following day was New Years Eve; Tom woke early, leaving Sara to lie in. He washed a load of potatoes and put them in the oven ready for later then had a shower before taking a coffee up to Sara

"Good morning love, am I forgiven?"

"For what?" asked Sara

"For yesterday"

"Yes come here and give us a cuddle"

Tom lay on the bed next to her

"I've put the jacket potatoes in the oven and I've taken the chilli out of the freezer so we're all set for tonight"

"How many are actually coming tonight Tom"

"Well—with the neighbours I should imagine twenty"

"Twenty and you have bought two extra bags of potatoes, all that meat for the barbecue?"

"Well—yes"

"You bloody fool, but that's what I love about you Tom Gardener, come here and give us a kiss"

"I can give you more than that"

"Oh yes, I don't know what you mean"

"Well I will just have to show you"

"But Tom I haven't had a wash yet"

"Shut up and I'll give you a bed bath"

Tom disappeared beneath the quilt

"Tom that's what I call a bed bath, if you turn round I can wash you at the same time," Sara said very excitedly.

Tom did not need telling twice.

Their guests arrived around nine, Tom set up the Barbeque and Sara showed them to the drinks, the night went extremely well.

At fifteen minutes to twelve Tom turned on the radio at full volume for the sound of Big Ben, at one minute to twelve Paul lit the fuse for the fireworks knowing it would take precisely one minute for the fuse to reach the board design, keeping his fingers crossed and on the eleventh strike of Big Ben both Tom and Paul held their breaths staring at each other.

"Yes"

Shouted Tom as Big Ben struck twelve and the display lit up with the words HAPPY MILLENNIUM, he threw his arms round Sara kissing her then exchanging kisses with the others, Sara tried to ring her dad, but his mobile was engaged so she rang her brother

"Happy millennium David"

"Happy millennium Sara, I've just spoken to Chris" said David

"David tell dad I've tried ringing him, his phones engaged and give Jessica a kiss from me"

"O.K Sara"

Sara went over to her mother who was talking on her mobile seeing Sara coming towards her she quickly ended the call.

"Hello mum and who were you on the phone to?" Sara said in a knowing voice

"Just a friend, Sara dear"

"Yes mum, Oh look my mobiles ringing and its dads number, do you know what both me and Chris have been trying to ring him for ages, (Eileen's face went bright red) you end your call and dad rings me" said Sara teasing her mum and answering her phone

"Hello dad, happy millennium"

"Hello Sara what are you doing to celebrate?" asked James

"I told you the other day Tom's, done a party in the back garden, mums here"

"Yes I've just—"

"Yes dad you've just what?"

"I've just spoken to her"

"So like the other day when I tried to ring you for an hour. I also tried ringing mum"

"Yes Sara"

"Well dad I'll hand you over to mum, she's here at the side of me, by the way, I love you, here's mum"

Sara handed her phone to her mum, kissed her on the cheek and left her talking to her father Sara went over to Christine and Sam who with Tom was looking at the mass of colour coming from the sky

"Give us kiss sis" said Christine in a rather drunk voice

"Chris I've something to tell you" said Sara taking Christine taking her to one side, she told her what she knew or at least suspected.

"Bloody hell, it's not a wonder I can never get her on the phone these days"

"What do you reckon Chris?"

"Well I think it's great, let's hope something comes of it"

"Yes so do I". Eileen brought Sara's mobile back to her

"I was going to tell you and Christine when the time was right"

"Mum you don't need to explain to us, we are both very happy for you"

"Thank you Sara"

"Mum there is one thing, and I'm only being nosey?"

"What's that Sara dear?"

"How long have you and dad been ringing each other for?"

"Since Sam's birthday party on bonfire night and we've spoke daily since"

"I hope you're on the pill my girl" laughed Christine

"Silly bugger"

"Ignore her Mum. We both had our suspicions, mum we so happy for you"

"He says he coming down soon, but he has got to tell David about us first, so if David says anything pretend you don't know".

The celebrations carried on until four in the morning fireworks could be heard for miles and by the end of the night all apart from Eileen were very worse for drink.

With the big day fast, approaching Sara spent all of her spare time sorting out their wedding. She chose the bridesmaid dresses, David came down with Jessica, Denise and Danny brought Alice and Thomas down so they could all be measured and try on their clothes.

Neither Tom nor Sara could decide on a honeymoon location so Tom suggested and Sara agreed that he should make the location a surprise.

Eileen and James kept in touch daily. James making several visits to Bourne stopping with Eileen, James told David about him and Eileen, although David wasn't very happy about his dad and Eileen, he accepted it.

All the wedding invitations had been returned so they now knew there would be a total of sixty-three people at their wedding. Sara informed the caterers, telling them she would need to know the price. She was then told by them that a woman had requested that all bills were sent to her and she would sort them. Sara didn't need to guess who this woman was, she rang her mother immediately

"Mum have you asked for all the bills for the catering to go to you?"

"Yes Sara I have"

"But mum"

"But nothing you're my daughter and I'm paying for your wedding and I mean all of it, in fact I need to ring Tom to find out about the honeymoon"

"Mum there's no need for you to"

314

"Sara I gave you and Christine a shit childhood, so I'm sure you are going to have the best I can give you now"

"Thanks mum".

March soon arrived with the first flowers forcing their way through the soil and the leaves formed on the trees.

The final arrangements had been put into place for the big day; Tom had sorted out their honeymoon destination keeping it a total secret from everyone. Sara had had the final adjustments done to her dress.

Tom arranged a bit of a stag night at his house while Sara had a quiet drink at Eileen's new bungalow on Holland Park.

Two weeks before the wedding Tom reluctantly agreed to go and listen to their banns being read at the Parish church. Although both Tom and Sara were very much in love, what with everything going on, the wedding, adapting to the new family members and the apprehension of her mother and fathers growing relationship was causing stress for Sara. Tom spent hours trying put Sara's mind at rest, assuring her, everything would be fine and as the big day closed in the more nervous Sara got.

"Sara I love you and I'm telling you sweetheart everything will be fine"

"I know, I'm just worried, I keep thinking of what could go wrong, What if dads late, or if he doesn't turn up? And what if the wedding plans go wrong"

"Sara they won't and your dad will be there, lets face it your mums going to be there, you try keeping your dad away"

"I know Tom, I'm just worried"

"Don't things will be fine"

"I love you Tom"

"I love you to Sara, I promise you it will all turn out O.K"

Chapter Twenty-Eight

The big day arrived Sara had spent her last night of being a single girl at her mother's home. She woke at eight to the sounds of her mother entering the room holding a mug of coffee.

"Come on Sara love time you were up"

"What's the time mum?"

"Just turned eight and your dad rang an hour ago to say he would be here by nine, so come on get this down you. I'll make you breakfast"

Just then, the doorbell rang and Eileen went to answer it

"Morning mum isn't she up yet?" asked Christine with Sam by her side

"She's in the spare room"

"Come you idle bitch get up" said Christine

"I am I'm just going to drink this, anyway the weddings not till three"

"Yes I'm well aware of that but its your wedding day and you should be up and about, by the way sis I've asked the hair dressers to be here for around eleven, she said she will do the bridesmaids first, I'm just hoping that your godchildren will be here by then"

"It's alright Chris I spoke to their mother last night; they stopped at Holbeach last night in a hotel. Sam have you spoken to Tom?"

"Yes Sara, I rang him this morning at six"

"God I'll bet he was pleased" said Sara

"He had been awake since five" said Sam

"Bloody pondering on what he was about to let himself in for" laughed Christine

"Well he's definitely the biggest April fool I've ever met" added Sam

"Yes Sam that's a point, who the hell in the right mind chooses April fools day to get married on?" laughed Christine

"An April fool" both Christine and Sam said together

"Go on you pair leave me to get up, go and wind up mum instead, better still go and wind Tom up" said Sara getting out of bed

"That's a nice pair of pyjamas can I feel them?" asked Sam joking

"Come on you slapper she's not your type, lets go and see mum" said Christine leading Sam out the room.

James, David and a very excited Jessica arrived just after nine, five minutes later the phone rang, it was Denise

"We will be a bit later than I said last night Sara, Alice was sick in the night"

"Oh no, bless her will she be alright?" asked Sara

"Yes it's just excitement, but Danny is out looking for another hotel for tonight"

"Why's that Denise?"

"The manager got funny when we asked for some clean sheets; I thought Danny was going to hit him. We walked out this morning not paying"

"I said to you last week we can put you up, in fact you can stop at my old flat, It's empty I know there's only one bedroom, but that won't matter for one night"

"I'll see what Danny says when he gets back" said Denise.

Over the next few hours, all the girls had their hair done and James, David and Sam went to see Tom, finding him busy

"God I'm pleased you lot have arrived I was just going to ring Simon and Paul" said Tom opening the door to them

"What's up Tom?" asked Sam

"I'll show you come with me into the bedroom" replied Tom

"And you were going to ask Simon and Paul to help you in the bedroom, the mind boggles, you're a braver man than me, or is there something I should know" said Sam.

"You will have to excuse our Sam she never stops taking the piss" laughed Tom

Tom led them into the master bedroom where he showed them the problem.

"I can't get those top boards on without someone holding these posts"

"A four poster when the hell did you have this delivered?" asked David

"This morning and I'm not at all happy I was under the impression it came erected"

"So Tom let me get this right you were going to ask Simon and Paul to come round here to give you an erection in your bedroom with this new four poster bed on your wedding day. I'm sure they could have managed it. Tell me dearest Tom what do you think your Sara would have said if ever she had found out?" asked Sam winding Tom up

"God Sam you are something else, tell me James what do you make of her?" said Tom shaking his head trying to keep a straight face

"Well she's one hell of a character," replied James laughing

"Yes Tom and that's why you love me, so come on Tom show me what you want me to do to complete your erection" said Sam helping Tom with the bed soon having it together.

"That looks great" commented David

"Yes it's not to bad I just didn't realise it came as a flat pack, but never mind it's together now curtains up the lot, come on I'll put the kettle on

"Tom why have you got the four-poster?" asked Sam

"It's a surprise, Sara saw it in the shop window and ever since she hasn't stopped talking about it" said Tom just as the doorbell rang

"It's the florist, I don't want them here" said Tom

"I'll get it Tom" said Sam answering the door explaining to the girl carrying a large box of white Carnations buttonholes and a large bouquet, removing two of the buttonholes for herself and Tom.

"Well Tom we don't mean to be rude, but David and I had better get back to the others we'll leave Sam with you"

"Thanks a bunch James, cant you drop her somewhere, like over the bridge in town, there are some weights in the garage, tie them to her legs" said Tom laughing and shaking their hands as they left.

"So Tom it's you and me and I'm hungry"

"Go on then, I'm a bit peckish, I'll make some sandwiches and we can sit outside and eat them, it's a lovely day".

The taxi arrived to pick Tom and Sam up at two thirty. Tom dressed in a pure wool black three piece suit, white shirt with a silk burnt orange tie and a pair of hand made black leather shoes, all chosen by Sara.

"Your Sara definitely knows what to choose when looking for clothes, Tom you look great, if I had been straight, even I could fancy you dressed in that"

"I don't know whether to take that as a compliment or not. Sam you don't look too bad yourself. I think if I had been a lesbian I would have taken you up on the offer, thinking about it I could be a lesbian, I like the same things as you".

"Yes you have a point there, bloody fool"

Sam dressed in charcoal pin stripe trouser suit with a longline jacket, a burnt orange blouse to match Tom's tie and black ankle boots she looked gorgeous.

"Tom—the photographer, I think he wants you" said Sam as a chap with a rather large camera walked over to Tom

"Mr Gardener could I get a couple of photos of you with your best man" asked the photographer

"Of course you can, come on Sam, where do you want us?" asked Tom

"Mr Gardener I said the best man"

"This is my best whatever" said Tom with Sam laughing

"I'm sorry—I see, over by the front of the church then please" said the photographer

"That's hell of a weapon he has in his hand there Tom" said Sam jokingly

"Shut up you silly sod, he'll hear you and he looks a bit of a gruesome bugger" Tom said in a whispery voice standing next to Sam posing for the camera.

Tom and Sam made their way into the church to be greeted by the vicar, Tom and Sam shook his hand.

"You can remember what to do Tom can you?" asked the vicar

"Yes I think I got the gist of it only I'll try not to fall over like I did on Wednesday's rehearsal" said Tom causing Sam to burst into laughter

"Oh dear it appears we've set this young lady off again" commented the vicar smiling at Sam

"It doesn't take a lot. Come on Sam I don't know why you're laughing it was your foot I fell over"

"I know I just can't get the picture of you rolling in the aisle holding your shin out of my mind," said Sam trying to contain her laughter

They received an order of service from David who along with Danny had accepted the job as usher, before making their way to their seats.

At Eileen's house, the wedding cars had arrived to collect Sara and the children, nerves where high

"You look beautiful Sara absolutely beautiful"

"Thank you dad".

Sara was dressed in a ivory 1930s style dress made of silk, her head dress was a circle of "WHITE LILIES" and orange freesias with ivy that matched her bouquet, she was a picture of beauty as was Christine dressed in a burnt orange colour full length bridesmaid dress made of silk taffeta, Jessica and Alice looking absolutely adorable, in their burnt orange colour three quarter length bridesmaids dresses.

Christine carried a bouquet of orange lilies and Jessica and Alice each carried old style brown teddies.

Eileen decided on a pale blue suit and matching hat, James also looked smart dressed in a three piece navy blue suit white shirt and blue tie,

"Come on Sara dear, its time you and your dad made a move the bridesmaids have already gone and I should be at the church, so come on in the car" said Eileen

Eileen kissed Sara on the cheek gently so as not to disturb her light covering of makeup and then kissed James on the lips. Before hurrying off to the church. She handed the door key to the neighbour so she could lock up after they had gone.

Tom was waiting nervously in the church with Sam

"What's the time Sam?"

"A minute later than you asked before. Stop bloody shaking especially with your hands in your pocket, people will think you're playing with yourself" Sam said whispering

"Perhaps I am" replied Tom grinning

"Silly sod, anyway you ought to be saving that for tonight"

"What's the time Sam?"

"Look at your own watch, hang on I think they're here".

Tom could feel his stomach knot up as the church organist played the wedding march and they all stood up looking to the altar.

It seemed to take ages for Sara and James to reach them, the look on Tom's face as he turned to look at his beautiful young bride. He couldn't help but to say,

"Sara you look beautiful" Sara just smiled not answering him.

The service began then they exchanged rings before being pronounced man and wife. They signed the registrar after which they all congregated outside the church for photographs. The reception took place at Glen Side Manor West Pinchbeck, a beautiful eighteen century manor house that had been converted into a hotel and restaurant surrounded by two acres of beautiful gardens.

In the car, Tom didn't stop telling Sara how beautiful she looked.

Tom, Sara along with Sam, Eileen, James, the bridesmaids and the pageboy, greeted the guests before the caterers served the meal, then the speeches Sam was first to speak thanking everyone for their attendance and helping make the day special

"I would also like to say how beautiful Sara looks and what a handsome couple they are, finally can I just say to Tom how honoured and thrilled I was when he asked me to be his best man or should that be woman"

Sam then asked them all to raise their glasses to toast the bride and groom and went on to read the cards before asking Tom to take over

"Thank you Sam, in all the time I've known you that's the most serious I've seen you. First of all I must say how beautiful this young lady I can now call my wife looks, Thank you all for coming a special thanks to Eileen for everything (the head caterer came over to Sara carrying a large bouquet of White Lilies, Sara handed them to her mother and kissed her and Eileen thanked her). Now this young lady Sam, what a character, I've only known her and her partner Christine, now my sister-in-law for just over a year and I can honestly say they are both two lovely people, and very lucky to have each other and Sam thank you for today, your humour kept me going (the caterer then came up to Tom carrying another bouquet of White Lilies, Tom gave them to Sam), Tom then went on to thank the bridesmaids and the page boy asking everyone to toast them all. Sara give the three bridesmaids a gold necklace and the pageboy a watch. Tom then asked James to give a speech, James told them all about finding Christine again only to find out he had another daughter Sara. He went on to say how delighted he was when Sara asked him to give her away.

"Thank you Sara, I'm really proud you (turning to look at Christine) and I'm proud of you to Christine"

After James finished Sam stood up and asked for Tom to let them all into the secret of their honeymoon destination. Tom pulled from his inside pocket of his jacket an envelope and handed it to Sara

"Open that sweetheart" some said

"Tom, Tom thank you" said Sara excitedly

"Well come on Sara tell us, where's the romantic old devil taking you?" asked Sam

"Paris and a trip, on the Orient Express" said Sara almost in tears leaning to hug Tom

"Yes we leave tonight a taxi is picking us up at nine and Sam helped pack your clothes so blame her" said Tom laughing

"You didn't Sam did you?" Asked Sara

"No, ignore him, anyway you wont need any will you" laughed Sam.

They then decided to cut the cake while the D.J set his equipment up and Sara and Tom wondered round chatting to their guests. Sara went over to see her mother who herself looked happy in the presence of her father.

"Thank you mum, thanks for all you've done"

"Don't even think about it Sara, I'm just so happy for you both, and thank you for my bouquet it's lovely, but where did you get the idea of White Lilies from?"

"Ask dad"

"I might have guessed, so that's why you also put them in your head dress and bouquet, because you knew they were my favourite flower (Sara nodded and Eileen hugged her) that's lovely, thank you Sara dear, thank you".

When it was time for Tom and Sara to leave all the guests went to wave them off. As they, all watched the lights of the taxi fade into the distance James turned to Eileen,

"So where would you like to go on our honeymoon?"

THE END...